THE DIPLOIDS

Wildside Press Science Fiction Classics

THE DIPLOIDS

Katherine MacLean

WILDSIDE PRESS
BERKELEY HEIGHTS, NEW JERSEY

THE DIPLOIDS

Published by:

Wildside Press
P.O. Box 45
Gillette, NJ 07933-0045
www.wildsidepress.com

ISBN 1-58715-128-6

First Wildside Press Edition: April 2000

THE DIPLOIDS

I

"LOOK OUT!" The shout was almost in his ear, and with the shout came another sound, a flat crack like two boards slapping together. He moved instinctively, grasping Nadine's arm and making three rapid strides to the shelter of a store doorway. Then he turned as the flat echoes of sound rang back from the stone fronts of the buildings across the street. He expected to see something fallen from a window, or a car out of control veering up over the curb.

At first glance there was nothing. The traffic moved by silently and swiftly as usual, but the people on the sidewalk milled oddly, and then straightened to stare all in one direction down the street. The light had changed a few seconds ago, and the traffic sped by more rapidly, accelerating.

He picked out voices.

"Did you get his number?"

"Some nut waving a gun from a taxi."

"But he shot at us!"

He glanced at Nadine; they exchanged a half shrug and walked on.

Then "Mart" Breden remembered that something had brushed his neck roughly as he heard the shout. He had assumed it was the sleeve of a waving arm, but . . .

"So as I was saying—" he continued stubbornly, determined to finish a half-finished witty point. While he spoke he put his fingertips up to feel the spot on his neck, then brought them down again. There was a dampness on his neck and a red smear of color on his fingertips—blood.

Nadine halted. "As you were saying, brother—you're just too dumb to know when you've been hurt."

She moved quickly around to his other side where she could see the side of his neck. "It's only a scratch. The bullet just

5

touched you," she reassured him, groping in her handbag. "Hold still! I'll fix it."

He stood still. It was a pleasure to stand and have Nadine fussing over him. She was indisputably lovely, and he was conscious of envious glances. Streams of brightly-dressed, handsome people returning to work from lunch passed by, their feet soundless on the green resilient sidewalk. Some of them were talking quietly and laughing in conversation as they passed; some were listening to music spools with ear-buttons that touched his hearing with a faint faraway strain of music as they passed. He was pleased they looked at her, and had no attention for him.

Standing still under Nadine's ministrations, he said appreciatively, "You're the perfect partner to take along to an accident."

She smiled up at him. "Well, if you're going to make a habit of being shot at, I'll buy more band-aids." The wail of a police patrol copter throttled down to a growl as it touched the road and swung in to where the crowd clustered. She glanced back doubtfully. "Should we go back and tell them?"

He touched the small flesh-colored bandage on his scratch, looking at the reflection in a window. "Hardly worth going back. All we'd prove is that someone was shooting, and they know that already."

They walked on together through the shade of the tall trees that lined the avenue. "When your Revision Committee for the Patent Code testifies before Congress," he said, remembering what he had been saying, "you should be spokesman in that tight green and gold suit you're wearing. They'd agree to anything."

She picked up the thread. " 'Gentlemen,' I'll say—"

"Undulating slightly," he added.

"Invention has become a form of restriction. The law has been diverted from—"

"*Seduced* from!"

"Seduced from its original intention, which was to guarantee sufficient profits to the inventor to encourage and stimulate invention. Instead, research now has as its main purpose the desire to invent something first and patent it first, not for use, but to prevent its use, to preserve the status quo for the industry."

A small tube elevator whooshed them up to the sixtieth floor, "Lawyers' Row." They were at the door of his office.

PAUL BREDEN
PATENT LAW

Nadine's office was further down the corridor. Paul pushed his door open, hoping to extend their lunchtime together a little more, beguiling her with the imaginary speech. "At this point your claque in the gallery claps and cheers and stomps, and while they are being ejected you pull out your compact and put on more lipstick."

They walked into the inner office past the secretary, ignoring the fact that lunch was over and they both had work to do. Nadine continued the speech, gesticulating with mock earnestness. He considered her from a standpoint of an imaginary audience of lascivious Congressmen. She was beautiful—yes, but too perfectly dressed, too crisp and finished and unapproachable. It was probably an effect carefully calculated to keep the minds of her business associates on the subject of business.

"You should muss your hair a little," he interrupted, getting a frown for his efforts.

"The competition, not to be outdone, pours its money into research to find *other* ways of doing what it needs done. This, gentlemen, is . . ."

He looked at her with a familiar question coming up in his mind, quickening his pulse. She probably had a private life of friends and lovers, but he had never dared let himself approach that side of her, although they had known each other for six months. She could choose among many men—men without his handicap—yet she seemed glad to be with him as a law collaborator, and welcomed any free time they could escape from business lunches to eat together. Yet . . . .

". . . . does not make the inventor any richer, for he draws only his research salary from his company. Actually, the prime result is duplication of research, so that instead of each day bringing hundreds of brilliant new inventions, the patent office is flooded daily with hundreds of brilliant new ways of doing the same damned thing, each one tying up the patent office with its red tape—each one no better than the other!"

He sat down behind his desk and propped his elbows on it, smiling. "Add this. 'There are nine and ninety ways—Of constructing tribal lays, And every—Single—One—Of them—Is *right!*'"

"As Kipling wrote—" she began, then stopped to frown at him. "Would Congressmen know that lays are a form of poetry?"

He laughed. "All the better if they don't." It was not often they had lunch together or extended their lunch hours like this. She probably would have been surprised to learn how much these occasional lunches meant to him.

The televiewer chimed.

Paul muttered a "damn," reaching for the right phone, and Nadine gave him a farewell salute and moved toward the door. "Wait a minute," he asked her, "and we'll see who this jerk is." He pushed a button and a screen on the wall opposite him sprang to life in color, showing a lean old man in a snappy pearl gray suit, waiting with restless impatience. "Yardly Devon." Breden identified him without pleasure, remembering the things Devon had said before switching off the last time they had seen each other.

"His last two inventions were not patentable, Nadine, and I told him so, but he insisted I try to get patents on them anyhow. When they were rejected he claimed I'd sabotaged them. He probably took them to another consultant, got the same opinion, and wants to apologize now." He indicated the chair beside the desk. "Sit there a minute. You're out of range of the scanner. He won't see you."

She smiled and sat down. The bell chimed again impatiently, and Breden switched on the scanner that put him on Devon's screen. "Yes?"

A light came into the eyes of the dapper old man as he saw Breden. With a quick move he jumped to his feet, bringing a gun up from somewhere below screen range. "I've got you now, Breden. I suspected it a long time, and now I know what you are."

For a half second of time Breden started to laugh, then he remembered the shot on the street a quarter hour before with a sudden cold jolt. Devon was not kidding.

"Careful there, old boy, you'll break your scanner," Nadine called.

He couldn't see her, and the tailored neat old man was childishly startled. "Who said that!" He leaned forward, peering, then turned to inspect the partially visible room showing on the screen, the gun waving in his hand. "I've got to kill him," he said clearly to no one in particular. "He's a diploid." He dwindled and came into full view further away, peered around, and then wandered out of screen view.

"Crazy," Breden muttered. He felt weak. That last meaningless word had been a shock. "Have the police trace the call. I'll try to hold him." He handed her one of the phones.

The old man had wandered back to his screen and he glimpsed the motion. He whirled, gun leveled. "Don't try to escape!"

Breden pulled his hand back and arranged his features in an expression of respect and interest. He felt shaken. *Diploid.* Judging by Devon's voice it meant something different from a human. It had been a long time since he had heard that inflection in anyone's voice. The meaningless word rang in his ears as if he had been called something animal. He forced himself to think. What would hold an inventor's interest long enough for the police to reach him? "I gather that that gun shoots through television screens. Could you give me an idea how it works, Mister Devon?"

Nadine was murmuring into the phone, "Yes, with a gun. It looks like a private room he's calling from." She turned and whispered, "What's your number?"

"Lascar B-1063," Breden said, without turning his head. On the screen Devon was looking down at his automatic.

"It's an invention—" he said, looking up at the sound of Breden's voice—"a new Devon invention." The old man stroked it fondly with his left hand, without turning it from its perfect pictured aim at Breden's face. It looked startlingly deadly pointing at him from the screen.

Breden pulled his eyes from it, resisting an irrational impulse to switch off the screen. "How does it work?"

If only he could keep this conversation going for a while, the police would come on to the screen in the room behind Devon and take him away.

The inventor's voice began to rise. "I won't tell you. It's secret. And you're not going to stop me from patenting it like you did the others. You sneaking diploids are trying to get in everywhere. But I won't let you have the Earth. You can't fool me! I know what you are. You're not going to hold up progress by keeping people from getting patents—" His voice had risen to a shriek; his face was distorted, *"I'll stop you! I'll kill you. . . . I'll kill you right now!"* The shots came with a shocking crack of sound. The screen was too clear, too tri-dimensional, too much like an undefended open window through which a yammering madman poured shots at him. Instinctively Breden threw himself to one side.

The vision of the shouting old man cracked across like a broken mirror and still moving, began to waver in ripples like something seen in disturbed water, then abruptly shattered to darkness. They heard a shriek, "Got you!" just before a final tearing sputter and the dull *pfut* of a blown fuse as Devon's sound system went dead.

Nadine had been staring, but now there was nothing to stare at but the smooth grayness of the viewer screen. "He just shot his televiewer all to hell," she said into the phone, still staring, fascinated at the screen. "It blew out . . . that's right. We'll leave it on." She put the phone back in its cradle with a sigh. "They said not to switch it off."

Her expression changed as she looked at him. "What is it, Mart? What's wrong?"

"Nothing." Another spasm of depression hit him. "Oh hell yes—everything. You heard him call me a diploid?"

She took out a cigarette case and opened it, selecting a cigarette with unnecessary care. She was concerned. "One of those little green men, you mean? Smoke?"

"No thanks."

She untelescoped a long cigarette holder and fitted the cigarette into it, speaking thoughtfully, "I heard him. It was nothing personal, Mart. For a paranoid there always has to be the heroes or the spies or the Martians, and the big conspiracy somehow against him. It had to be someone, and you were elected. You must see enough nuts coming in here with lunatic inventions and delusions of grandeur to be used to it."

He leaned forward and lit her cigarette. "Too used to it. Beginning to wonder." He put away his cigarette lighter and held up his hand, looking at it. Five fingers and a thumb. Too many fingers.

"Right up to high school they called me 'Marty' for 'Martian Breden'—and it wasn't a friendly nickname. I was with a gang, but I was its goat. If we played cops and robbers —I was the robber, and got arrested or electrocuted or shot resisting arrest. If we played cowboys and Indians—I tried to burn people at the stake and got my throat slit by a hero with a bowie knife, and bit the dust. In high school they started getting smarter, and I had friends who *were* friends, but for them I was 'Marty' too. By that time it was my name. I like it now, but that's where it came from."

He put his six-fingered hand down on the desk. "When a new client comes in, now, I mention that the simplest inventions are the best, like the safety pin—or the small laborsaving device I invented which makes it easier to play the piano and carry four beer bottles in each hand. 'What is it?' they ask. . . . I hold my hand up. 'Extra finger,' I say. 'It is patented.' That always tickles them."

He had given her the same line when they had first met. He remembered that he had felt the same first hostile alertness and expectation of hurt for her as for any other stranger, and had concealed his tension behind the usual line of entertaining talk. She had been just another beautiful woman to him, a lawyer like himself, but more poised and bland than he was —and too beautifully dressed, too efficient, probably critical and unforgiving and egotistical, someone who could hurt you if you dropped your guard.

That was before he knew her. His guard was all the way down now. There was no pretending and no caution when he talked to Nadine. "I'm not just being sensitive, Nade, I need jokes like that. I have to use them, and use them carefully. So they'll get a lift and a laugh every time they notice a detail

that's different. That Mart! Always a character. Everything
with him has to be original— If I don't point it out and make
jokes about it, sooner or later people begin to fidget and grow
uncomfortable with an instinct of something being wrong.
There are too many subtle physical oddities that disturb with
a feeling of misproportion. The only thing I can do to stop
nervousness and tension from building up in them is to bring
out my differences and display them like a collection of card
tricks, so whenever they get the wrong feeling again, it's part
of the joke, just Mart being a character again."

II

FOR A TIME Nadine sat back, something close to pity on her
lovely face. Then she grinned and mimicked him from memory,
with a proudly bent arm and clenched fist, demonstrating
the muscles. "My own invention. . . ." She quoted words he
had said, flexing her arm as she had seen him do, with a precise back and forth motion. "I'm the only *genuinely* self-made
man. Self-made—self-assembled—" A rusty hinge noise began
in perfect time with the motion of the flexing arm, and she
glanced at the arm with dismay and tried to stop it. It kept
moving stiffly, the rusty squeak growing louder. Hastily she
grabbed it and brought it to a halt with her other hand, and
then apologetically took an imaginary small object from her
pocket. "Of course, I was pretty young at the time . . . might
have slipped and gotten some parts in from the wrong stack
. . . not enough light. . . ." Nadine's voice faded to an apolo-
getic mumble as she carefully oiled her elbow with an imaginary oil can.

He was laughing. This was the first time he had seen anyone
else do his act. He had seen clients laugh, but this was the first
time he had seen what they were laughing at from the outside,
and, well, it *was* funny.

She looked up from oiling her elbow, her eyes round and
solemn. "You were saying?" she asked innocently, putting the
invisible and imaginary oil can carefully back into her pocket,
and then smiled. "I wondered about that end-man effect,
Mart. It's amusing and starts a talk off in a good mood, but

it isn't exactly like you, not when a person gets to know you better. Are you sure you need it?"

For an instant a crowd of painful incidents pushed against the unlocked door of memory. The time, when he was twelve, visiting the city and he had wandered into a strange neighborhood where the kids did not know him; the fight he had lost. And other times. "I've lived long enough to find out what happens if I don't."

"Are you sure that still applies?" she asked, her cool green eyes showing interest and concern.

Breden went on talking as if he hadn't heard her question. His eyes held a faraway look as he remembered people's past reactions to his difference.

"Take my face—ears set higher than normal and tipped back more—a difference easy to sense, hard to focus on. It makes my face look foreign, but what race? I can see the re-action to it even in the faces of people who pass on the sidewalk —the usual quick unseeing glance, then a double-take and a puzzled expression. Then they're past and they forget about it. It doesn't lead anywhere with adults. No one spits at me anymore or stops me to ask who the hell I am and why don't I go back to wherever I came from, but the reaction is always the same. None of them can classify me. It must be a genuinely strong feeling of something alien." He laughed suddenly and harshly, surprising himself with the sound. "By the law of democracy the majority is right. Maybe I *am* a Martian, if that's what they think!"

She blew a plume of smoke reflectively, not commenting, then picked up the phone. "Let's see if the police have our paranoid friend yet."

"A Martian." Saying that hateful word to Nadine made it sound like a joke and not like something that had been dreams and nightmares ever since he was a kid and they had dubbed him "Martian" Breden, and he'd known something secret about himself that the others did not know.

Nadine's voice, vibrant and soft, said, "Calling in for Paul Breden about a threat to him we reported . . . yes, did you? Oh . . . no . . . of course. Thank you." She hung up thoughtfully. "You can switch off now."

He switched off the scanner that had held connection with Devon's blown televiewer. "What'd they say?"

"They didn't get him. When they got there there was nothing but a smashed televiewer and the neighbor in the next room complaining about the racket—that must have been his gun."

"Anything else?"

"They want you to drop down to the local station house today or tomorrow and swear out a complaint. I said yes."

"Check."

She smiled. "Let's hope he sticks to trying to kill you by television."

Then when he thought she had let it pass, Nadine looked at her gold-tinted nails, and asked, "What did you mean about being a Martian?"

She had known it was more than a gag.

It would have been better if she had not been so understanding.

"Could you spare me fifteen more minutes?" he asked, hoping she had a business appointment in her own office.

She settled back and crossed her legs. "I'm listening."

He hesitated a moment, his hands flat on the desk top, looking for easier ways of saying what he was going to say. Stray fugitive thoughts scurried around the fringes of consciousness like a dusty frightened nest of mice looking for escape from a suddenly opened closet—mice that could have grown to full scale monsters if he had waited longer before telling someone of this. And the tightening feeling in his chest warned of coming fear, the ghost that always comes out of mental closets that have been locked too long.

It would be better, he decided, to speak rapidly and bluntly, or he might not get it out at all. There was no real trouble, it was just that this was the first time he had explained to anyone. What are you afraid of? This just needs airing out.

"Let's take it item by item," he said slowly, still holding his palms flat against the desk top, feeling their slight tremor. "I've got six fingers, right?"

"Sure," she said with a touch of defiance. "Six good fingers."

"Ever notice something odd about my walk?"

"Yes." She smiled reflectively. "Individual . . . a slightly crouched springy look. I'd recognize you by it."

"My feet are different."

"Oh?" She exhaled a translucent puff of smoke, looking at it, then met his eye. "In what way?"

He swung in his chair so that she could see his legs and shoes. "They're long in the arch, and abnormally narrow. I can't keep my heel on the ground, it doesn't feel right there. Go on my toes instead." He considered his deep rubber soles, checking their normal appearance. "My shoes are built up inside—up in the back—down in the front, so inside I'm standing on my toes the way I like it. The angle brings my shoe down to normal length." He looked up at her, challenging her to answer. "Remind you of something?"

"Hocks," she said reluctantly. "Do they hurt?" It was a key question.

"No." He knew what she meant. An abnormality should be imperfect. Feet hurt vehemently at the slightest trace of imperfection. His feet felt fine.

"What else?" she asked grimly. He could see the conclusions forming in her mind.

"What race would you say I am, Nadine?"

The long grey-green eyes wandered over his face. "I don't know. A nice, handsome blend—definitely worth staring at. If you're sensitive about stares—try being ugly and peculiar both. People will look away in droves. . . . Probably some Japanese for those good, broad cheekbones and the set of those ears. Mongoloid skull, Caucasian nose, extra wide chiseled mouth, Hindu almost. I'd guess American Indian, or high caste Brahman. That orangy olive skin doesn't tell me anything." She smiled. "I give up."

"My parents were straight Caucasian—white midwestern Americans from Omaha."

"Anyone else in the family look like you?"

"No."

"What else?" She was forgetting to smoke.

He bent his right arm, clenching his fist near his shoulder. "My arms. The proportion of forearm to upper arm is wrong. They should be about equal. My fist should come level with my shoulder." His fist was five inches above his shoulder. "My upper arm is shorter and thicker than my forearm."

"Handicap?" The question was automatic now. She knew what the answer would be.

"Advantage, I think. My arms are unusually strong." Abnormalities should be crippling defects, but these weren't. People had told him that he was one of the strongest and most vital persons they had ever met. He wondered how much of this Nadine had noticed herself, and how much she had shrugged off. She wasn't shrugging now.

"What else?"

He hesitated. There was something else—a fact that came into his mind reluctantly as if it were something that was half untrue, a private fairy tale that had no meaning except for him. He had hidden it too long. It was a repression now. His fingers whitened against the desk top. He could feel them trembling. "I've got a soft spot in the back of my head." That's what he had told the other kids when they had bumped it accidentally and he had cried. His hair covered it, and he hadn't let them look at it. He had fought instead.

"On the left side," he said. "The doctor said it looks like it was starting out to be an eye." He watched her face and saw it go hard and expressionless in defense against whatever was coming, reflecting his own sudden tight control. He continued levelly without change of tone. "I'm lying to you, Nadine. It *is* an eye!"

After he had told her, he sat frozen. This brought the fact to full reality in one blow. *An eye in the back of his head. What was it doing there?*

After a pause she said, "I believe you." Her cigarette had burned down to the holder. She stubbed it out.

"Want to see it?" They had to bull through now it was begun.

"No—yes." She got up and moved behind him. "Show me."

He reached back and parted his hair in the place where he let it grow long.

There was a moment of silence. "Does it open?" she asked behind him.

He opened it. The unaccustomed glare of the light in the

room was painful, a blinding blend of tans and blues. A pinkish blur came into focus in the shape of a face. He shut his eye again, gratefully shutting out the light.

Nadine walked back in front of the desk looking younger and more flustered than he had ever seen her. "Not the right place for an eye," she muttered confusedly. Fumblingly she took out a cigarette, juggled and dropped it. "It blinked at me," she said, picking up the cigarette and trying with trembling fingers to fit it into her holder.

Her confusion was amusing. He had never seen her even slightly flustered before, and the sight distracted him from his own reactions. The tremor left his hands as he began to smile. Self-consciously, Nadine made an effort to say something controlled and practical. "Why don't you have it taken out?"

He looked at her without answering for a moment, then said, "Why don't you have one of your eyes taken out?"

She looked up at him, seeing him as a person, thinking how he would feel, and suddenly had back her balance and wisdom like picking up a purse she had dropped. "Sorry. You gave me the right answer to that one."

He grinned, snapping on his cigarette lighter and holding it out for her, his hand steady, and she remembered the cigarette in her hand with a start and looked from it to him, beginning to grin back, and leaned forward putting it between her lips. When the cigarette caught she straightened. "All right, so I'm a sissy."

They shared smiles. "Okay, I've shown you the inventory. How does it add up?"

She sobered abruptly and took the holder from her lips and looked at the cigarette's glowing tip, delaying speech. Then she took a deep breath and forced herself to look at him and reply. "All right. *What gives you the idea that you're human?*"

For a moment he didn't breathe or think, then his mind raced like a squirrel trapped in a cage. It was almost unbelievable how long he had managed to avoid the elementary question that had trapped him at last. Why should he think he was human? Why should any *man* have so many freakish differences, and yet feel no pain from any of them at all? Automatically he gasped out the stock answer he had used to fool himself with all those years. "My parents are normal."

"How do you know that they are your parents?"

Here was another shattering question. They were obviously *too* normal, no physical peculiarities at all. They could not possibly be his parents, and yet he had wanted them to be his parents when he was a kid, wanted it desperately enough to fool himself into believing it. The shock of the idea when he heard it now was appalling. It was the effect of the tremendous effort by which he had always avoided that awful question. It was incredible how long he had managed to suppress it, and how cleverly he had been able to fool himself, he thought dully.

All right, so he wasn't human.

Then damn all humans! The hatred flamed like a blow torch. He could hate them now, all these puny, two-eyed five-fingered people who were the same race as the kids who had jeered and tormented him through his bitter childhood. Somewhere there were people like him—people for whom three eyes and six fingers were *right*, who could be friends and accept him without thinking anything about him was wrong—or ugly—or *inhuman*.

"All right," he said thickly. "So I'm a Martian. Now what?"

Nadine held up a perfectly manicured five-fingered hand. "Not so fast!" She was recovering from the shock and thinking now as he'd seen her concentrate when they were working on a tough case and the opposition had them in a tight corner. She was on his side, battling against his conclusions. "You don't have to go all the way into a padded cell with our friend there." She jerked her head at the televiewer screen. "We don't need extra-terrestrials to account for a non-human anthropoid type race. You're obviously Earth adapted, so you have to be a member of a race natural to Earth."

For a moment Breden was held by the sight of her hand. It had five fingers, five lovely fingers, and he couldn't hate Nadine. He couldn't hate his "father" or his "mother" either, and they were human. Even some of his clients were good guys and honest dealers. He clenched his hands and unclenched them in frustration. Was there nothing in the world that was simple? Nothing that a person could be wholeheartedly either for or against? He smiled wryly. A tolerant sense of humor was supposed to be the mature reaction to such impulses. But it was a pale substitute for the pleasure of a knock-down, drag-out fight.

He forced his attention back to what Nadine was saying. Other races on Earth. . . . "There isn't any other—"

She interrupted, restraining a knife-edge of impatient logic. "No other known species of mankind *surviving*. But paleontologists have already dug up almost a hundred extinct species. Apparently the conditions were so favorable back in the early days that every species of tarsier, monkey, lemur, baboon and gorilla existing started evolving an offshoot branch of man, and homo sap got there firstus with the mostus and wiped the others out. But perhaps he hasn't wiped *all* the others out. There may be a few small tribes of a different kind still surviving in the hills and jungles."

He had wanted to meet and know people like himself, but this presented only a depressing vision of a patent lawyer foolishly out of place on some distant mountainside, trying to communicate in six-fingered sign language to a bunch of six-fingered savages.

"If there are any people like myself around," he said emphatically, "they'll be running things."

"Like that, eh?" she looked him up and down, measuring him for a strait-jacket. "The diploid conspiracy?"

"Like that," he snapped, uneasily defiant.

She stood up and touched her fingers to the top of his desk, looking at him with irritated affection. "Let's bring it down to common sense, Mart. If there's any group running things, it's obviously a group of low grade imbeciles. The world has never been in such a mess. We've been walking the plank towards an atomic blow-up for fifty years, and the longer we take to get there, the bigger the blow. Or put it this way . . . granted your I.Q. is high, and maybe high I.Q. goes with six fingers—are *you* running things? There are a million people every bit as intelligent as ourselves. We meet them every day in this line of work. Are they controlling the world?" Her vehemence grew, adding force to her words and brightness to her eyes. "Now add them up. If all the political experts, intellectuals, economists, sociologists and general geniuses who ought to know how to run things better, plus all their brains, success, money and power, can't get control of what's going on—then a hypothetical handful of conspiring three-eyes has about as much chance of seizing power as a package of Jello has of stiffening up the English Channel for dessert!"

He grinned and cowered down behind his desk. "Cease fire! You're right."

She smiled, holding out her hand. "All right, Mart. The war's over. Now I have to get back to work."

He took her hand, standing up. "Sorry you can't stay."

"I'm sorry too. We had a nice lunch." She looked at him slantwise from under her long dark lashes, suddenly provocatively helpless and appealing. "Remember, any time you want someone to talk to while you're being used for a target, or any time you feel confessional and want to tell someone about a few extra things like a third arm, or how you walk through walls. . . ."

"I'll call on you." He finished the sentence as she let it trail off wistfully, and he hustled her toward the door, grinning. She had taken it the way he had hoped she would, as something casual. There was no discernible difference in the easy relationship they had established.

She poked her lovely head back in a moment after he had closed the door after her. "If you find out that there really is a Martian conspiracy, tell me so I can help. I like conspiracies."

Suddenly fear and loneliness came again. *"I like conspiracies,"* she had said. His spirits sank. But what of Martians, of freaks? How could she like a freak? Perhaps it was all pretense. The old wave of doubts assailed him. A spasm clenched somewhere in his chest and he rose, trying to think of something to say—some question that would somehow bring an answer he could trust.

Nadine stood in the doorway in her green suit, looking at him, seeing something in his expression. She came back into the office and put her hand on his arm, looking up into his face with an intent and puzzled gaze. Something changed.

He felt the warmth of her hand on his arm as if it were fusing into his body, as if in some subtle way their bloodstreams had grown into one. For a long joined moment they stood in silence, their gazes locked together, and then she said in an oddly quiet voice, "Well, there's work."

With an effort they stepped away from each other. "I'll see you, Nade," he said as she walked away.

"Yes," she said, for he had stated something that had to happen. They could not help but see each other. The thought of remaining apart had become an impossible, ridiculous thought.

He had been given his answer, and it was magnificently more than he had hoped for.

He postponed thinking on the subject, letting it remain in the back of his mind as a source of warmth and happiness, and got down to his delayed stack of work. An interview with a client was due in five minutes and he had to brief up on the legal twists he was planning to use to get the man's patent through. Concentration shut out from his universe everything but patents and technical details for the time that was necessary. But before the man came in, Mart lifted his head and let his mind range back over the discussion, just once. Maybe there was some explanation for his differences, some pleasant explanation that he could tell Nadine with pride. *Mart Breden wants to know where he came from, what his real name is, and why he has an extra finger on each hand and an extra eye in the back of his head.*

Put that way, it hardly seemed too much to ask.

III

ON THE WAY over to the police station at four-thirty he heard a shot. It came from God knows where, and it missed, but there was no telling how close it had come. He didn't stop to investigate; he merely hurried his stride down into the nearest belt entrance and merged himself into the crowd. No one turned to see what the sound was. There was enough noise in the quiet city in the first home-going rush to partially muffle it and make it seem like a normal street sound, and there was no reason for anyone else to think of a possibility of shots. Violence was too unusual to be expected.

Stepping on a belt the crowd dispersed over the local and express strips, and for a moment Mart was exposed again before the belt carried him out of shot range of the platform. There was no shot, but he was sweating as he found a chair and sat down. It would be easy to be killed that way. The unwary passersby of the city could not defend him; they simply provided an innocent camouflage and ambush from which Devon could take easy aim without being noticed.

The rest of the way he was wary, but there were no more shots.

At the station the police informed him that they had not managed to locate Devon in his usual haunts, but they had alerted hotels and airlines to watch for him.

"If you set someone to follow me," Mart said, "you'll probably follow Devon too. He's probably waiting for me somewhere along my usual route home. He tried to get me again today." He began to have the futile feeling that the police were not particularly interested. The reply confirmed that feeling.

"We don't do much bodyguarding anymore Mr. Dev—Mr. ah—Breden. We're pretty busy, and there aren't as many cops as there used to be. Automatic alarms take care of protection against burglary and housebreaking. Hypno-questioning has made it pretty difficult for professional crooks, because they find themselves on the suspects' line-up every time there's a crime in the city, and if they did it, they find themselves saying so. There's no profit in the business, and there aren't so many crooks as there used to be. We have things to do, but most cops are college trained specialists. We route the traffic of the city on all levels, on different loads and flow directions at different times of day; we calculate the maximum load limit of each route and how to reroute from it if it breaks down. We keep things moving and keep jams from piling up. We keep people from getting hurt around fires and power failures and broken water mains, things like that. The city is a big machine and we have to know where all the controls and keypoints are, and keep the wheels turning. You see—" he spread his hands—"we just don't have any dumb lug with nothing better to do than guard one single man."

It sounded like a speech he had made often to plaintive citizens. "You see our position?"

Doggedly Mart asked, "But you have some department to investigate shooting, don't you?"

"Of course. We have Homicide and Crimes of Violence

sections—mostly plainclothes investigation." The officer smiled. "No matter how unprofitable it is, people still get mad enough to try to kill each other."

"How do I attract its attention?" Mart asked. "By getting myself killed?"

The officer was amused and patronizing. "Don't worry. If he's as far gone as he sounds from your story we'll probably pick him up tomorrow for taking off his clothes and sitting in the middle of Times Square blowing bubbles. He won't be around long enough to bother you."

Breden remembered Devon's trim appearance, and his pride when apparently he had been sane. He had probably been close to paranoia for a long time, and vanity and surface self-esteem held him back from any conspicuous oddity. Probably he'd be witty and poised to the end, and go to the mental hospital with his sandals shined, his Phi Beta Kappa key impeccably in place and his wristwatch wound, the picture of a sane man being led away by lunatics.

Except for a small obstacle like trying to kill by television, Devon was his choice for the murderer-most-likely-to-succeed. If the police wouldn't protect him, he would have to protect himself.

"I guess I'll buy a gun," he said to the policeman with malicious pleasure. It was legal, but almost unheard of, for a man to carry a weapon for self-defense. Let them have their attention attracted by a gun battle in the streets, if nothing else would do it.

The fattish officer blinked, his smile fading slightly. "This is a crowded town, mister. You can't go shooting guns off in a city, because you'd be mowing down bystanders six to a slug. I can't stop you, but if you're licensed, how about borrowing something from us to shoot at him, something not so dangerous?"

Mart was suddenly interested, remembering the spectacular police weapons in the hands of the screen heroes. He'd been watching them enviously for years. "How about a fizz pistol? I've always wondered if they really work like they do on TV shows—"

"No! Those aren't for civilians. You'd gas crowds at every

shot. You know the penalty for unauthorized use of hypno-drugs—sixty-years-to-life, or even death. If I loaned a hypno-loaded pistol out to a civilian we'd both be behind bars before you were out the door. We can't use them ourselves for questioning without being under bond and having three witnesses and a tape recording of every word." He seemed genuinely upset. Apparently someone in the department had been rated down for the misuse of hypno recently, for he paused and wiped his forehead with a paper handkerchief, and then tried a feeble smile. "No, all I've got for unauthorized types like yourself is a curare automatic. It won't hurt anybody if you handle it carefully. Just aim low; try not to shoot anyone in the eye, huh?"

Mart walked out feeling better able to defend himself. In one pocket was a button push that would put a directional call for help on the radios of patrol wings, and in the other a small flat automatic that threw a hollow bullet filled with a harmless drug of the curare type that made its victim instantaneously limp and unable to move. Two shots would cause unconsciousness, and three, death. He had been warned to shoot for the legs where a puncture would cause little damage, and to stop when one bullet had penetrated.

Back on the subsurface belt conveyers he kept alert for the sight of a slim old man in an iridescent pearl grey suit. He would have to see Devon first or no weapon would help him. . . .

In his apartment he called his parents, or the people whom he had always loved and thought of as his parents. They were retired on one of the Florida Keys. As tactfully as he could, he asked about his birth.

"I'm sorry you found out about that, Marty," said his father over the televiewer. He stood on the screen, tanned and healthy with wrinkles weathered deep into his face. A flaming orange shirt with fluorescent green seagulls flying across his chest put a strain on the screen's color system, and the seagulls wavered from bluer to yellower green as the scanner struggled to approximate its shade. Through a window behind him was visible a view of deep blue sky and white sand. "We thought it might hurt your feelings, if you found out. But I guess you're old enough to know that it doesn't matter."

"Could you tell me who were my real parents?"

"I don't know, Marty—it never seemed important to us. The only one who knew was my brother Ralph—he helped arrange the adoption—but he wouldn't say, except to say that they were good people. He'd promised not to tell, I guess. He was a doctor, and doctors have to keep their secrets."

"No reflection on you, Dad, but I'm curious. I'd like to find out. Could you tell me how to get in touch with Uncle Ralph?"

"Why, he died about two years ago. We mentioned it to you in a letter, but I guess you forgot."

They talked pleasantly about other things for a while, and then he switched off thoughtfully, his problem coming up in his mind. Doctor Ralph Breden had known who his parents were, but he had been dead for two years.

If there was an unknown species of man, what was it doing in Omaha? And if these men traveled among ordinary men, how did they manage to keep their existence a secret? The ability to keep the secret required money, intelligence and organization. And why did they want to stay secret? His imagination drifted toward the idea of a conspiracy again, and he smiled and rejected it. All the tenuous deductions were based on the idea that he was of an alien species, and that was merely an unproven hypothesis. There probably could be some other explanation of his physical peculiarities.

His thoughts were broken by a sound like someone turning the knob of his apartment door. It was locked of course, and it would be no use to anyone to turn it. He finished his shower and dressed hurriedly, scanning the corridor through the door viewplate before stepping out. No intruder was lurking there, and he began to wonder if the sound had been imagination. When he got to the street a feeling of being watched suddenly came with complete conviction. Casually he put his back against the nearest wall and inspected the street, checking each person.

Many people walked by. Some noticed him and glanced at him with the usual disconcerted reaction deepening to suspicion as they noticed his searching eyes, and the tension of his hands in his pockets.

He noticed the change in their expressions and wondered bitterly how little provocation it would take to have them decide he had done something and call the police. Sourly he gave up looking and walked on his way, taking his chances on a bullet. The feeling of being watched continued.

In the airbus waiting room he had a chance to look around without attracting attention to himself and being stared at. People always looked around in waiting rooms, searching for first sight of whoever they were waiting for. His careful inspection of the room went unnoticed. There was no one in evidence who looked like Devon. Apparently Devon was not following him after all.

Mart picked up a newspaper from a mechanical vender. The headlines were much the same as yesterday's. As he flipped toward the back pages an ad in a lower corner caught his eye.

It was a picture of a hand, held out flat, the fingers separated, and it reminded him of his problem. The ad was nondescript, easy to pass without seeing. It could have been selling anything—astrology—palm reading—insurance. "Worried?" the caption read. "Dissatisfied? Seeing. . . ."

People began to stream down from the upper level exits. The airbus had come in. *Worried?* Smiling wryly he folded the newspaper, dropped it into a trash dispenser and watched the draft suck it away into darkness. *Dissatisfied?* Smiling more broadly he went slowly home.

The feeling of being watched was with him again, but he hadn't seen anyone who looked like Devon, and he was beginning to get used to the feeling.

When he stepped into his office the next day the viewer was chiming. He switched it on while taking off his overshirt, and Nadine appeared on the screen. "Hey, the Martians are advertising for you."

"What do you mean?" He took the curare gun and the alarm button the police had given him from his pockets and carefully placed them in a desk drawer.

When he glanced back at the screen she was holding up a magazine with a full-page ad showing a well drawn hand, almost two thirds life size. "Did you see this ad?" It looked like an enlarged replica of the one he had glanced at in the newspaper the day before.

"I noticed it," he admitted. "Didn't read it."

"Notice the hand?"

"Yeah, what's it about? Palm reading?"

"Count the fingers."

The hand was well drawn and looked normal, but this time he didn't have to count. He could see the difference. Six fingers.

This was it. The thing he had been looking for. He wondered how often the ad had run. How many years had he been passing it by? He tried to control the eagerness in his voice. "What does it say? Read it!"

She read clearly. "Restless? Dissatisfied? Seeing dots before your eyes—too many fingers on your hands? Call Wesley C-06320. *We might be what you're looking for.*" She glanced up eagerly. "And at the bottom here it says, 'National Counseling Service, 1862-A Halshire Avenue.' That's right in the city!"

"We can check on it this lunch. Have the time free?"

"I can fit it in. I don't want to miss any of this."

They found that the address on Halshire Avenue was a huge, beautiful white building with a three-story-high webbed-bronze archway opening on exclusive Halshire Place. Recessed inconspicuously into the white stone wall a long way from the main door was a private entrance. It was padded in morocco leather, studded with bronze studs and labeled with a small bronze plate. *National Counseling Service.* Through a porthole window inset in the door they could see a waiting room which was luxurious with the expensive Spartan simplicity of modernistic furniture.

Nadine touched his arm. "Going in?" People passed them in orderly separate streams on the wide green sidewalk. Some glanced at them with faint interest. Some glanced back at him after they had passed, with that expression of puzzlement that he always noticed.

He glanced at his watch. It had taken them fifteen minutes to reach the address, and they both had appointments at one. "No. We have to save a little time for lunch."

A well-dressed man came out, flagged a taxi, and drove away without giving them a glance.

"Martian going to lunch," murmured Nadine.

They ate in a nearby drugstore, sitting at a counter looking at the impassive white stone face of the towering building across the street. The separate entrance was a luxury for which the building must have charged high rent. Apparently the National Counseling Service could afford such expensive whimseys. They ate hastily, considering the implications of what they had seen. The National Counseling Service had money and power, and they were interested in him for some reason. That advertisement was obviously directed at him and others like him. He wondered how many others there were to see the ad.

"Power. . . ." he mused. "A big organization, too. . . ."

Nadine set a sliding pointer on the menu and pushed a button at its base. "We don't know how much space they've taken behind that swank front. Maybe it's just intended to look expensive to frighten off people who are attracted by the ad and genuinely come for counseling." She sipped a malted milk that came out of the automatic mixer and continued thoughtfully. "If I were using a front like that, I think I'd give a little genuine counseling to make it stand up."

She had bought another magazine on the way over, and she began flipping through it as she talked. Pictures in fluorescent inks glowed vividly as she flipped past them. Suddenly a page turned up in cool black and grey, the familiar spread hand. "Here it is!" Nadine flattened the magazine and they looked at it together.

"Puzzled?" He read the black letters, "Discontented? We don't read palms, but we can tell you about yourself—call the National Counseling Service. We find unusual situations for unusual people."

"Now they are threatening you with an unusual situation," Nadine remarked skeptically. They had finished their lunches and it was time to go back to work. "What are you going to do, Mart?" They dropped their meal tabs in the slot and paid the amount the machine rang up. The turnstile yielded and passed them through. They stood on the sidewalk looking at the towering, impassive building across the street.

"Go in and look around, I guess. I'll have to wait till after work. Would you like to come in with me?"

"No." She looked up at him soberly, the sunlight touching

her face in sprinkles of light as it filtered through the elms
overhead. "This looks secret, Mart. They probably wouldn't
tell you anything if you had anyone with you, or even said
you'd confided in anyone about this. I want to hear about it,
but I'd better just spend the time looking some stuff up in the
science and technology room at the library. Call me there
when you find out anything, will you Mart?"

"Right." He made his face solemn and asked, "Date?"

"Date," she smiled. Hurrying together they went down the
belt entrance and back toward the afternoon's work.

IV

FIVE HOURS LATER, with his hand on the bronze knob of
the leather-covered door, he hesitated briefly, looking in
through the small window set in the door. There was still no
one inside the waiting room as far as he could see. Was the
whole organization waiting for him as a trap waits for a
mouse?

Then he thought of Devon, free somewhere, and looking
for him with a gun. He glanced anxiously over his shoulder.
There was only the stream of brightly-clad people, looking
wilted in the dusty late afternoon heat, going wherever people go after work. Women, girls, young men, old men—no one
familiar, but there was no use standing there like a target.
He turned the knob, pushed through the door and was inside.
The door shut after him softly.

As it closed, the sounds of the city dwindled and vanished,
and he was in a sound-proofed silence as still and remote as
the room of a deserted house on some distant hillside.

It was the pine scent that made him think of mountains,
he realized after a moment. A cool drift of air brushed against
his face as if somewhere near there were wide windows open
to a breeze that had come through an evergreen forest.

The waiting room was comfortably darkened, with recessed
lights in the small bookcase, and wide stylized chairs in
polished wood and rough dark green cloth with small adjustable spotlights clamped to the left arm of each chair for easy
reading.

He felt almost hidden standing in the half-dark, and his

tension faded. Under the glass coffee table an indirect light
shone on a lower shelf, glowing on a scattering of varicolored
pamphlets and bound booklets with the name *National Counseling Service* in script on the cover.

The waiting room remained soundless and peaceful. Apparently no one was going to interrupt or ask him why he was
there. Through a small archway he could look down a softly
lighted corridor and see the blank wall where it turned. Breden
sat down and picked up a pamphlet. The back section was
filled by a reassuring collection of honest-looking graphs and
statistics. He turned to the front and stared at the first page.

A single slogan was blazoned across it: SQUARE HOLES
FOR SQUARE PEGS. A small block of print at the bottom,
placed like a footnote, stated, "The National Counseling Service is approved by The American Psychometric Association,
the Association for Corrective Psychotherapy, and works in
co-operation with the Human Engineering Laboratories of
Stevens Institute, Columbia University and the University of
Chicago. We have available on request all personal data of
public, State and Federal psychometric tests already individ-
ually taken."

All the organizations mentioned were of unassailable integ-
rity. Feeling impressed, he turned the page to the next, a
glowing montage of full colored tri-dimensional photographs of
faraway landscapes, and able-looking people working with
unusual machines. Large glowing white letters superimposed
across the middle of the page stated aggressively: WE'LL
TELL YOU WHERE TO GO—AND YOU'LL LIKE IT!

He turned to the next page. It was an exaggerated drawing
of a small nervous man sitting in an electroencephalograph
that was built like an electric chair, with a huge metal head-
piece over his head and wires streaming from it in all directions:—EVEN IF IT'S TO A HOSPITAL TO HAVE YOUR
HEAD EXAMINED.

The outside door opened and a timid woman came in,
looked around hesitantly and then, taking courage from his
example, took a pamphlet, sat down and began to read. There
was nothing visibly unusual about her. Breden began to wonder

if he had merely let himself in for a total psychological check, and a diagnosis of what his abilities best fitted him to do. The six fingered hand could be merely a coincidence, a copywriter's inspiration.

He turned to the next page. On it a man stood triumphantly with his arms flexed, bulging startlingly with muscle, grinning with enthusiasm and radiating health, vigor and vitality in big orange rays: *Our technique* WORKS.

The nonsensical cheer of it was infectious. Someone came in and said, "Doctor Sheers will see you now." Breden looked up with a grin reflecting the grin in the cartoon. The receptionist had apparently spoken to him rather than to the mousy woman, so he rose. "Could I keep this pamphlet?"

"Yes indeed." She smiled professionally as a nurse smiles, warm but distant. "The office is right down the hall."

He followed, still grinning. The receptionist reminded him of Nadine in the incongruity of her pretty face and figure, and her efficient businesslike air. If nothing happened now he'd take his counseling like a man, and have a good laugh with Nadine when he came out.

They turned the blind bend in the corridor and it widened with doors on either hand for thirty feet before making another turn. The receptionist stopped before an open door to let him pass, and then closed it after him as he went in.

He found himself in a mellow, wood-paneled room with the relaxing half-dusk of indirect lighting focused on the shelves of books. Good books with thoughtful titles, and reference books he recognized as old friends, books he had for his own reference in microfilm.

The man who greeted him was spare, with a slight scholarly round-shoulderedness. He came forward and took Breden's hand with confident hospitality. "How do you do. I'm Doctor Sheers, and you're—"

"Paul Breden."

"I'm glad to meet you, Mister Breden," he said, seating himself behind his desk. "Have a chair."

Breden sat down, trying to judge Sheers's face. The diffuse desk light lay in a pool of orange brown on the mahogany and lit up the counselor's face from below with a ruddy light that should have made him satanical, but instead merely made his face look round and childish. He looked at Breden, waiting for him to speak.

"I saw your advertisement," Breden said, "and I was interested. Could you tell me more about it?" He moved his hands, slightly shifting their position. The reading light that was clipped to the chair was focusing diffusely in his lap, spotlighting his hands.

The room's atmosphere of safety and concealment was the result of having one's face in shadow. It was probably very relaxing to the shy, self-conscious misfits, and the hostile types that came in, needing counseling. But the concealment was an illusion, for the counselor could read expressions and reactions in the small unconscious motions and tensions of the spotlighted hands.

He should also be able to notice a deliberate conscious motion made to call his attention, such as Breden had made. Breden waited, wondering if it would mean anything to him.

The counselor's own hands under the desk light were white and large knuckled, with blue lines of veins showing through. They lay there quietly, white and inexpressive, schooled to perfect relaxation.

"What is your profession, Mister Breden?"

"I'm an attorney—my specialty's patent law."

"And what complaint against life attracted you here?" There was a slight smile in his voice, and he interrupted before Breden could reply. "You needn't answer that one. I'm not completely unobservant." He stood up, smiling, and said regretfully, "I would have liked to have given you a few tests and made at least a surface diagnosis. You're an interesting case, and rather well integrated considering the stress. Interesting. . . . But you didn't come for that, and I can't take up your time, of course."

He held out his hand.

With excitement building in him, Breden rose and shook hands. "What you want is right down the hall," the counselor said regretfully. He escorted him to the door and opened it, then reached into a recess of a bookcase shelf and pulled out a box of fig bars. "Here, have a couple of fig bars. You need to fortify your blood sugar. You're probably going to get something of a shock. . . ."

Breden accepted them with an inward smile. Some diagnosis! He was hungry all right. That sandwich for lunch hadn't been enough, and he was growing shaky with so much excitement.

The counselor leaned out from his office and pointed. "Just turn right and keep straight ahead until it stops at a door."

"Right," Breden started off, taking a quick bite from a fig bar.

"And remember, I'd like to diagnose you sometime," the counselor said after him wistfully. "You diploids are always fascinating."

Breden had rounded the turn and was walking along a remarkably long, featureless corridor before the full explosive impact of that struck him. "You diploids!" Then diploids were real; it was not just a gibberish word from Devon's imagination! It meant something! *Diploids*. What in the name of Howling Entropy *was* a diploid?

He wolfed the second fig bar and licked his fingers, walking steadily down a doorless corridor where every step looked just like every other step, like a corridor in a dream. What was a diploid? There was an answer to that question, but it was a joke. *He* was a diploid.

So far, being a diploid was no different from being a Martian.

Ahead, terminating the corridor, was a small door. He felt the floor-level change subtly from one stride to the next and realized that he had just walked out of one building into another. The corridor had been going straight back through the building, and it was longer than the building itself, more than half a block long. The door was closer, just ahead now.

Doctor Sheers was a pleasant man, he thought irrelevantly. Too bad there wasn't time . . . he opened the door and stepped through.

He stepped through into a shock of light. The corridor had been dimmer than he thought. Blinking, he stood still, letting his eyes adjust. To his left a woman was writing at a desk. There was an odd sweetish smell in the air. A form dimly seen moved beside him and the sweetish smell increased and mounted to his brain and swirled there with the thin singing of a dream, and he could not turn or look in the direction of the person moving beside him.

From that direction a voice asked patiently, *"Ever hear of MSKZ?"*

"I read something about it once," answered a voice that sounded like his own.

"Are you a super, or directed by supers?"

"I don't know."

"Never heard of supers, all right. Have you been given hypnotic instruction for any special behavior while here?"

"No."

"Do you intend any damage while here?"

"No."

"Okay." The smell changed to something sharp and acrid, and the figure on the side of his vision moved blurrily, fading back. *"You'll forget this. When you wake, you'll feel and act as if you'd just come in."* The smell was gone, and after some vague time the swirling feeling stopped abruptly.

He'd just stepped into the room. It was lighter than he had expected. He stood blinking, waiting for his eyes to adjust. A woman was writing at a desk on his left. This was another office, but this one was bright and aseptic in white and grey, with the scientific look of a hospital—everything in clean precise squares and angles, with heavy medical books and scientific journals arranged neatly in grey metal shelves. *Medical and Biochemical*, he thought, classifying automatically. He glanced behind him. The door he had come through was flat and inconspicuous beside another door which stood between two banks of open shelves.

It looked like the door to a closet. Secret passage?

The desk was beautiful in grey ruled metal, with the weightless, floating effect of expensive design. A lucite light hose had been pulled out from its wall coil and arched back above the desk, sending down its beam of brilliance like a transparent cobra suspended in the act of striking.

The woman at the desk said, "Just a minute," without looking up, and continued writing for a moment.

Then she looked up. She was middle-aged and small, with an air of restless energy and a thin pointed face with large eyes that her friends would probably call pixy-like. Her gaze was impersonal, her eyes flickering across his face and down to his hands then back to his face again thoughtfully, as if she were making an effort to place an old acquaintance.

"E-2 control." She nodded. "You look like the pure type, too. I didn't think there would be any."

After a second he decided that he had not been mistaken for someone else who would have understood her.

"My name is Breden," he said. "I saw an advertisement."

"Six fingers," she nodded again. "We run that one once a year. It pulled in a few people last year too." She looked at him speculatively again. "The extra eye is recessive. You do have it, don't you?"

Again he mastered the jolt that came with mentioning the thing which he had hidden so long. "Yes," he said, forcing the word out. And then the full implication of what she had said came through. There were others like him. They had seen the advertisement and come to this place before him. And they were important, very important, judging by the expense and secrecy used in locating them. He was the pure type, she had said.

"How old are you?" she asked.

He answered mechanically through the surge of his excitement. "Twenty-eight." Leaning forward, he was unable to conceal his eagerness, and he no longer wanted to. "You mean that there are other people like me? I'm not the only one?"

She leaned back, beginning to smile. Her chair was metal, he saw with one corner of his mind, and cunningly designed metal joints in the chair gave with the motion.

Money, he thought again, automatically fitting facts together. *Inconspicuous swank. This place sells something medical.* Then he thought, in the first touch of rising fear, *This is routine to her. She doesn't treat me as if I were important.*

"The only one?" she repeated. Abruptly the woman laughed. "To put it bluntly—no." Smiling, she reached into a desk drawer and took out a heavy catalogue. He glimpsed the cover, MSKZ LIVE BIOLOGICALS, as she found a place in the thumb tab index and flattened it open, turning it so that he could see what was on the page. A double spread of twenty-four diagramatic chromosomes were spaced across it, like twenty-four vertical strings of black and white beads, each bead numbered and explained in a listing at the bottom. At the upper left of the left page was an insert circle with the photograph of a small curled fetal figure.

Looking up at him with a smile she said, "You might be the only adult copy in existence. Except for that, Mister Breden, you are probably the least unique being in existence." She dropped her hand emphatically on the diagram of numbered chromosomes. "That's your chromosome set right there. At this moment there are probably several hundred thousand identical embryo copies of you from that chromosome set in use in all the genetics, cytology, endocrinology and geriatrics laboratories in the world. *Embryos*—not legally persons—being used as experimental animals, under the premise that they will never be men. In thirty years of use, hundreds of thousands of them have gone down the drain, advancing the knowledge of medicine and genetics immeasurably, and we are prepared to make and sell millions more. You are our diploid standard model E-2."

Smiling with a touch of impishness, she waited for him to speak.

So this was the great secret.

He was a laboratory fetus accidentally grown up to be a human being. A laboratory animal! A million fetal copies of him were being experimented on, damaged, injured and mutilated in the experiments—dissected and casually thrown away as junk at each experiment's end! For a moment he could feel the scalpels and needles in his own flesh, the probes moving in his brain, the hypodermics plunging in deep with germs and poisons. *Flesh of my flesh, blood of my blood . . . a million mangling deaths, and it's what we were designed for legally, not for life. . . .*

The woman still leaned back pleasantly, showing mild friendliness and attention. She had told him cheerfully and without feeling, either not knowing or not caring what the information would do to him. The only emotion that he had seen in her since he entered was intellectual interest—an experimenter, one who experimented on E-2s.

He stood with his hands resting at his sides and let the fury go off inside him like a silent explosion of firecrackers, rockets and pinwheels. When it died down he found himself still standing in the same position, lightly dewed with cold sweat, damp in the palms of his hands and shaking slightly, but he had not moved, and to the woman he could have just looked thoughtful. He had probably changed color, but the artificial lights helped conceal that.

A habit of self-control was a good thing, he thought. It can even carry you through an attack of madness.

"I didn't get the name," he said smoothly, hating the woman's aging pixy face and graying, curly hair. *Why are you doing this?*

"Mirella Sorell."

"Doctor?"

"—of Philosophy—Biochemical." She was smiling slightly.

"Why are you doing this?" His voice seemed to have no connection with himself. It was urbane and polite, as if the question meant nothing.

She was still smiling. The overhead light left her eyes in shadow. "I could have said 'for money,' Mister Breden. That's always considered an honorable and adequate motive for any act. As long as one stays inside the law that answer is enough —no further questions are asked. It's only when one becomes tainted with beliefs or ideals or purposes that one becomes dangerous and an object of suspicion and ridicule and hostility. . . . Is that not so, E-2?"

He took the name stoically, and after a moment realized that by it she had meant a compliment. It indicated that she expected some extra quality of understanding or special insight from him by virtue of his being born to a letter and a number instead of a name. A compliment of a sort, but she had not answered what he wanted to know. He touched his lips with his tongue. "Why are you doing this?"

Sorell made a gesture of deprecation. "I'll tell you this much, Mister Breden—your genes were selected from some of the cream of humanity, the top men and women in atom power and radioactive tracer research, with I.Q.s of one hundred seventy and over. We managed to get our hands on these by taking a government research contract, where the

government wanted to know if the genes of their scientists
who had been exposed to sublethal radiation over long periods
had more recessive lethal mutilations. The sperm and ova we
took to answer the question we kept, and it gave us a good
start in our classified gene bank."

"My abilities, I know about," he said. "Regardless of their
history. What interests me is why these—these—"

"We wanted abnormalities. We needed a good control for
crosses before we could go ahead in any other genetic research.
Your characteristics had to be tagged with slight abnormalities
and mixed racial differences which were plain enough to be
visible in embryo. That way we could see what we were doing
and judge the properties of each outcross into E-2 by watching
the embryo develop and checking the number of E-2 alleles
showing. Once we had the control gene set selected we not
only used it ourselves, but we began to sell it. It has been
priceless in a thousand laboratories. Almost thirty years of
genetics research is based on E-2." She smiled. "We suspected
that some geneticists might be tempted to follow their test
crossbreeds past the embryo stage, even though it's strictly illegal. And they were tempted—obviously. Here *you* are, a
sample of the pure strain, indicating that someone needed
you for a control check on another child."

They had trademarked him with peculiarities simply for
purpose of recognition. He began to wonder if his question had
any meaning. Could they be doing everything she described
for mere scientific curiosity, without purpose, indifferent to the
cost? Or was there some purpose hidden behind her evasions
of his question? He asked, "You have me now—E-2, adult
version. What do you want me for?"

"You could answer some questions first, and take a physical examination. You don't object?" There was a trace of
mockery in her voice, and something quizzical in her expression, almost as if she were interested in his reactions, and ob-
serving them closely.

"Anything you say," he replied with bitterness. How much
of this could he tell Nadine? And what good would it do him
to tell her? Even if other things had not driven her away, this
new knowledge of what he was would certainly do it. *A lab-*

oratory guinea pig. "How much secrecy is there in this business?"

"Very much secrecy," Sorell replied gravely. "We will explain later." She touched a button on her intercom box and switched off her desk light. "I'm leaving for the day, but I'll have someone show you around." She gathered up things from the desk and moved toward the door, adding absently, "There's a diploid meeting going on upstairs. I don't think many of them have left yet. If you can spare the time. . . ."

"I think so," Breden said. He remembered Nadine, waiting at the library for the news, and added, "I can't stay long."

"Long enough to be introduced around, anyway," Sorell said at the door, and as a young man came in she introduced him hastily. "Zal, this is E-2 control standard. Mr. Breden, this is Ea-crossZ, he can explain anything you want to know. If you don't mind, I have to leave now."

Zal shook hands firmly, saying over his shoulder to Sorell as she left, "G'night Mirella." He turned back to Breden. "Glad to meet you," he grinned. "She's a monomaniac. People aren't real to her, they're just carriers for genes. I also have a name, besides a gene file. Zal Elberg."

"Mart Breden," he said, puzzling over an odd familiarity in the young man's appearance. "What's going on upstairs?" he then asked curiously.

"Sort of a party." Zal Elberg was shorter than Breden, but broad in the shoulders. He was handsome with rugged features, slightly slanting blue eyes and dark hair bristling up in a stiff crew cut. He was wearing a defiantly gaudy pink sport shirt. "Come on upstairs and join in. I'll answer your questions like a tourist guide."

V

ON THE WAY UP in the escalator Mart saw that there was something odd about Zal Elberg's hands, and realized suddenly that there had been something odd about the feel of his handshake. Their fingers had meshed. Six fingers.

And the familiarity of Elberg's face—it was like his own, like a brother would look if he had a brother.

While Mart was absorbing the realization and trying to

frame a question about it, they came to the right floor and walked towards the sound of mingled voices. They entered through a half open door into a big room with desks, file cabinets, computers and a standard laboratory work-table with a sink down the middle. It was filled with a mild babble of voices.

Mart's first impression was like a blare of colors; there were so many completely different personalities there, and they were so dissimilar. Most of them were eating sandwiches, drinking beer, and talking with intensity and excitement.

He took a deep breath and looked around more carefully, but his first impression was confirmed. They were all individuals—characters. They all deviated, and they all deviated in different directions, setting off each other's differences by the contrast of their own.

There was a long, drawn-out individual seated cross-legged on a table in a meditative pose listening to a very short individual who was telling a funny story. There was a short chubby girl of about fourteen, with buck teeth and the face of a happy baby, loudly arguing some obscure mathematical point with a short, square, thick-armed young man who looked as if he had a dash of gorilla blood.

In the middle of the room was a lanky young man with a beaked nose that could have been used to slice bread. His hair was too long, and he sat on a stool quietly reading a magazine, eating a sandwich, and swizzling from a bottle of beer. Two doll-like children on short stools drank milk and root beer and talked excitedly in shrill fluting voices about the Doppler effect.

Somehow this wasn't what he had expected.

"These are diploids?"

"Sure."

"But," he hesitated. He had expected that they would all look something like him or Zal, but the expectation suddenly seemed foolish. "Then what the blue blazes are diploids?"

Zal grinned and stepped forward to tap the lanky fellow on the shoulder. "Plink Plunk, what's a diploid? E-2 wants to know."

"Please," said the one addressed, putting down his beer bottle and turning his beaked face to them with slow dignity.

"The name is Max P. Planck, or Planck-Planck, if you prefer, and the answer is *I'm* a diploid. Who did you say wants to know?"

"E-2 control standard," Zal said, reaching up and putting a hand on Mart's shoulder. "He's just come in."

The thin one offered his hand gravely. "I'm glad you found us. Do you know that E-2 has been the anchor to windward of an entire generation of biological research? The world owes the E-2 set a great deal. What's your real name, by the way?"

"Mart—er—Paul Breden."

"Mine is really Max Planck-Planck, but these discourteous characters have no concept of dignity." He indicated Zal. "They call me Plink Plunk, or Plunk Plink or Plunk-Plunk. What have you been called?"

"Martian."

The skinny young man made a slight bend of the shoulders that implied a bow. "Thank you, Mr. Breden. I take it, being a newcomer, that you are eager for an explanation." He glanced at Zal. "Mister Elberg, would you see that our guest is properly provided for?"

"Sure. Swiss with white or rye?" Zal asked Breden. "Beer or ale?"

The sight of the food around him had set his stomach gnawing at itself for minutes.

"Ale," he said gratefully. "Swiss on white."

"Right away," said Zal and went off toward a big white refrigerator. Planck-Planck continued.

"Although I do not work with MSKZ I am almost uniquely provided among diploids to explain the process of diploiding. The others being kept in the dark as to their individual inheritance, to avoid any influence of expectation on their behavior, I am one of the few fully able to explain precisely my own origins."

Nearby, the two children of doll-like incredible beauty were now arguing dogmatically about the latest stellar evolution theory, and Max Planck-Planck raised his voice slightly to compensate. "I'm the only one who thus has his proper name, and these buffoons are jealous."

Zal returned with a cold plastibottle of ale and two sandwiches. He set them down on the laboratory table beside them.

Breden remembered what he had read of the great mathematician and physicist. "Are you related to Max Planck?" he asked with respect, peeling the pliofilm shell from his sandwich.

"Closely," said the skinny young man with precision, hitching himself around in his stool and closing his hand on the neck of his beer bottle. "He's the one person that I am related to. To be exact, I represent half of his chromosome set, doubled up to a full set, so that some of his characteristics I have in double strength, and others, dominant genes which shaped him, I don't have at all, just the other of the gene pair, doubled in me so that it comes out, while it was just an unused recessive for him. MSKZ was probably trying to double the genius genes and get a double genius, but my friends say that obviously they doubled the wrong half."

He paused and took a thoughtful swallow from the bottle. "The number of different people with different combinations of traits you can get from one man's genes, after nature has done its job of haploiding—randomly selecting one set of twenty-four, from two sets of twenty-four—is, I think, factorial twenty-four, or twenty-four times twenty-three times twenty-two and so on. It comes to some incredible number. I can't say precisely because I'm no mathematician; I'm a musician. *She* could tell you." He indicated the plump, baby-faced girl who was still discussing something incomprehensibly mathematical with the gorilla-like young man. "I suspect that May, there, is another diploid Planck set. I think she represents the opposite half set, allowing for embryo mortality to weed out the doubled lethals. I think she is probably the Hyde to my Jekyll. Neither of us look at all like Max Planck." He waved a hand from her to himself. "Can you explain why one of us is fat and the other thin?"

Breden thought of suggesting that she might eat more, but decided that it was a remark inappropriate to an academic discussion of heredity. He found himself liking the courtly, ugly young man he was talking with, and possessed of a strong desire to call him Plunk Plunk.

The gorilla-like young man and the girl who was probably a sister of Max Planck-Planck were now engaged in detaching

the two little children from their root beer bottles and their
argument and herding them toward the door, still arguing.
"Aw, that's not right." "It is too!" Seen in motion they were
even more unreally pretty, a Hollywood idealization of children.

"Who are those kids?" Breden indicated them as they went
out.

"Sales Package," Zal answered for Planck-Planck. "They're
for people who want beautiful children. Will Your Child Be a
TV Star? If the customers have no brains of their own that's
all they'll want, but brains and health and all the mutant im-
provements we can collect from all the populations of the
world will be in the same package. We'll need a wide selection
of different kinds of beauty to have sets that will closely match
the purchasers. The customers won't mind that they have quiz
kids, as long as they are born naturally to Momma and look
like Momma or Papa and are pretty enough to compete with
movie kids. They'll think of them as their own kids and be
flattered by any extra abilities that are thrown into the bar-
gain. Trouble is, beauty is something we can't check in embryo
to see how the crosses come out. It will take fifty more years.
We'll need plenty more test kids like Em and Ben before we
can advertise."

"These scientist characters work themselves like Simon Le-
gree worked Uncle Tom," commented Planck-Planck. "Fifty
more years of work he mentions like planning a weekend. My
work plans extend to the age of thirty when I shall retire to a
hammock and fiddle or compose music in a recumbent position. All this work, and for what?"

"For supermen," Zal said in a very low voice, so that
Breden barely heard him. The word was a shock, although
he had been touching the edges of the idea for days. It sounded
like something for the far future, not to be casually mentioned
as a project.

"Supermen we have," Planck-Planck said mildly. "At least
that is what the supers claim to be, and so far they . . . ."

Zal interrupted, speaking to Breden hurriedly. "Would you
like to meet another fourth of MSKZ?"

Breden felt a surge of hostility. MSKZ had him in its cata-
logues. MSKZ sold gene duplicates of him for experimental

purposes. "That's rather a large order," he said casually, concealing his resentment. "I haven't time to meet the whole organization. It's . . . ."

Zal laughed. "It's not an *it*, it's a *them*. MSKZ are the initials of the team that runs MSKZ. You've met Sorell. She's S." He indicated a man sitting on the other side of the room. "That's K over there—Keith. He's in town this week. I'll introduce you to him."

The pale blond man sitting across the room had been easy to ignore, but now that he had been pointed out Breden could see that he was not a diploid. He was too normal, and he lacked some extra charge of vitality that made the others relatively conspicuous. When they walked over he looked up inquiringly, and Breden saw that he was greying and considerably older than anyone in the room. The diploids were all young.

"Mart," said Zal, "I want you to meet Anson Keith, one of the guys responsible for this outfit being started. Responsible for you being here, too." He put his hand on Breden's arm. "And Keith," Zal continued, "I want you to meet Mart Breden. He's the first E-2 to show up."

Keith rose to shake hands. He was big and thick-boned, the kind built to carry muscle and fat, but there wasn't any fat on him, and not much muscle. His hand was bony in Breden's hand—he was thin in the same way Sorell had been thin, wasted out in the fires of too much work without enough food or rest, with enthusiasm giving a life and energy to his face that denied its lines. "E-2, are you?" Interest shone in his eyes, and he pulled a note pad and pencil from his pocket with a practiced motion. "Do you have wisdom teeth?"

Another person to whom he was just E-2. Breden smiled faintly. "No." Another diploid, a tall sturdy girl, entered the room through a swinging bookcase that was evidently a secret door, and sat down quietly with a magazine and a sandwich. Breden was not surprised by the door. It fitted with the signs of secrecy that he had observed, and with the way Zal had just interrupted Planck-Planck to prevent him from giving some information that had to do with the incredible word— supermen. There is something obviously undercover about the organization of MSKZ, and something illegal about its activities.

"Good. We hoped you might have that allele." Smiling, Keith made a note. "It had been one chance in four. I'm glad you came in. You settled something we were in doubt about with the E-2 set. We can follow up that line now. Any dental work ever needed?"

"No." Breden found himself hating the greying blond man, hating his normal Caucasian face, his narrow five-digited hands and his evident intelligence, just as he had hated Mirella Sorell. He hated them as a chess pawn would hate the players who moved the pawns. He was just an experiment with a number to them. As a long range result of their experiment he had lost Nadine—lost any chance of any kind of marriage. They had done it by making a freak of him.

Keith made a note. "That seems to be hopeful. There's a faint probability that one of the E line got a gene for self-repairing teeth in the shuffle. We couldn't check that in embryo, and even if your teeth continue in good shape we can't be sure it isn't coincidence unless one of them is knocked out and we see whether it grows back in."

"I'll have someone knock one out for you," Breden said without expression.

Looking at him more sharply, Keith folded his notebook and put it away. "Is there something I could do for you—something you might like to discuss?"

He had decided what he would do. Mart Breden took a deep breath and said softly, "I'd like to know what is there in your program that justifies my being born with an extra astigmatic eye? It seems to me I owe you nothing for that. Life itself is a meaningless gift, for no one misses life when it is not given. It's the quality of life that's important, and for that *you* were responsible. But you don't acknowledge your responsibility. You don't ask what your distortions may have cost me, or what I may have lost by them."

Breden had always angered slowly; he was angering now. "If your routine plans had their way, the geneticist who incubated me—supposedly for his experiments—would have sent me the usual way of the scalpel and the ashcan. I don't owe you anything for that either. Oh yes, I accidentally escape the ashcan, and so you greet me cheerfully and ask about the condition of my teeth, inquiring in effect what more I can do for you." Although he kept his voice at conversational pitch the words were intense, and, as Keith listened, Breden got the impression that everyone in the room was listening, keeping up their previous activities and conversation without change, but bending an interested ear to the remarks the newcomer was making to Keith.

"Do any of these experiments—" he indicated those in the room—"who are taken in by this good-of-humanity mish-mash actually owe you anything?"

Zal, leaning against a table reading a technical journal said, "Diploids of the world, arise." He turned a page blandly. "Go on, Mart."

"For the sake of the future of mankind—" Keith began mildly.

"Propaganda! Does the white rat owe any duty to mankind because he is the subject of experiments? No; he owes duty to his own kind—to humanity he owes only hatred, because he is being used and sacrificed by humanity. An enemy."

He had maneuvered himself back against the bank of filing cabinets and he could feel the reassuring weight of the curare gun in his pocket. The gun which was also a radio signal mechanism to call the police if it were fired. The police would probably be very interested in secret doors and whatever lay beyond them. "You know," he said, suddenly mild, "I could cause you people a lot of trouble."

There was a vague kind of motion in the room, a slight reshifting of positions so that there were more people between him and the door, though they still were not looking at him. Zal glanced around and suddenly laid down his magazine, his expression changing.

Keith sat down, seeming politely attentive, his expression a mask hiding his thoughts. "I find your viewpoint interesting, Mr. Breden. Other people have tried to convince me to see things in that light before, but not quite so rapidly as you seem to have arrived at your conclusions. Would you say you have chosen sides, then?" The urbanity was not natural to the man; it was camouflaging something else.

Very clearly, speaking to Breden alone, Zal said, "Mart,

look; this isn't good. You're going off half cocked. You're in some kind of bad mood." His voice was low, but the repressed urgency of his tone made what he meant as emphatic as a shout. "Before you do anything, how about going out and walking it off? You're not thinking clearly right now."

As he became aware of it, Mart could hear the pulse pounding in his ears and the stiff tension of his hands, the way he had been leaning forward on the balls of his feet unconsciously in anticipation and hope that someone would attack him. What he wanted was a good stupid old-fashioned brawl. He wanted to work off his rage and pain against something tangible. He had been talking through a fog of hatred for what seemed like hours, like a drunk precariously giving the impression that he was sober.

"We can talk it over later," Zal said softly, watching him with eyes that had doubtless seen similar expressions in the mirror on his own similar face. Keith watched the two of them without remark or motion.

With an effort of decision Breden pulled his hand stiffly from his pocket and relaxed. "I have an appointment," he apologized to Keith.

To Zal he muttered, "See you sometime." People between him and the door hesitated briefly as he walked toward them, and for a moment he hoped they would try to stop him. His hands clenched, but there was no sound from Keith and his fellow diploids stepped aside.

VI

Now HE WAS OUTSIDE, still walking in his private fog. *Nadine,* he thought. Then in an ironical flash that seemed to come from some separate place in himself that didn't ache like the rest, *You're in love, brother.*

Judging by the way it felt, people in love should be locked up to beat their heads against white padded walls until the fit passed. There was a tiny element of doubt that made it worse, for that meant he would have to force her to say it herself. Being sure what her reaction would be wasn't enough; he would have to hear it.

Then he was in a televiewer booth with Nadine looking at

him, close, very close, but nothing, but only a picture with the
hard touch of glass. She was far away in the library, out of
reach. "Are you all right, Mart? It was bad news, wasn't it."

He didn't speak for a moment, looking at her; then he said,
"Secret."

"Secret," she repeated, with a small motion of crossing her
heart. It was a promise not to tell.

"I'm some sort of a lousy genetics experiment," he said
bluntly. "Not even anything special, just a test run." He
looked at the screen image of Nadine—the beautiful hair and
eyes, the slim five-fingered hands, the notebook and library
cards she was carrying, the cards scrawled on in larger, more
irregular letters than usual, her hair slightly mussed on top
from a habit she had of running her fingers into it when
nervous. Signs of waiting. "Don't wait for me when you get
through, Nadine, go on home."

"Is it hereditary?" The picture looked at him. It was hard
to tell with a picture, but it looked white, and it looked as if
it might be crying.

"It's hereditary."

Then it seemed they were going to switch off, and suddenly
he had to know, he had to be sure.

"Nade, would you marry a three-eyed freak, a lousy laboratory experiment?"

Her voice came controlled and dead-sounding. "No, Mart, I
wouldn't."

Then both screens were blank and he sat in the dark televiewer booth, trying to remember who had hung up first. "See
you," he said absently, but the connection was cut and she
could not hear him now.

"I'd marry for children." Had she said that? She had said
it once in a discussion of something else several months ago,
and he could hear her voice as if she had just said it. "I'm
sorry for myself, Mart, losing you." That was a good thing
to have said, he hoped that she had really said it.

Numbly, Mart Breden left the televiewer booth and began to
walk. He walked carefully, balancing his numbness and trying
not to disturb it, as a man would carry a fragile vase. Whatever his feelings were, he would feel them later; for now, for
the moment, he had no emotions. He could see the things

around him very clearly—buildings, sidewalk, people, trees—
and he could think with an odd effect of being distant from
himself, seeing the point of view of Keith and Sorell. MSKZ
Biologicals.

Scientists are not trained to consider individuals. Their
philosophy and practice included a daily practice of inflicting
small immediate losses to win long range large gains. The
MSKZ team of biologists, when they had added a line of ster-
eotyped human fetuses to their selection of standardized stereo-
typed laboratory animals, had probably done so with the full
expectation that some of them would be carried illegally to
term in the incubators by purchasers, and birthed as physical
misfits into a world of people differently shaped from themselves. The results in psychological loss could easily have been
predicted, and probably was something the biologists took into
account and disregarded as not particularly important. . . .

Traffic hummed in the sky over the skyscrapers, circling
in changing interweaving patterns as radar control patterns
changed with the gradually diminishing load, and the com-
muters' 'copters streamed away from the city. The sky had
darkened to a transparent deep blue, and the street lights were
beginning to glow. A little way behind him a man in a gray
overcape was walking almost in step with him, but Mart ignored him and walked blindly, trying to keep himself walking
away from the thing that had happened to him. Hating was no
good as a solution, and letting it hurt was no good either. He
had to think, to grasp and understand it as a pattern of
events that was natural, something that was inevitable and had
to be—before he could let himself feel.

He had to keep thinking, asking logical questions. What
had Sorell said was the reason for them giving the E-2s the
extra eye?

There were few pedestrians now, and only one convertible
air-ground car parked on the block between himself and the
door to MSKZ. It was a business section without restaurants,
and so always almost totally deserted during the dinner hours.

As he came opposite the parked car he saw that there were
some people sitting in it, and simultaneously a hand touched
his arm. "Are you sure you want to go back to MSKZ?"

Breden turned. He had assumed indifferently that the follower was some arrangement of MSKZ, but now this stranger's presence became something that rang along his nerves like the clangor of an alarm bell. The presence of the follower implied that MSKZ and the National Counseling Service had enemies to whom their secret purposes were known and familiar, enemies as secretive as their own hidden goals.

The man insisted. "You shouldn't go in there without knowing something about it." Out of the sides of his eyes Mart could see the black air-road convertible at the curb. Inside, shrouded in the half darkness, was the pale blur of two faces and the twin small glows of cigarettes.

Waiting for me, thought Mart. The follower had waited and had not spoken to him until they were both opposite the car. A quick silent shot from an illegal hypno-gun and a quick ordering of him into the car—and then what? Why should anything of the sort happen? His only known enemy was a lunatic inventor who had singled him out as the source of his demented persecution. A madman who thought he was either a Martian or a diploid.

But he was a diploid! Did that make a target of him in some way he couldn't conceive? Was the mere fact of his existence a provocation for murder? Why hadn't Keith explained this and warned him? Mart measured the distance to the door of MSKZ and considered the amount of time it would take the man beside him to free a hypno-gun from under his cape. There was time enough if he ran. But running would be ridiculous; you don't run from a surmise. And pulling out his curare pistol, or pushing the buttonpush that would summon the police, would seem equally ridiculous to rational outsiders.

"If you could give us a few minutes—" a tense voice interrupted his thoughts— "you could find out what we have to say," the man continued, watching his face as if looking for hesitation. "There are things about MSKZ you should know."

He was a small man, with sharply cut features, and the skin was tight over the bones of his face as if he were in fear, holding in check a great fear of the door labeled MSKZ BIOLOGICAL SUPPLIES. Looking at Mart's hesitation, he smiled, and his face changed and seemed younger, until he seemed less than twenty, perhaps a kid who had learned to pass as an adult. He held out his hand.

"My name is John Eskhart." The smile seemed friendly and eager.

Beginning an answering smile Mart grasped the extended hand.

And felt the needle with its hypnotic contents sink into his palm.

He had about five seconds before the hypnotic would return in the circulating blood from his arm and reach his brain. He reached for his pocket to push the button in the radio signaler and summon the police. John Eskhart gripped his arm and stopped the motion. The man was small and light, but the full weight of even a small person clinging to his arm would make it impossible to get his hand into his pocket. With a sudden yank Mart pulled free and ran for the doorway of MSKZ. There were only a few seconds left.

There was no sound of anyone running after him, but when he was ten feet from the door John Eskhart's voice reached him very clearly.

"There's no hurry. You don't have to go in just yet."

No hurry. He found himself slowing as he reached for the door. *No hurry . . . don't have to go in. . . ."* He hesitated, trying to remember why he had been hurrying.

Behind him Eskhart's voice said, "You do want to find out what we can tell you about MSKZ before you go in there. Don't fight it, man, we're friends."

Friends. He could have laughed at that, but then as the hypnotic swirled darkly up into his mind, he believed, and turned to walk back. They held the car door open for him. . . .

The only thing of which he was conscious was a voice, or was it several voices?

"No human could genuinely love you. People who said they loved you were pretending. Your parents. . . ."

"No." He tried to pull away from the awful words, knowing they were not true, but they came into his mind in a steady flow, each sentence with its own burning belief and pain.

"Only your own kind, only those of the diploids who have not been misled to favor humanity can be your friends."

"No," he thought, but the ideas burnt their way in. He tried to wake up, to escape from the voice, but it came remorselessly.

"Compared to average humanity you are a freak. You are only at home among your own kind. The friends you have had were not your friends."

Nade . . . no. He struggled to pull himself up out of the dream, and suddenly there was the sight of a gray ceiling and a male arm. He had succeeded in opening his eyes. He lay looking at the ceiling, victorious, but oddly without any wish to look around.

"He learns resistance to drugs like learning to recite 'Mary Had A Little Lamb,'" said a voice disgustedly. It sounded like the same voice, but this time it was a real voice, outside of him, and not a voice in his mind.

"Okay, switch to octo-hypno and take him down again. It's a good thing we blacklisted the E strain—I never would have believed it without seeing this." It was another person, but this voice sounded like the other, like the man or youth who had called himself John Eskhart.

"We can't have these recalcitrants and immunes—they're dangerous."

"Diploids must control." These voices were younger, but still alike.

"He's a diploid too. You mean supers must control."

"You two are talking like hypno indoctrination formulas." This was an older voice. "*You* don't have to take that literally. Words are just words. We follow what we feel."

Obligingly Mart held still for an injection, feeling friendly and tolerant, because these were his friends. As his senses ebbed again, he wondered of what famous man all these John Eskharts were the diploid descendants. These anti-MSKZ diploids had called themselves "supers" in his hearing, but even as supers, what would they do with this "control" if they had it? Who could genuinely control any part of such a jumble of events? An image of Nade, her face flushed and earnest, leaning forward with her hands planted on his desk. "*If all the political experts, intellectuals, economists, sociologists, and general geniuses who ought to know how to run things better— plus all their brains, success, money, and positions of power can't get control of what's going on—*"

"Package of Jello—" he murmured to himself, smiling. Then he felt an inexplicable wave of loss and desolation, and escaped from it into the drugged darkness.

MSKZ BIOLOGICAL SUPPLIES said the lettering on the door. It was much later in the evening, about nine-thirty, and he was hungry again, but before eating there were important things he had to do for the supers and for himself. Some time during the evening he would use his curare pistol, and some time during the evening he would use the button push in his pocket to call the police. It would have to be done with a careful timing that was vague to him now.

But he knew he would remember when the time came.

The door was unlocked and there was a light in the hall. He wedged a matchbook cover into the lock to make sure it would stay unlocked and left the door slightly ajar for *someone* who would be following. Then he switched on the escalator and went up to the second floor, where he could hear the distant sound of conversation.

There were fewer people than before, and the conversation had grown more subdued. Breden looked around and was suddenly let down from a tenseness he had not recognized in himself. He had been ready to do something in connection with Keith being there. What it was, he did not know.

The fluorescent pink shirt drew his eye to where Zal was holding forth to Planck-Planck and the tall heavy girl who had come in through the secret door when he was last there. Zal was explaining, gesturing occasionally with a technical magazine he had clutched in one hand. "Or, better yet, a small operation on the father will replace his sperm manufacturing tissue with our own improved gene-carrying substitute, and permit him to take care of fertilization in his own way. A rather more complicated operation will do the same for a woman." He added regretfully, "We need to make it all easier than that before we can sell on a large scale. These operations are too expensive, and people are generally afraid of operations anyhow."

Zal grinned at him as he approached. "Hello Mart, how'd it go?"

"I cooled off," Breden said, smiling briefly. He liked this

husky slant-eyed kid who looked like him. But he had to appear ignorant and innocent, as if he had not learned things and chosen sides against MSKZ while he was gone. "By the way, Zal, what's the secret door for?"

"For ourselves." Zal waved at it casually. "We just like to have it handy. It leads to a secret room where we keep things we don't want stolen, and work on gadgets we don't want made public. We need defenses, and we don't want to broadcast the fact or get the police in on it."

"Defenses against what?" Asking the question he realized that he did not know much of the answer. He knew which side he was on, but the reason for the fight. . . . MSKZ was run by the team of MSKZ, biologists—human, non-diploid human, and for some reason they opposed direct action by diploids who were interested in some kind of political activity. It was all vague and sketchy, though he could have sworn the details had been explained to him and he had been persuaded by logic.

"Some of our diploid geniuses go a little wild. They go all out for being supermen with a capital S and want to conquer the world—manufacture a million type copies of themselves for an army." Zal grinned at Breden with some friendly mockery in his expression. "There must be a lot of pleasure in the idea of shaking hands with yourself and forming a mutual admiration society, huh?"

"A lot of pleasure," Breden agreed gravely. Brothers closer than brothers, fellowship and understanding to end the loneliness of being different and separate and unable to join wholeheartedly with the people around you. Loneliness can become so basic that a whole personality is built on it. Who would know better than a diploid?

Of all mankind, only MSKZ had the power to make duplicates.

Soberly Zal said, "Diploiding as a process brings out all kinds of hidden hereditary weaknesses in the strain. We can weed out the physical defects by spotting them in the embryo, but we can't see the mental defects until the child is born. Some of our incross geniuses have turned out sort of nuts. They've organized together in a separate faction, and they've tried to steal their egg files from the gene bank a couple of times, and they tried to take the MSKZ team once when all four of them were here, to hold them hostage until the organization produced and birthed a half army of baby duplicates and found homes for them at random."

Breden blinked, reconsidering the last casual statement. "What help could they get from babies?"

Zal nodded, "No help at first. But we can't kill off babies, once they are developed, and babies grow up. The chances are good that every one would grow up just like his adult proto-type—a genius. But from the strictly humanoid point of view, more than half crazy, with drives completely tangent to the main line of human ambition, born enemies to everything that's human. For them it's a straight-out issue of dominate or be dominated. They'd make an army all right." The other two were listening soberly to this recital of a situation they all knew. They looked grave and thoughtful, as if they foresaw danger and possible defeat. Zal went on seriously:

"It's been something of a private war between us. We fight each other quietly with hypnosis and gadgets that won't attract police attention. Both factions have invented some good gadgets, too. It's not a big war, but it's serious enough. If the public ever got wind of any of this, all hell would break loose. And if the renegades were to get hold of Self Perfection, they could plant their own type copies on a million women, to be born normally instead of incubated, and the country would be swamped with them."

Breden remembered a similarity of voices he had heard somewhere recently, and his curiosity about them. "Are many of the supers the same type copy. I mean, from the same person?"

VII

THERE WAS NO DOUBT in Breden's mind that he was for the supers and would help them as much as he could, but he needed to know something about them. It had to seem like a casual question.

Zal did not seem to have noticed anything different about his manner. He answered slowly, "Let's see. . . Keith and Mac don't spill much. We don't know our own eggs, generally, but Keith told me something about this line when it started making trouble. He needed a good, healthy outcross to mix in, because most of the star genius lines have traditionally moved around the world so much and outcrossed so much that there hasn't been any inbreeding in their background which would weed out the accumulation of lethal recessives, so diploiding shows up too much physical weakness. For the cross, Keith scouted around and picked up a batch of gamete-producing tissue from a healthy inbred high I. Q. family from one of those inbred southern small towns that get into the sex and scandal novels. The crossing strengthened the other strains, but those kids mostly grew up with an odd personality, all misfits the same way, not liking anybody but each other. Their organization has pulled in other misfits, but the kids of the F line of crosses have been the nucleus and center of it. That southern family strain personality was as dominant as the Hapsburg lip."

"Probably," commented Planck-Planck, "the reason why the town had been inbreeding and staying to itself. All a bullheaded lot who don't like strangers and won't marry anyone but cousins."

Breden glanced at a catalogue lying open on the table. "*MSKZ original house for genetic identicals since 1968. If you need precise standardized animal reactions for comparison experiments, and are dissatisfied with the variability of ordinary inbred animals, we can accept any special strain of experimental animal you find suitable, and from it provide you with two strains of genetically homogeneous males and genetically homogeneous females, one or more of each, all of whose progeny will be genetically identical male twins. You can breed them to any quantity you require.*" There was a repeating frieze of tiny identical rabbits bordering the page. Breden remembered the page with the curled embryonic figure that was E-2 . . . *experimental animals.* . . .

He shut the catalogue hastily.

"When is Keith coming back?"

Zal was still talking. "Naturally Keith discontinued the F strain and started looking for another for a base. That's what started most of the fighting. They want MSKZ to make more of the F type crosses like themselves, and we won't."

Planck-Planck said, "Frankly, if this is the way superhumanity is going to behave, I don't see that the world of the future will be any calmer than the world of the present."

"Who wants calm?" Zal observed.

"*Superman*," Mart said, as though he had not heard. The word still sounded fantastic. "I thought only the supers used that word."

"Oh, we use it too. It's just that we're not so looping superior about it." Planck-Planck glanced down at his skinny length with a wry smile. "I'm a superman—you're a superman, anyone over I. Q. of 140 is enough of a superman to do in a pinch. They're using Wallace corn technique in breeding. Incrosses are always frail and idiosyncratic compared to what comes next. If you want what you would call supermen, just let MSKZ go along selecting the cream of the world's health and ability and incrossing—diploiding them—letting selection weed out weakness—and see what happens when they start combining what's left into outcrosses."

Zal made a mystic sign of propitiation to luck. "That's my job," he breathed reverently. "Keep your fingers crossed; we've already started. In fact, we have some kids adopted out. Brother, the F strain outcrosses haven't a chance! If they can't figure a way to capture or stop MSKZ now, they'll be calling themselves subs."

The tall heavy girl came in the front door and set a large plastic container with a spigot on the table beside them. "Hot coffee," she announced to the room. "Anyone who wants it, come ladle it out."

"Look," Mart said, trying to get the attention of the two friendly halfwits as they reached for coffee. "Could you tell me when Keith is coming back? Someone was supposed to give me an examination."

Somewhere in the room behind him Keith said distinctly, "Ahem." He was standing near the secret door, and looked as if he had been standing there for some time. "I am examining you, Mr. Breden." He smiled slightly. "You move like a

dancer—you seem to have more vitality than anyone here. Is it
something you learned how to do? Self-training?"

Mart hesitated, trying to understand the question of the
tall man with pale hair who should have known him in advance as the E-2 pattern. Keith read his hesitation, and
stopped moving in the midst of reaching for a coffee cup.

"Man, do you mean to say that you are genuinely not
crippled? That all those structural abnormalities *work*? I expected some kind of physical and mental wreck. The kind of
topblowing you were doing in here earlier was about what I
expected psychologically, but Doctor Sheers reported that you
were more stable than I am, friendly and accessible even with
all that included rejection stress." He drew himself some coffee
and walked over to his desk to sit down. "And Mirella reports
that you were hellishly poised. What's the trick, man? Nothing
should have been strong about you but those teeth, and here
you are back gabbing with my zoo, healthy as a gorilla and
more sure of yourself than I am."

"I'm only poised from five to nine and alternate weekends."
Mart allowed himself a slight grin. He couldn't afford to like
Keith—Keith was the enemy—but it was getting difficult not
to. "I'm only friendly on hours whose names begin with T." It
was time. Abruptly he walked over to the wall and put his
back against the filing cabinets. He raised his voice. *"Nobody
can leave the room."* He took the curare gun out of his pocket
and leveled it at Keith.

"I've already chosen sides," he explained boldly to the
suddenly silent room. "I chose the supers."

"Oye!" Zal clapped himself on the forehead exclaiming in
an undertone. "I let him go out alone and the supers got him!"
There was dismay behind the joke.

Mart smiled at that. Someone moved stealthily, and he
swung the curare pistol a little towards him, saying clearly,
"I would like to point out that if I find it necessary to fire, a
radio signal from the gun will bring the police. Don't forget
that there are laws against human experimenting. The Anti-
Vivisection League would carry the case to court and stand
guard over all the post-five-month embryos to see that they are
birthed when they come to term. That would give me fifty

duplicates or so." He smiled around the room at unsmiling faces.

"You'd destroy all of MSKZ for a lousy fifty replicas?" asked the gorilla-like young man who had not previously spoken to him. He was angry. "What would you do with them when you had them, play ring-around-the-rosey?"

In Breden's pocket the button push that would call the police was growing slippery from contact with the fingers of his left hand. He was trying to push it, but something seemed to be holding his tensed hand back from completing the motion.

Planck-Planck hiked himself gangling up on the edge of a table facing him. "We can talk it over. You want to give MSKZ unfavorable publicity in order to have your replicas birthed. You have decided that MSKZ owes you something, and you want to take it out in replicas, right?"

That wasn't what he wanted. Breden hesitated. What did he want? He remembered Nadine again. He had lost her. There was nothing like knowing the truth, even if knowing it never helped. "Mister Planck-Planck," he said coldly, "I don't need a reason, I'm just expressing my feelings. Somebody owes me something for making me a freak, and if I don't take it out in replicas, I'll take it out in hide." If only someone would attack him, he thought wistfully; if only he had an excuse for hitting someone, preferably Keith. He made another try at pushing the button and this time succeeded.

With an odd mingling of satisfaction and depression he realized that he had called the police. If he didn't let them shut the secret door, if he made them remain to be questioned, MSKZ as an organization was dead. And then he knew that the whole thing was unreal. Something else was going to happen. The door to the hall, the door downstairs that opened to the darkened street both stood ajar, open and waiting. For . . . he found his finger too tense on the trigger and relaxed it, turning the gun carefully away from Keith's face.

The members of MSKZ and the diploids did not know that he had sent a call signal.

Zal was saying seriously, "Don't argue with him. Can't you see that he's been hypnoed?"

"He can't be, Zal. The supers' wouldn't have him calling

the police; not if they hypnoed him. The police hypno questioning would be too likely to show up what they had done to him, and you know there's a penalty in the anti-hypnotic law for making people catspaws. They have more to lose by it than we have."

"If he's catspaw for them, they don't have to give him the inside dope on what he's doing. Any story will do." Zal turned to him. "Mart, as a favor, could you tell me where you went between six and nine?"

"I was met by some supers," he answered, feeling that he was breaking some obscure instructions in answering, yet easily able to do it. "They persuaded me to enlist on their side."

"How much did they tell you? Can you remember what arguments they used to persuade you?" Zal was earnest, leaning forward with interest.

He hesitated, a vast confusion flooding into his mind and subsiding again. He had been sure he had discussed the subject with the supers for a long time and been informed and chosen his own side reasonably, but— "I can't remember any specific arguments." The supers were still his friends and these were his enemies, but it was better to know the facts.

"He was hypnoed," Planck-Planck said. "That makes him completely unpredictable. We don't know what he's standing here with his gun for, because he doesn't either. Not only do we have to look after ourselves now, but we have to look after him."

"You're probably quite right," said Breden, suddenly liking him without caring which side he was on. There was an odd stir in the room. Planck-Planck looked at him directly and keenly, without stirring. "Mister Breden, you know that people with post hypnotic commands on them are also commanded to forget what has been done to them. You are not supposed to be able to admit that you can't remember, and you are definitely not supposed to recognize any possibility that you have been influenced to do what you are doing. How do you account for your own behavior?"

Breden remembered something. It was a disturbing memory, but the sound of the words was quite clear. "They said I learned resistance to drugs like learning a nursery rhyme." He found the gun muzzle was pointing at Keith's face again and shifted it, remembering the police warning not to shoot any-one in the eye. His gun hand was growing tense, and there was a feeling of instructions he was about to remember. . . .

Keith had been leaning back in his desk chair, watching Breden with a cool, studying expression. "It's probably true. In all the hundreds or thousands of generations of division and selection of the E-2 cells within our incubators the only possible evolution that could have gone on was evolution in the direction of chemical adaptability, since only the chemical environment varied. If this happened, Breden, it means that biochemically you are something like twenty thousand years ahead of the rest of us. At that rate I think you should be able to pull yourself out of any effect from external drugs with-out any help from us."

Breden found himself swallowing painfully. "This is good news. . . ." It came out as half a whisper, and he pulled him-self together with an effort, trying to forget what he had just heard, and to remember what he was supposed to do. He shifted the direction of the gun absently away from Keith's face.

"If this is so," Keith continued, his eyes straying from Mart's face to the gun and back, "then it answers the ques-tion of why you are so healthy. That kind of adaptability could probably fit any random kind of physical structure to-gether and make it work."

Mart suddenly felt the health of his body as a physical sensation, and the gun in his hand which he was pointing at this quiet room full of people seemed totally incongruous. He was following instructions, but he had no enthusiasm for it now. He was doing it only as a favor to the supers. They were his friends, they were with him in his fight against humanity. Fight against humanity. . . .

A second of silence had passed and Zal exploded impetu-ously, "For heaven's sake, Mart! Put that damn gun down. Don't you see you're holding us for some kind of a trap?"

"The supers are my friends. I'm doing what they want."

"That's hypnosis talking. Fight it."

"I don't want to fight it," Breden said reasonably. "I want to help them." If the button push was to have brought the police, they would have been here minutes ago. Something prickled along the back of his neck. Just what kind of a trap had his friends prepared for MSKZ? Why hadn't they told him? He hoped it was no worse than hypno-conversion.

"I suggest," Planck-Planck said softly, "that the F line of supers know something about the E-2 abilities and are afraid of being displaced. They have worked out some plausible way of eliminating Breden, who is E-2's only living representative."

"This was to be a trap for him, and not for us."

"Mart," Zal's voice was strained. "For God's sake, take care of yourself. Don't just stand there."

He was fighting now, trying to open his hand and drop the gun. He could feel the tension straining the muscles of his arm right up to the shoulder, and the surging and growth of the feeling of obligation, the feeling of obedience to the supers, that fought to keep the gun in his hand, wavering, pointing. . . .

Pointing in the general direction of the lined face of the big blond man who was sitting so close, leaning back in his desk chair, occasionally glancing from Breden's eyes to the gun. They probably could have jumped then and taken the gun away from him, but everyone in the room knew that they could not risk the chance that his finger would contract on the trigger, for one shot would bring out enough of the story to retrograde forty years of MSKZ's work in genetics and make it once more into a simple supply house for laboratory animals.

It was up to him. "I don't believe they are against me," he said, "but I . . . ." He tried. His eyes fogging with the effort, he glanced up at a sound, looking past Keith's face toward the half open door on the far side of the room.

Yardly Devon stood there, a slim old man dressed in pearl grey. A hat was rakishly on the side of his head; his face was smoothly shaven and pink, and in his hand was the blue-steel glimmer of an old fashioned automatic. "I heard you," he told Breden.

For a moment he clearly remembered his instructions. He was supposed to shout and start pulling the trigger of the curare pistol wildly in Devon's general direction. None of the bullets would strike Devon, but one of the bullets was to go,

as if by accident, into the face of Keith, penetrating one of
his eyes. If he did this, they had told him, he would be perfectly safe and have his revenge against MSKZ for what it
had done to him. Murder. Keith's eyes were a cool grey-blue
color. *Murder.* . . .

Mart Breden shut his own eyes tightly, with a knot of
terror that leaped in his chest, twisting intolerably. Then it
was gone and he could breathe and his heart could beat again.
With immeasurable relief he felt the gun fall from his fingers
and heard it thud on the floor. He opened his eyes, looking
back at Yardly Devon, who stood across the room regarding
him triumphantly, ready to shoot.

It had been a double catspaw. They had primed him so
that he would do a murder for them, apparently by accident,
and then never be able to reveal that it was a catspaw murder,
or that he had been hypnoed—because he would be dead,
killed by Yardly Devon, a paranoiac who had probably been
easily set off in his direction by a few carefully keyed casual
remarks. Devon made a handy killer, for he would kill with
perfect innocence, convinced that his choice of time and place
was his own, convinced that he had learned of Breden's
whereabouts by accident and able to tell the police no more
than that. Mart felt he ought to warn the others in the room.

"Mr. Devon's business is entirely with me," he said, leaning
back against the filing cases and feeling the handles and knobs
push against his back. Filing cases aren't comfortable to lean
against, but there had been too many cross-currents of melo-
drama, and he was tired. "I think it is his contention that I
am a diploid or a Martian or something. He has been trying
to kill me." He added wearily, "If I have been irritable today
you can blame it on that."

All the tiny normal motions of the people in the room had
suddenly stopped, even the motion of breathing diminished. A
madman with a smile and a shave and a gun full of bullets
is not the person to bring confidence and relaxation. Devon
said, "I had my detectives follow you. I told you that you
couldn't get away."

Breden could feel the light weight of the curare pistol
against his toe. It was supposed to be there to protect him,
but it might as well have been on the moon for all the chance

he would have to get it. He leaned against the filing cases, watching Devon's gun, wondering if a person could see the bullet flash out.

Someone was stirring slightly in a stealthy movement. "He's a good shot," Breden warned quietly, remembering the creased neck in a shot from a moving cab. He looked into the dark hole of the muzzle. It was like a small dark eye that would expand to cover the world with darkness. His own voice seemed to come from a distance. "If I'm going to hell I don't want an escort. Just take it easy and hold still, and in a minute E-2 will stop complaining and giving you trouble and go back to being just another label on an egg compartment."

"But I *like Mart,*" said Zal plaintively after a moment. He stood up, a solid-shouldered nineteen-year-old in a defiantly gaudy pink sport shirt, carefully stuck his thumbs into his ears and wiggled his fingers at Devon. His *excessive* number of fingers. Breden saw it from the side of his vision as something fantastic but unimportant. At the center of focus he saw the most important thing in the universe, the automatic and the hand that held it jerk slightly, and then begin to waver in an arc. He wondered why Devon neither spoke nor fired.

"You're *all* Martians," wailed Devon.

That was when the tension broke. Everyone began to move rapidly at once, apparently all acting on the same simple impulse that Breden was acting on, that there was no profit in waiting for Devon to shoot them all down. The shots were too loud in that enclosed room. The sound had an impact like a succession of blows, distorting everything.

Zal was clinging to Devon's gun arm, and then was on the floor on his hands and knees while the tall stout girl held the thrashing figure in a tight desperate clasp with his arms partially pinned, and the convulsively squeezing hand pumped shots into the floor.

Breden had instinctively circled out of the line of fire and come in from behind, his eyes ranging for the gun in the struggling tangle of heads and arms and hands. The convulsively squeezing hand began pulling the trigger randomly again, and the impact of the sound stung his ears and skin as he spotted it. He slapped at the deadly shiny thing with an open palm, and it suddenly thumped on the floor and skidded away. . . .

The tall stout girl picked it up and suddenly the room was quiet. Only Devon continued to struggle against the restraining arms.

She waved the gun in a sweeping hurried gesture, holding it by the barrel. "Everybody get out through the passage and close the door. Pick up the bottles and sandwich wrappings and take them along so it won't look like there was a crowd," she called. "Keith will take care of this madman."

The big blond man approached the group and locked himself to Devon with a wrestling grip as the others unpeeled from their struggling captive one by one and darted through the open door.

Zal had uncurled from his hands-and-knees position and rolled over on his side. There was a small pool of blood where he had crouched. "Gut wounds aren't dangerous," Keith told him, bending down. The diploids hardly glanced at Zal as they passed him and crowded through the open catalogue rack, but Planck-Planck said, as he passed, "Take it easy Zal. Look out for those doctors. They'll get curious and claim they have to open you up and take out something—just for a look inside." The tall girl lagged behind last and handed the gun to Breden.

"Take over, boy," she called, her lips close to Breden's ear. Devon had wriggled free except for one wrist, and he was pulling and jerking at the end of his held arm like a hooked fish flopping on a line. His whimpers were rising to a keening wail, like a banshee warming up. The girl raised her voice. "Shut the door behind us and leave us out of the story." Sirens in the street and air outside were adding to the racket. She vanished through the door, and he closed the swinging rack hastily.

VIII

DEVON WAS STILL PULLING away from Keith's placid grip on his wrist, jerking and shrieking thinly with every breath, apparently under the impression that the Martians were going to murder him. It was hard to think, like being in the same room with a fire siren, and the sound of feet pounding up the escalator and a whistle blowing on the sidewalk added to the din. Holding the gun turned in Devon's direction, Mart moved toward the door, and through it abruptly caught a glimpse of two policemen. They were wearing flesh-colored pads over their noses. He recognized their intention just as the first startling noise of a fizz bullet sizzled past his face; but it was too late to stop the breath he was drawing and some of the gas went into his lungs.

There were three other sharp sizzling sounds. He saw Keith and Devon slow to a stop, just as his own desire to move faded. When Devon stopped screaming it left the air empty.

The gas-ice bullets had shattered against the walls and filing cabinets, and the shattered small pieces lay on the floor sizzling and dwindling into gas.

He felt like a cataleptic, perfectly able to think, but with no desire to move or speak. The fizz pistols shot some standard hypnotic suspended in a compressed gas-ice pellet.

The police waited a cautious minute and a half and then they stepped into the room. "You won't move or talk unless we ask you to," said the one in the uniform of a sergeant, speaking with slight difficulty because of his nose pad. He walked up to Breden and efficiently removed the gun from his hand, wrapped it in a handkerchief and dropped it in his pocket. The other one was busy at a desk opening out and arranging a sound recorder. He switched it on and stepped back. "Okay," he told the sergeant.

The sergeant turned his head and said matter-of-factly into the recorder, "These are preliminary questionings taken under hypnosis at the scene of the incident and do not constitute voluntary confessions unless later sworn to in free-will state, and a condition of sanity."

He turned to Breden and gestured at Zal on the floor. "Who's that?"

"Zalmeyer Elberg."

"What's your name?"

"Paul Breden."

"Are you responsible for his injury?"

It was a debatable question. "Indirectly," he said, after hesitating.

The sergeant looked faintly annoyed. "Did you fire at him with intent to kill?"

"No."

"Did you fire at him with intent to kill?"

"No."

"Did you fire at him accidentally?"

"No." There was some disadvantage in this method of questioning, for though he answered willingly, he felt no desire to save the man questions by explaining that he had not had the gun.

The sergeant belatedly put two and two together. "Who did the shooting?"

"Yardly Devon." Mart knew he could fight the drug and lie if he had to.

"With this gun?"

"Yes." So far no lies had been necessary.

"Point him out." The cop glanced at the other two. "Which is he?"

Breden pointed, and the cop followed his indication and addressed Devon, who stood passively, looking pathetic, his thin sandy hair rumpled, his overshirt ripped and his hat knocked off. "What's your name?"

"Yardly Evert Devon," answered Devon obediently, and the recorder took down the sound of his voice.

"Did you shoot this man?"

"Yes."

"Why?"

"He was trying to get my automatic. I had to stop him."

"Why did you have a gun?"

"Because they are—I think they are Martians. They call themselves—"

"Cuffs," said the sergeant. While the other was snapping cuffs on Devon's wrists he checked the time on his watch, unclipped a small mike from his belt and spoke into it. "Everything under control. Gas cleared. Send up a stretcher and the med for one gut wound and a violent case." He hung the mike on his belt again and walked over, switching off the recorder.

Breden found his powers of motion returning as the hypnotic suddenly wore off. He knelt beside Zal. "You all right?"

"You wanna trade places?" muttered the husky young diploid who looked like him. "Say the word." A doctor appeared and motioned Breden away, opening his kit. Another policeman came in with a five-lens motion picture camera and began moving around with it in routine fashion, taking pictures of the scene.

"They're Martians," Devon stated suddenly as he recovered his ability to speak. "There were a lot more of them and they escaped before you got here."

The sergeant swung on Breden with his expression hardening. "How about that? You know that the people involved in a shooting have to stay around to be questioned. Did somebody leave?"

Here was the perfect moment to do what he had once intended, destroy MSKZ in a blast of publicity. The moment was spectacular. The cameraman taking pictures, the wounded man on the floor, the doctor working over him, a policeman holding the door for two attendants carrying a stretcher, the madman making strange accusations. . . .

All Breden had to do now to add the crowning touch of sinister fantasy was to walk over to the catalogue rack that concealed the hidden door and swing it open. After that he could make whatever accusations he chose, and they would be believed.

Suddenly Breden found that he no longer wanted to tell the police about the secret door. He had forgotten what his reasons had been for threatening it.

His lag in answering had been only an instant. "Nobody else was here," he lied.

The sergeant gave Devon a disgusted glance and nodded. "Okay. Do you want to go down to the station with this Devon character now and make a statement of what happened? We'll give you a lift." He glanced at Zal's fingers as he was carried past on the stretcher, then spoke as if from some shadowy uncertainty, "I take it you two are related."

"Cousins."

"Yeah." The sergeant gave Devon another disgusted glance. "Let's go."

They went out and down the escalator, and behind them

Devon pushed back against urging hands, his voice growing hysterical. "No, you have to listen to me. Believe me, the Martians were here. They went out a secret door. It's behind that bookcase." His voice was pleading now. "You can't take me away without listening to me. At least look at the—" The policeman with him gave him an impatient shove to the head of the escalator. Devon clung to the side with manacled hands, his voice shrill.

"For the love of justice! Look at that bookcase! You can't . . . not without even. . . ." A rough shove dislodged him from the railing, and the screaming began again while the irritated young policeman held him still and the police doctor passed Keith and Breden, running up the moving escalator with a pacifying hypo in hand. It was the sound of terror.

"You can't—no, you're with them! You're with the Martians. They've hired you. I see it now. You're against me too. No, don't. It's poison. Help!"

Behind them the shouting choked off to a mumble as the hypo took hold. The escalator delivered them, silent and pale, to street level. A crowd had assembled outside, Keith and Breden climbed into the waiting police patrol wing. . . .

After they had given their testimony and signed the record of their statements they paused on the station house steps, reluctant to separate.

"Quite a day!" Mart said.

"It was interesting enough," Keith agreed. He hesitated oddly. "If you don't mind my saying—I'm sorry about—ah—your troubles. E-2s weren't really meant to be birthed, but I can arrange that if you have children they shan't be like you —that is—?"

"That they won't be *too much* like me anyhow?" Mart supplied the words, grinning.

"That's it." Keith shook hands with embarrassed vigor as they parted. "Take care of yourself. Remember that you are my star line now."

"Thanks," Mart said, meaning it.

They walked away from each other, and it was a warm friendly summer night that seemed to Mart to be just for him.

When he stepped out of the elevator on his own floor

Nadine flew into his arms. "Mart. Are you all right? I called everywhere and you weren't there. You weren't home—"

She was crying. He wrapped his arms around her comfortingly, and she tilted her face back from his shoulder to look at him, and everything was fine. It was wonderful, and he couldn't understand how he could ever have been unhappy. "Mart . . . I wanted to tell you. We don't have to have children."

"Oh yes we do," he said firmly before kissing her. "And they'll all grow up to be President." He'd explain later.

DEFENSE MECHANISM

THE ARTICLE was coming along smoothly, words flowing from the typewriter in pleasant simple sequence, swinging to their predetermined conclusion like a good tune. Ted typed contentedly, adding pages to the stack at his elbow.

A thought, a subtle modification of the logic of the article began to glow in his mind, but he brushed it aside impatiently. This was to be a short article, and there was no room for subtlety. His articles sold, not for depth, but for an oddly individual quirk that he could give to commonplaces.

While he typed a little faster, faintly in the echoes of his thought the theme began to elaborate itself richly with correlations, modifying qualifications, and humorous parenthetical remarks. An eddy of especially interesting conclusions tried to insert itself into the main stream of his thoughts. Furiously he typed along the dissolving thread of his argument.

"Shut up," he snarled. "Can't I have any privacy around here?"

The answer was not a remark, it was merely a concept; two electro-chemical calculators pictured with the larger in use as a control mech, taking a dangerously high inflow, and controlling it with high resistance and blocs, while the smaller one lay empty and unblocked, its unresistant circuits ramifying any impulses received along the easy channels of pure calculation. Ted recognized the diagram from his amateur concepts of radio and psychology.

"All right. So I'm doing it myself. So you can't help it!" He grinned grudgingly. "Answering back at your age!"

Under the impact of a directed thought the small circuits of the idea came in strongly, scorching their reception and rapport diagram into his mind in flashing repetitions, bright as small lightning strokes. Then it spread and the small other brain flashed into brightness, reporting and repeating from every center. Ted even received a brief kinesthetic sensation of

71

lying down, before it was all cut off in a hard bark of thought
that came back in exact echo of his own irritation.

"Tune down!" It ordered furiously. "You're blasting in too
loud and jamming everything up! What do you want, an
idiot child?"

Ted blanketed down desperately, cutting off all thoughts,
relaxing every muscle; but the angry thoughts continued coming in strongly a moment before fading.

"Even when I take a nap," they said, "he starts thinking
at me! Can't I get any peace and privacy around here?"

Ted grinned. The kid's last remark sounded like something a little better than an attitude echo. It would be hard
to tell when the kid's mind grew past a mere selective echoing
of outside thoughts and became true personality, but that last
remark was a convincing counterfeit of a sincere kick in the
shin. Conditioned reactions can be efficient.

All the luminescent streaks of thought faded and merged
with the calm meaningless ebb and flow of waves in the
small sleeping mind. Ted moved quietly into the next room
and looked down into the blue-and-white crib. The kid lay
sleeping, his thumb in his mouth and his chubby face innocent
of thought. Junior—Jake.

It was an odd stroke of luck that Jake was born with this
particular talent. Because of it they would have to spend the
winter in Connecticut, away from the mental blare of crowded
places. Because of it Ted was doing free lance in the kitchen,
instead of minor editing behind a New York desk. The winter
countryside was wide and windswept, as it had been in Ted's
own childhood, and the warm contacts with the stolid personalities of animals through Jake's mind were already a pleasure.
Old acquaintances—Ted stopped himself skeptically. He was
no telepath. He decided that it reminded him of Ernest
Thompson Seton's animal biographies, and went back to typing, dismissing the question.

It was pleasant to eavesdrop on things through Jake, as long
as the subject was not close enough to the article to interfere
with it.

Five small boys let out of kindergarten came trooping by
on the road, chattering and throwing pebbles. Their thoughts
came in jumbled together in distracting cross currents, but Ted

stopped typing for a moment, smiling, waiting for Jake to show his latest trick. Babies are hypersensitive to conditioning. The burnt hand learns to yank back from fire, the unresisting mind learns automatically to evade too many clashing echoes of other minds.

Abruptly the discordant jumble of small boy thoughts and sensations delicately untangled into five compartmented strands of thoughts, then one strand of little boy thoughts shoved the others out, monopolizing and flowing easily through the blank baby mind, as a dream flows by without awareness, leaving no imprint of memory, fading as the children passed over the hill. Ted resumed typing, smiling. Jake had done the trick a shade faster than he had yesterday. He was learning reflexes easily enough to demonstrate normal intelligences. At least he was to be more than a gifted moron.

A half hour later, Jake had grown tired of sleeping and was standing up in his crib, shouting and shaking the bars. Martha hurried in with a double armload of groceries.

"Does he want something?"

"Nope. Just exercising his lungs." Ted stubbed out his cigarette and tapped the finished stack of manuscript contentedly. "Got something here for you to proofread."

"Dinner first," she said cheerfully, unpacking food from the bags. "Better move the typewriter and give us some elbow room."

Sunlight came in the windows and shone on the yellow table top, and glinted on her dark hair as she opened packages.

"What's the local gossip?" he asked, clearing off the table. "Anything new?"

"Meat's going up again," she said, unwrapping peas and fillets of mackerel. "Mrs. Watkin's boy, Tom, is back from the clinic. He can see fine now, she says."

He put water on to boil and began greasing a skillet while she rolled the fillets in cracker crumbs. "If I'd had to run a flame thrower during the war, I'd have worked up a nice case of hysteric blindness myself," he said. "I call that a legitimate defense mechanism. Sometimes it's better to be blind."

"But not all the time," Martha protested, putting baby food in the double boiler. In five minutes lunch was cooking.

"Whaaaa—" wailed Jake.

Martha went into the baby's room, and brought him out, cuddling him and crooning. "What do you want, Lovekins? Baby just wants to be cuddled, doesn't baby."

"Yes," said Ted.

She looked up, startled, and her expression changed, became withdrawn and troubled, her dark eyes clouded in difficult thought.

Concerned, he asked: "What is it, Honey?"

"Ted, you shouldn't—" She struggled with words. "I know, it is handy to know what he wants, whenever he cries. It's handy having you tell me, but I don't— It isn't right somehow. It isn't *right*."

Jake waved an arm and squeaked randomly. He looked unhappy. Ted took him and laughed, making an effort to sound confident and persuasive. It would be impossible to raise the kid in a healthy way if Martha began to feel he was a freak. "Why isn't it right? It's normal enough. Look at E. S. P. Everybody has that according to Rhine."

"E. S. P. is different," she protested feebly, but Jake chortled and Ted knew he had her. He grinned, bouncing Jake up and down in his arms.

"Sure it's different," he said cheerfully. "E. S. P. is queer. E. S. P. comes in those weird accidental little flashes that contradict time and space. With clairvoyance you can see through walls, and read pages from a closed book in France. E. S. P., when it comes, is so ghastly precise it seems like tips from old Omniscience himself. It's enough to drive a logical man insane, trying to explain it. It's illogical, incredible, and random. But what Jake has is limited telepathy. It is starting out fuzzy and muddled and developing towards accuracy by plenty of trial and error—like sight, or any other normal sense. You don't mind communicating by English, so why mind communicating by telepathy?"

She smiled wanly. "But he doesn't weigh much, Ted. He's not growing as fast as it says he should in the baby book."

"That's all right. I didn't really start growing myself until I was about two. My parents thought I was sickly."

"And look at you now." She smiled genuinely. "All right, you win. But when does he start talking English? I'd like to understand him, too. After all, I'm his mother."

"Maybe this year, maybe next year," Ted said teasingly. "I didn't start talking until I was three."

"You mean that you don't want him to learn," she told him indignantly, and then smiled coaxingly at Jake. "You'll learn English soon for Mommy, won't you, Lovekins?"

Ted laughed annoyingly. "Try coaxing him next month or the month after. Right now he's not listening to all these thoughts. He's just collecting associations and reflexes. His cortex might organize impressions on a logic pattern he picked up from me, but it doesn't know what it is doing any more than this fist knows that it is in his mouth. That right, bud?" There was no demanding thought behind the question, but instead, very delicately, Ted introspected to the small world of impression and sensation that flickered in what seemed a dreaming corner of his own mind. Right then it was a fragmentary world of green and brown that murmured with the wind.

"He's out eating grass with the rabbit," Ted told her.

Not answering, Martha started putting out plates. "I like animal stories for children," she said determinedly. "Rabbits are nicer than people."

Putting Jake in his pen, Ted began to help. He kissed the back of her neck in passing. "Some people are nicer than rabbits."

Wind rustled tall grass and tangled vines where the rabbit snuffled and nibbled among the sun-dried herbs, moving on habit, ignoring the abstract meaningless contact of minds, with no thought but deep comfort.

Then for a while Jake's stomach became aware that lunch was coming, and the vivid business of crying and being fed drowned the gentler distant neural flow of the rabbit.

Ted ate with enjoyment, toying with an idea fantastic enough to keep him grinning, as Martha anxiously spooned food into Jake's mouth. She caught him grinning and indignantly began justifying herself. "But he only gained four pounds, Ted. I have to make sure he eats something."

"Only!" he grinned. "At that rate he'd be thirty feet high by the time he reaches college."

"So would any baby." But she smiled at the idea, and gave Jake his next spoonful still smiling. Ted did not tell his real thought, that if Jake's abilities kept growing in a straight-line growth curve, by the time he was old enough to vote he would be God; but he laughed again, and was rewarded by an answering smile from both of them.

The idea was impossible, of course. Ted knew enough biology to know that there could be no sudden smooth jumps in evolution. Smooth changes had to be worked out gradually through generations of trial and selection. Sudden changes were not smooth, they crippled and destroyed. Mutants were usually monstrosities.

Jake was no sickly freak, so it was certain that he would not turn out very different from his parents. He could be only a little better. But the contrary idea had tickled Ted and he laughed again. "Boom food," he told Martha. "Remember those straight-line growth curves in the story?"

Martha remembered, smiling, "Redfern's dream—sweet little man, dreaming about a growth curve that went straight up." She chuckled, and fed Jake more spoonfuls of strained spinach, saying, "Open wide. Eat your boom food, darling. Don't you want to grow up like King Kong?"

Ted watched vaguely, toying now with a feeling that these months of his life had happened before, somewhere. He had felt it before, but now it came back with a sense of expectancy, as if something were going to happen.

It was while drying the dishes that Ted began to feel sick. Somewhere in the far distance at the back of his mind a tiny phantom of terror cried and danced and gibbered. He glimpsed it close in a flash that entered and was cut off abruptly in a vanishing fragment of delirium. It had something to do with a tangle of brambles in a field, and it was urgent.

Jake grimaced, his face wrinkled as if ready either to smile or cry. Carefully Ted hung up the dish towel and went out the back door, picking up a billet of wood as he passed the woodpile. He could hear Jake whimpering, beginning to wail.

"Where to?" Martha asked, coming out the back door.

"Dunno," Ted answered. "Gotta go rescue Jake's rabbit. It's in trouble."

Feeling numb, he went across the fields through an outgrowth of small trees, climbed a fence into a field of deep grass and thorny tangles of raspberry vines, and started across.

A few hundred feet into the field there was a hunter sitting on an outcrop of rock, smoking, with a successful bag of two rabbits dangling near him. He turned an inquiring face to Ted.

"Sorry," the hunter said. He was quiet-looking man with a yet. It can't understand being upside down with its legs tied." Moving with shaky urgency he took his penknife and cut the small animal's pulsing throat, then threw the wet knife out of his hand into the grass. The rabbit kicked once more, staring still at the tangled vines of refuge. Then its nearsighted baby eyes lost their glazed bright stare and became meaningless.

"Sorry," the hunter said. He was a quiet-looking man with a sagging, middle-aged face.

"That's all right," Ted replied, "but be a little more careful next time, will you? You're out of season anyhow." He looked up from the grass to smile stiffly at the hunter. It was difficult. There was a crowded feeling in his head, like a coming headache, or a stuffy cold. It was difficult to breathe, difficult to think.

It occurred to Ted then to wonder why Jake had never put him in touch with the mind of an adult. After a frozen stoppage of thought he laboriously started the wheels again and realized that something had put him in touch with the mind of the hunter, and that was what was wrong. His stomach began to rise. In another minute he would retch.

Ted stepped forward and swung the billet of wood in a clumsy sidewise sweep. The hunter's rifle went off and missed as the middle-aged man tumbled face first into the grass.

Wind rustled the long grass and stirred the leafless branches of trees. Ted could hear and think again, standing still and breathing in deep, shuddering breaths of air to clean his lungs. Briefly he planned what to do. He would call the sheriff and say that a hunter hunting out of season had shot at him and he had been forced to knock the man out. The sheriff would take the man away, out of thought range.

Before he started back to telephone he looked again at the peaceful, simple scene of field and trees and sky. It was safe to let himself think now. He took a deep breath and let himself think. The memory of horror came into clarity.

The hunter had been psychotic.

Thinking back, Ted recognized parts of it, like faces glimpsed in writhing smoke. The evil symbols of psychiatry, the bloody poetry of the Golden Bough, that had been the law of mankind in the five hundred thousand lost years before history. Torture and sacrifice, lust and death, a mechanism in perfect balance, a short circuit of conditioning through a glowing channel of symbols, an irreversible and perfect integration of traumas. It is easy to go mad, but it is not easy to go sane.

"Shut up!" Ted had been screaming inside his mind as he struck. "Shut up."

It had stopped. It had shut up. The symbols were fading without having found root in his mind. The sheriff would take the man away out of thought reach, and there would be no danger. It had stopped.

The burned hand avoids the fire. Something else had stopped. Ted's mind was queerly silent, queerly calm and empty, as he walked home across the winter fields, wondering how it had happened at all, kicking himself with humor for a suggestible fool, not yet missing—Jake.

And Jake lay awake in his pen, waving his rattle in random motions, and crowing "glaglagla gla—" in a motor sensory cycle, closed and locked against outside thoughts.

He would be a normal baby, as Ted had been, and as Ted's father before him.

And as all mankind was "normal."

THE PYRAMID IN THE DESERT

(formerly AND BE MERRY)

The tusks that clashed in mighty brawls
Of mastodons are billiard balls.
The sword of Charlemagne the Just
Is ferric oxide, known as rust.

The grizzly bear whose potent hug
Was feared by all, is now a rug.

Great Caesar's bust is on the shelf
And I don't feel so well myself!
Arthur Guiterman

IT WAS AFTERNOON. The walls of the room glared back the white sunlight, their smooth plaster coating concealing the rickety bones of the building. Through the barred window drifted miasmic vapors, laden with microscopic living things that could turn food to poison while one ate, bacteria that could find root in lungs or skin, and multiply, swarming through the blood.

And yet it seemed to be a nice day. A smoky hint of burning leaves blurred the other odors into a pleasant autumn tang, and sunlight streaming in the windows reflected brightly from the white walls. The surface appearance of things was harmless enough. The knack of staying calm was to think only of the surface, never of the meaning, to try to ignore what could not be helped. After all, one cannot refuse to eat, one cannot refuse to breathe. There was nothing to be done.

One of her feet had gone to sleep. She shifted her elbow to the other knee and leaned her chin in her hand again, feeling the blood prickling back into her toes. It was not good to

79

sit on the edge of the bed too long without moving. It was not good to think too long. Thinking opened the gates to fear. She looked at her fingernails. They were pale, cyanotic. She had been breathing reluctantly, almost holding her breath. Fear is impractical. One cannot refuse to breathe.

And yet to solve the problems of safety it was necessary to think, it was necessary to look at the danger clearly, to weigh it, to sum it up and consider it as a whole. But each time she tried to face it her imagination would flinch away. Always her thinking trailed off in a blind impulse to turn to Alec for rescue.

When someone tapped her shoulder she made sure that her face was calm and blank before raising it from her hands. A man in a white coat stood before her, proffering a pill and a cup of water. He spoke tonelessly.

"Swallow."

There was no use fighting back. There was no use provoking them to force. Putting aside the frantic futile images of escape she took the pill, her hands almost steady.

She scarcely felt the prick of the needle.

It was afternoon.

Alexander Berent stood in the middle of the laboratory kitchen, looking around vaguely. He had no hope of seeing her.

His wife was missing.

She was not singing in the living room, or cooking at the stove, or washing dishes at the sink. Helen was not in the apartment.

She was not visiting any of her friends' houses. The hospitals had no one of her description in their accident wards. The police had not found her body on any slab of the city morgue.

Helen Berent was missing.

In the corner cages the guinea pigs whistled and chirred for food, and the rabbits snuffled and tried to shove their pink noses through the grill. They looked gaunt. He fed them and refilled their water bottles automatically.

There was something different about the laboratory. It was not the way he had left it. Naturally after five months of the stupendous deserts and mountains of Tibet any room seemed small and cramped and artificial, but there were other changes. The cot had been dragged away from the wall, towards the icebox. Beside the cot was a wastebasket and a small table that used to be in the living room. On top of the table were the telephone and the dictation recorder surrounded by hypodermics, small bottles cryptically labeled with a red pencil scrawl, and an alcohol jar with its swab of cotton still in it. Alec touched the cotton. It was dusty to his fingers, and completely dry.

The dictation recorder and the telephone had been oddly linked into one circuit with a timer clock, but the connections were open, and when he picked up the receiver the telephone buzzed as it should.

Alec replaced the receiver and somberly considered the number of things that could be reached by a woman lying down. She could easily spend days there. Even the lower drawers of the filing cabinet were within reach.

He found what he was looking for in the lowest drawer of the filing cabinet, filed under "A," a special folder marked "ALEC." In it were a letter and two voice records dated and filed in order.

The letter was dated the day he had left, four months ago. He held it in his hand a minute before beginning to read.

Dear Alec,

You never guessed how silly I felt with my foot in that idiotic bandage. You were so considerate I didn't know whether to laugh or to cry. After you got on board I heard the plane officials paging a tardy passenger. I knew his place was empty, and it took all my will power to keep from running up the walk into the plane. If I had yielded to the temptation, I would be on the plane with you now, sitting in that vacant seat, looking down at the cool blue Atlantic, and in a month hiking across those windy horizons to the diggings.

But I can't give up all my lovely plans, so I sublimated the impulse to confess by promising myself to write this letter, and then made myself watch the plane take off with the proper attitude of sad resignation, like a dutiful wife with a hurt foot.

This is the confession. The bandage was a fake. My

foot is all right. I just pretended to be too lame to hike to have an excuse to stay home this summer. Nothing else would have made you leave without me.

New York seems twice as hot and sticky now that the plane has taken you away. Honestly, I love you and my vacations too much to abandon the expedition to the unsanitary horrors of native cooking for just laziness. Remember, Alec, once when I was swearing at the gnats along the Whangpo, you quoth, "I could not love you so, my dear, loved I not science more." I put salt in your coffee for that, but you were right. I am the wife of an archeologist. Whither thou goest I must go, your worries are my worries, your job, my job.

What you forget is that besides being your wife, I am an endocrinologist, and an expert. If you can cheerfully expose me to cliffs, swamps, man-eating tigers and malarial mosquitoes, all in the name of Archeology, I have an even better right to stick hypodermics in myself in the name of Endocrinology.

You know my experiments in cell metabolism. Well naturally the next step in the investigation is to try something on myself to see how it works. But for ten years, ever since you caught me with that hypodermic and threw such a fit, I have given up the personal guinea pig habit so as to save you worry. Mosquitoes can beat hypos any day, but there is no use trying to argue with a husband.

So I pretended to have broken one of the small phalanges of my foot instead. Much simpler.

I am writing this letter in the upstairs lobby of the Paramount, whither I escaped from the heat. I will write other letters every so often to help you keep up with the experiment, but right now I am going in to see this movie and have a fine time weeping over Joan Crawford's phony troubles, then home and to work.

G'by darling. Remember your airsick tablets, and don't fall out.

Yours always,
Helen

P.S. Don't eat anything the cook doesn't eat first. And have a good time.

After the letter there were just two voice records in envelopes. The oldest was dated July 24th. Alec put it on the turntable and switched on the play-back arm. For a moment the machine made no sound but the faint scratching of the needle, and then Helen spoke, sounding close to the microphone, her voice warm and lazy.

"Hello, Alec. The day after writing that first letter, while I was looking for a stamp, I suddenly decided not to mail it. There is no use worrying you with my experiment until it is finished. I resolved to write daily letters and save them for you to read all together when you get home.

"Of course, after making that good resolution I didn't write anything for a month but the bare clinical record of symptoms, injections and reactions.

"I concede you that any report has to include the human detail to be readable, but honestly, the minute I stray off the straight and narrow track of formulas, my reports get so chatty they read like a gossip column. It's hopeless.

"When you get back you can write in the explanatory material yourself, from what I tell you on this disk. You write better anyhow. Here goes:

"It's hard to organize my words, I'm not used to talking at a faceless dictaphone. A typewriter is more my style, but I can't type lying down, and every time I try writing with a pen, I guess I get excited, and clutch too hard, and my finger bones start bending, and I have to stop and straighten them out! Bending one's finger bones is no fun. The rubbery feel of them bothers me, and if I get scared enough, the adrenalin will upset my whole endocrine balance and set me back a week's work.

"Let's see: Introduction. Official purpose of experiment—to investigate the condition of old age. Aging is a progressive failure of anabolism. Old age is a disease. No one has ever liked growing old, so when you write this into beautiful prose you can call it—'The Age-Old Old-Age problem'."

"Nowdays there is no evolutionary reason why we should be built to get old. Since we are learning animals, longevity is a survival factor. It should be an easy conquest, considering that each cell is equipped to duplicate itself and leave a couple of young successor cells to carry on the good work. The trouble is, some of them just *don't*. Some tissues brace themselves to hang on fifty years, and you have to get along with the same deteriorating cells until death do you part.

"From Nature's point of view that is reasonable. The human race evolved in an environment consisting mainly of plagues, famines, blizzards, and saber-toothed tigers. Any man's chances of staying unkilled for fifty years were pretty thin. Longevity was not worth much those days. What good is longevity to a corpse?

"We have eliminated plagues, famines, and saber-toothed tigers, but old age is still with us. One was meant to go with the other, but evolution hasn't had time to adjust us to the change.

"That Russian scientist started me on this idea. Bogla-metz. He gave oldsters a little of their lost elasticity by injections of an antibody that attacked and dissolved some of their old connective tissue and forced a partial replacement.

"I just want to go him one better, and see if I can coax a replacement for every creaking cell in the body.

"You can see how it would be a drastic process—halfway between being born again and being run through a washing machine. There is nobody I dare try it on except myself, for I'll have to feel my way, working out each step from the reactions to the last step, like making up a new recipe by adding and tasting.

"Item: The best way to test your theories is to try them on yourself. Emergency is the mother of exertion.

"Thirty-eight is just old enough to make me a good guinea pig. I am not so old and fragile that I would break down under the first strain, but I am not so young that a little added youth won't show.

"One question is—just how many tissues of any kind dare I destroy at once. The more I clear away at once, the more complete the replacement, but it is rather like replacing parts in a running motor. You wonder just how many bolts you can take out before the flywheel comes off its shaft and flies away. Speed should help. A quick regrowth can replace dissolved tissue before the gap is felt. The human machine is tough and elastic. It can run along on its own momentum when it should be stopped.

"This winter I bred a special strain of mold from some hints

I had found in the wartime research reports on the penicillia. The mold makes an art of carrying on most of the processes of life outside of itself. Digestion and even most of the re-synthesis of assimilation is finished before the food touches the plant. Its roots secrete enzymes that attack protein, dismantle it neatly down to small soluble molecules, and leave them linked to catalytic hooks, ready to be reassembled like the parts of a prefabricated house.

"The food below the mold becomes a pool. The mold plants draw the liquid up through their roots, give it the last touch that converts it to protoplasm, provide it with nucleus and throw it up in a high waving fur of sporangia.

"But that liquid is magic. It could become the protoplasm of any creature with the same ease and speed. It could be put into the bloodstream and be as harmless as the normal rough aminos, and yet provide for an almost instantaneous regrowth of missing flesh, a regrowth complete enough, I hope, to allow the drastic destruction and replacement I need.

"That may provide the necessary regeneration, but to have the old cells missing at the proper time and place, in the proper controlled amounts, is another problem entirely. The Russians used the antibody technique on horses to get a selectively destructive serum. That is all right for them, but it sounds too slow and troublesome for me. The idea of innoculating a horse with some of my connective tissue doesn't appeal to me somehow. How am I supposed to get this connective tissue? Besides, I don't have a horse. The serum farms charge high.

"After watching a particularly healthy colony of mold melting down a tough piece of raw beef I decided that there are other destructives than antibodies.

"I forced alternate generations of the mold to live on the toughest fresh meat I could find, and then on the dead mold mats of its own species. To feed without suicide it had to learn a fine selectivity, attacking only flesh that had passed the thin line between death and life. Twice, variants went past the line and dissolved themselves back to puddles, but the other strains learned to produce what was needed.

"Then I took some of the enzyme juice from under a mat, and shot the deadly stuff into a rabbit—the brown bunny with the spot. Nothing happened to Bunny, she just grew very hungry and gained an ounce. I cut myself, and swabbed the juice on the cut. It skinned the callus from my fingertips, but nothing happened to the cut. So then I sent a sample over to the hospital for a test, with a note to Williams that this was a trial sample of a fine selective between dead and live tissue, to be used cautiously in cleaning out ragged infected wounds and small local gangrene.

"Williams is the same irresponsible old goat he always was. There was an ancient patient dying of everything in the book, including a gangrenous leg. Williams shot the whole tube of juice into the leg at once, just to see what would happen. Of course it made a sloppy mess that he had to clean up himself. It served him right. He said that the surprise simply turned his stomach, but the stuff fixed the gangrene all right, just as I said it would. It was as close and clean as a surgical amputation. Nevertheless he came back with what was left of the sample and was glad to be rid of it. He guessed it to be a super catalyst somehow trained to be selective, and he wanted to get rid of it before it forgot its training.

"When I asked about the old patient later, they said that he woke up very hungry, and demanded a steak, so they satisfied him with intravenous amino acids, and he lived five days longer than expected.

"That was not a conclusive check, but it was enough. I labeled the juice 'H' for the acid ion. 'H' seemed a good name somehow.

"The first treatment on schedule was bone replacement. Middle age brings a sort of acromegaly. People ossify, their bones thicken, their gristle turns to bone and their arteries cake and stiffen. My framework needs a polishing down.

"For weeks I had cut my calcium intake down to almost nothing. Now I brought the calcium level in my blood down below the safe limit. The blood tried to stay normal by dissolving the treated bone. For safety, I had to play with parathyroid shots, depressants, and even a little calcium lactate on an hour-to-hour observation basis, to keep from crossing the spasm level of muscle irritability.

"But the hullabaloo must have upset my own endocrines, for they started behaving erratically, and yesterday suddenly they threw me into a fit before I could reach the depressant. I didn't break any bones but I came out of the fit with one of my ulna uncomfortably bent. The sight of it almost gave me another fit.

"When one's bones start bending it is time to stop. I must have overdone the treatment a bit. There seems to be almost no mineral left in the smaller bones, just stiff healthy gristle. I am now lying flat on the cot drinking milk, eggnogs, and cod liver oil. I dreamed of chop suey last night, but until I ossify properly, I refuse to get up and go out for a meal. The icebox is within easy reach. Maybe my large bones are still hard, and maybe not, but I'll take no chances on bow legs and flat feet just for an oriental dinner.

"Darling, I'm having a wonderful time, and I wish you were here to look over my shoulder and make sarcastic remarks. Every step is a guess based on the wildest deductions, and almost every guess checks and has to be written down as right. At this rate, when I get through I'll be way ahead of the field. I'll be one of the best cockeyed endocrinologists practicing.

"I hope you are having a good time too, and finding hundreds of broken vases and old teeth.

"I've got to switch back to the notes and hours record now and take down my pulse rate, irritability level, PH and so on. The time is now seven ten, I'll give you another record soon.

"G'by Hon—"

Her voice stopped and the needle ran onto the label and scratched with a heavy tearing noise. Alec turned the record over. The label on the other side was dated one week later.

Helen said cheerfully:

"Hello, Alec. This is a week later. I took a chance today and walked. Flat on my back again now, just a bit winded, but unbowed.

"Remember the time the obelisk fell on me? They set my arm badly, and it healed crooked with a big bump in the bones where the broken ends knitted. That bump made a good test to check the amount of chromosome control in this replacement business. If it approaches true regeneration, the bump should be noticeably reduced, and the knitting truer, to conform better to the gene blueprint of how an arm should be.

"The minute I thought of that test I had to try it. Risking flattened arches I got up and took the elevator down to the

second floor office of Dr. Stanton, and walked right through
an anteroom of waiting patients to the consulting room, where
I promptly lay down on his examination table.

"He was inspecting a little boy's tonsils and said irritably:

" 'I really *must* ask you to wait your turn— Oh, it's Dr.
Berent. Really Dr. Berent, you shouldn't take advantage of
your professional position to— Do you feel faint?'

" 'Oh I feel fine,' I told him charmingly, 'I just want to bor-
row your fluoroscope a minute to look at an old break in the
right humerus.'

" 'Oh yes, I understand,' he says blinking. 'But why are you
lying down?'

"Well, Alec, you remember how that young man is—rather
innocent, and trying to be dignified and stuffy to make up
for it. The last time we spoke to him, and you made those
wonderful cracks, I could see him thinking that we were somewhat odd, if not completely off our rockers. If I tried to tell
him now that I was afraid my legs would bend, he would have
called for a padded wagon to come and take me away.

"I said, 'I am afraid that I have upset my parathyroids.
They are on a rampage. Just a momentary condition, but I
have to stay relaxed for a while. You should see my irritability index! A little higher and . . . ah . . . I feel rather twitchy.
Do you happen to have any curare around?'

"He looked at me as if I had just stabbed him with a hatpin,
and then pulled out the fluoroscope so fast it almost ran over
him, screened my arm bones and hustled me out of there before I could even say aha. Apparently the idea of my throwing
a fit right there didn't arouse his professional ardor one bit.

"Alec, when I saw those bone shadows it was as much as I
could do to keep from frightening the poor boy with war
whoops. I put both arms under together, and I couldn't see
any bumps at all. *They were exactly the same.*

"This means that cells retain wider gene blueprints than
they need. And they just need a little encouragement to rebuild
injuries according to specifications. Regeneration must be an
unused potential of the body. I don't see why. We can't
evolve unused abilities. Natural selection only works in life
and death trials—probably evolution had no part in this. It is
just a lucky break from being fetal apes, a hang-over bit of
arrested development.

"I wonder how wide a blueprint each cell retains. Can a hand sprout new fingers, a wrist a new hand, a shoulder a new arm? Where does the control stop?

"The problem is a natural for the data I am getting now. Next winter when I am through with this silly rejuvenation business I'll get down to some solid work on regeneration, and try sprouting new arms on amputees. Maybe we can pry a grant from the Government, through that military bureau for the design of artificial limbs. After all, new legs would be the artificial limb to end all artificial limbs.

"But that is all for next year. Right now all I can use it for is to speed up replacement. If I can kid my cells into moving up onto embryo level activity—they would regrow fast enough to keep the inside works ticking after a really stiff jolt of the bottled dissolution. I'd have to follow it fast with the liquid protein— No, if they regrew that fast they would be using the material from the dissolved old cells. I could telescope treatment down to a few hours. And the nucleus control so active that it rebuilds according to its ideal.

"Demolition and Reconstruction going on simultaneously. Business as Usual.

"Next stop is the replacement of various soft tissues. If I were not in such a hurry, I would do it in two long slow simple Ghandi-like fasts, with practically no scientific mumbo jumbo. The way a sea squirt does it, I mean—though I'd like to see someone starve himself down to a foot high.

"I have to start working now. The record is running out anyhow, so good-by until the next record, whenever that is.

"Having wonderful time.

"Wish you were here."

He took the record off hurriedly and put on the next one. It was recorded on only one face, and dated September 17th, about fifty days later, seven weeks.

Helen started speaking without any introduction, her voice clearer and more distant as if she were speaking a few feet from the microphone.

"I'm rather upset Alec. Something rather astonishing has happened. Have to get you up to date first.

"The fasting treatment went fine. Of course I had to stay indoors and keep out of sight until I was fit to be seen. I'm almost back to normal now, gaining about a pound a day. The embryo status treatment stimulated my cells to really get to work. They seem to be rebuilding from an adult blueprint and not a fetal one, so I am getting flesh again in proper proportion and not like an overgrown baby.

"If I am talking disjointedly it is because I am trying hard not to get to the point. The point is too big to be said easily. Of course you know that I started this experimenting just to check my theoretical understanding of cell metabolism. Even the best available theory is sketchy, and my own guesses are doubtful and tentative. I never could be sure whether a patient recovered because of my treatment, in spite of my treatment—or just reacted psychosomatically to the size of my consultant fee.

"The best way to correct faulty theory is to carry it to its logical absurdity, and then to use the silliness as a clue to the initial fault.

"Recipe: to test theories of some process take one neutral subject—that's me—and try to induce a specific stage of that process by artificial means dictated by the theories. The point of failure will be the clue to the revision of the theories.

"I expected to spend the second half of my vacation in the hospital, checking over records of the experiment, and happily writing an article on the meaning of its failure.

"To be ready for the emergency I had hitched one of the electric timer clocks to the dictaphone and telephone. If I didn't punch it at five-hour intervals, the alarm would knock off the telephone receiver, and the dictaphone would yell for an ambulance.

"Pinned to a big sign just inside the door was an explanation and full instructions for the proper emergency treatment. At every step in the experiment I would rewrite the instructions to match. 'Be Prepared' was the motto. 'Plan for every contingency.' No matter when the experiment decided to blow up in my face I would be ready for it.

"There was only one contingency I did not plan for.

"Alec, I was just looking in the mirror. The only mirror that is any good is the big one in the front bedroom, but I had put off looking into it. For a week I lounged around reading and sleeping on the lab cot and the chair beside the window. I suppose I was still waiting for something to go wrong, but nothing did, and the skin of my hands was obviously different —no scars, no calluses, no tan, just smooth pink translucent skin—so I finally went and looked.

"Then I checked it with a medical exam. You'll find that data in with the other notes. Alec, I'm eighteen years old. That is as young as an adult can *get*.

"I wonder how Aladdin felt after rubbing a rusty lamp just to polish it up a bit.

"Surprised I suppose. The most noticeable feature of this new face so far is its surprised expression. It looks surprised from every angle, and sometimes it looks pale, and alarmed.

"Alarmed. Einstein was not alarmed when he discovered relativity, but they made a bomb out of it anyhow. I don't see how they could make a bomb out of this, but people are a wild, unpredictable lot. How will they react to being ageless? I can't guess, but I'm not reckless enough to hand out another Pandora's box to the world. The only safe way is to keep the secret until you get back, and then call a quiet council of experts for advice.

"But meanwhile, what if one of our friends happens to see me on the street looking like eighteen years old? What am I supposed to say?

"It is hard to be practical, darling. My imagination keeps galloping off in all directions. Did you know your hair is getting thin in back? Another two years with that crew cut and you would have begun to look like a monk.

"I know, I know, you'll tell me it is not fair for you to be a juvenile when every one else is gray, but what is fair? To be fair at all everyone will have to have the treatment available free, for *nothing*. And I mean *everyone*. We can leave it to an economist to worry out how. Meanwhile we will have to change our names and move to California. You don't want people to recognize you, and wonder who I am, do you? You don't want to go around looking twice as old as your wife and have people calling you a cradle snatcher, now do you?

"Wheedling aside, it is fair enough. The process is still

dangerous. You can call yourself Guinea Pig Number Two. That's fair. We can sign hotel registers G. Igpay and wife. Pardon me, Alec, I digress. It *is* hard to be practical, darling.

"If the treatment gets safely out of the lab and into circulation—rejuvenation worked down to a sort of official vaccination against old age—it would be good for the race I think. It may even help evolution. Regeneration would remove environmental handicaps, old scars of bad raising, and give every man a body as good as his genes. A world full of the age proof would be a sort of sound-mind, sound-body health marathon, with the longest breeding period won by the people with the best chromosomes and the healthiest family tradition.

"Thank heavens I can strike a blow for evolution at last. Usually I find myself on the opposite side, fighting to preserve the life of some case whose descendants will give doctors a headache.

"And look at cultural evolution! For the first time we humans will be able to use our one talent, learning, the way it should be used, the way it was meant to be used from the beginning, an unstoppable growth of skill and humor and understanding, experience adding layer on layer like the bark of a California Redwood.

"And we need thinkers with time to boil the huge accumulation of science down to some reasonable size. It is an emergency job—and not just for geniuses, the rest of us will have to help look for common denominators, too. Even ordinary specialists will have time to learn more, do some integrating of their own, join hands with specialists of related fields.

"Take us, a good sample of disjointed specialties. You could learn neurology, and I could learn anthropology and psychology, and then we could talk the same language and still be like Jack Spratt and his wife, covering the field of human behavior between us. We would be close enough to collaborate—without *many* gaps of absolute ignorance—to write the most wonderful books. We could even . . . ah— We *can* even—"

(There was a silence, and then a shaky laugh.)

"I forgot. I said, 'Take us for example,' as if we weren't examples already. Research is supposed to be for other people. This is for us. It *is* a shock. Funny—funny how it keeps taking me by surprise.

"It shouldn't make that much difference. After all, one lifetime is like another. We'll be the same people on the same job—with more time. Time enough to see the sequoias grow, and watch the ripening of the race. A long time.

"But the outside of the condemned cell is not very different from the inside. It is the same world, full of the same hare-brained human beings. And yet here I am, as shaky as if I've just missed being run over by a truck."

(There was another uncertain laugh.)

"I can't talk just now, Alec. I have to think."

For some minutes after the record stopped Alec stared out of the window, his hands locked behind his back, the knuckles working and whitening with tension. It was the last record, the only clue he had. The quaver in her voice, her choice of words, had emphatically filled his mind with the nameless emotion that had held her. It was almost a thought, a concept half felt, half seen lying on the borderline of logic.

Before his eyes persistently there grew a vision of the great pyramid of Cheops, half completed, with slaves toiling and dying on its slopes. He stared blindly out over the rooftops of the city, waiting, not daring to force the explanation. Presently the vision began to slip away, and his mind wandered to other thoughts. Somewhere down in that maze of buildings was Helen. Where?

It was no use. Unclenching his stiffening fingers Alec jotted down a small triangle on the envelope of the record, to remind himself that a pyramid held some sort of clue. As he did it, suddenly he remembered that Helen, when she was puzzled, liked to jot the problem down on paper as she thought.

On the bedroom vanity table there was a tablet of white paper, and beside it an ashtray holding a few cigarette stubs. The tablet was blank, but he found two crumpled sheets of paper in the wastebasket and smoothed them carefully out on the table.

It began "Dear Alec" and then there were words crossed and blotted out. "Dear Alec" was written again halfway down the sheet, and the letters absently embroidered into elaborate script. Under it were a few doodles, and then a clear surrealistic sketch of a wisdom tooth marked with neat dental work, lying on its side in the foreground of a desert. Subscribed was the title "TIME", and beside it was written critically, "Derivative: The lone and level sands stretch far away." Doodles and vague figures and faces covered the bottom of the page and extended over the next page. In the midst of them was written the single stark thought, "There is something wrong."

That was all. Numbly Alec folded the two sheets and put them into the envelope of the record. A tooth and a triangle. It should have been funny, but he could not laugh. He took the record out and considered it. There was another concentric ribbon of sound on the face of the disk. Helen had used it again, but the needle had balked at a narrow blank line where she had restarted the recorder and placed the stylus a little too far in.

He put the record back on the turntable and placed the needle by hand.

"Alec darling, I wish you were here. You aren't as good a parlor psychologist as any woman, but you do know human nature in a broad way, and can always explain its odder tricks. I thought I was clever at interpreting other people's behavior, but tonight I can't even interpret my own. Nothing startling has happened. It is just that I have been acting·unlike myself all day and I feel that it is a symptom of something unpleasant.

"I walked downtown to stretch my legs and see the crowds and bright lights again. I was looking at the movie stills in a theater front when I saw Lucy Hughes hurrying by with a package under one arm. I didn't turn around, but she recognized me and hurried over.

"'Why Helen Berent! I thought you were in Tibet.'

"I turned around and looked at her. Lucy, with her baby ways and feminine intuition. It would be easy to confide in her but she was not the kind to keep a secret. I didn't say anything. I suppose I just looked at her with that blank expression you say I wear when I am thinking.

"She looked back, and her eyes widened slowly.

"'Why you're too young. You're not—Heavens! I'm awfully

sorry. I thought you were someone else. Silly of me, but you look just like a friend of mine—when she was younger I mean. It's almost uncanny!

"I put on a slight western drawl, and answered politely, as a stranger should, and she went away shaking her head. Poor Lucy!

"I went in to see the movie. Alec, what happened next worries me. I stayed in that movie eight hours. It was an obnoxious movie, a hard-boiled detective story full of blood and violence and slaughter. I saw it three and a half times. You used to make critical remarks on the mental state of a public that battens on that sort of thud and blunder—something about Roman circuses. I wish I could remember how you explained it, because I need that explanation. When the movie house closed for the night I went home in a taxi. It drove too fast but I got home all right. There was some meat stew contaminated with botulus in the icebox, but I tasted the difference and threw it out. I have to be very careful. People are too careless. I never realized it before, but they are.

"I had better go to bed now and see if I can get some sleep."

Automatically Alec took the record off and slid it back into its envelope. The penciled triangle caught his eye, and his hands slowed and stopped. For a long time he looked at it without moving—the pyramids, the tombs of kings. An ancient religion that taught that one of man's souls lived on in his mummy, a ghostly spark that vanished if the human form was lost. A whisper of immortality on earth. Cheops, spending the piled treasures of his kingdom and the helpless lives of slaves merely for a tomb to shield his corpse, building a pitiful mountain of rock to mock his name down the centuries. Hope—and fear. Hope brings terror.

There are wells of madness in us never tapped.

Alec put away the record and stepped to the window. The brown towers of Columbia Medical Center showed in the distance. Cornell Medical was downtown, Bellevue—"Hope," said Alec. "When there is life there is hope," said Alec, and laughed harshly at the pun. He knew now what he had to do. He turned away from the window, and picking up a classified telephone directory, turned to "Hospitals".

It was evening. The psychiatric resident doctor escorted him down the hall talking companionably.

"She wouldn't give her name. Part of the complex. A symptom for us, but pretty hard on you. It would have helped you to find her if she had some identifying marks I suppose, like scars I mean. It is unusual to find anyone without any—"

"What's her trouble?" asked Alec. "Anxiety? Afraid of things, germs, falls—?"

"She's afraid all right. Even afraid of me! Says I have germs. Says I'm incompetent. It's all a symptom of some other fear of course. These things are not what she is really afraid of. Once we find the single repressed fear and explain it to her—" He checked Alec's objection. "It's not rational to be afraid of little things. Those little dangers are not what she is really afraid of anyhow. Now suppression—"

Alec interrupted with a slight edge to his voice.

"Are you afraid of death?"

"Not much. There is nothing you can do about it, after all, so normal people must manage to get used to the idea. Now she—"

"You have a religion?"

"Vedanta. What of it? Now her attitude in this case is—"

"Even a mouse can have a nervous breakdown!" Alec snapped. "Where is the repression there? Vedanta you said? Trouble is, Helen is just too rational!" They had stopped. "Is this the room?"

"Yeah," said the doctor sullenly, making no move to open the door. "She is probably still asleep." He looked at his watch. "No, she would be coming out of it now."

"Drugs," said Alec coldly. "I suppose you have been psychoanalyzing her, trying to trace her trouble back to some time when her mother slapped her with a lollypop, eh? Or shock treatment perhaps, burning out the powers of imagination, eh?"

The young psychiatrist let his annoyance show. "We know our jobs, mister. Sedatives and analysis, without them she would be screaming the roof off. She's too suspicious to consciously confide her warp to us, but under scopolamine she seems to think she is a middle-aged woman. How rational is *that?*" With an effort he regained his professional blandness.

"She has not said much so far, but we expect to learn more after the next treatment. Of course being told her family history will help us immeasurably. We would like to meet her father and mother."

"I'll do everything in my power to help," Alec replied. "Where there is life there is hope." He laughed harshly, on a note that drew a keen professional glance from the doctor. The young man put his hand to the knob, his face bland.

"You may go in and identify her now. Remember, be very careful not to frighten her." He opened the door and stood aside, then followed Alec in.

Helen lay on the bed asleep, her dark hair lying across one cheek. She looked like a tired kid of nineteen, but to Alec there seemed to be no change. She had always looked this way. It was Helen.

The doctor called gently. "Miss . . . ah . . . Berent. Miss Berent."

Helen's body stiffened, but she did not open her eyes. "Go away," she said in a small, flat voice. "Please!"

"It is just Dr. Marro," the young man said soothingly.

"How do I know you are a doctor?" she said without stirring. "You'd say that anyway. Maybe you escaped and disguised yourself as a doctor. Maybe you are a paranoiac."

"I'm just myself," said the resident, shrugging. "Just Dr. Marro. How can I prove it to you if you don't look at me?"

The small voice sounded like a child reciting. It said: "If you are a doctor, you will see that having you here upsets me. You won't want to upset me, so you will go away." She smiled secretly at the wall. "Go away please."

Then, abruptly terrified, she was sitting up, staring. "You called me Miss Berent. Oh, Alec!" Her eyes dilated like dark pools in a chalk face, and then Helen crumpled up and rolled to face the wall, gasping in dry sobs. "Please, please—"

"You are exciting her, Mr. Berent," said the resident. "I'm sorry, but I'm afraid you'll have to leave."

It had to be done. Alec swallowed with a dry mouth, and then said in a loud clear voice, enunciating every syllable:

"Helen, honey, you are dying."

For a moment there was a strange silence. The doctor was looking at him with a shocked white face; then he moved, fumbling for an arm lock, fumbling with his voice for the proper cheerful tone. "Come, Mr. Berent, you . . . we must be going now."

Alec swung his clenched fist into the babbling white face. The jolt on his knuckles felt right. He did not bother to watch the doctor fall. It only meant that he would have a short time without interruption. Helen was cowering in the far corner of the bed, muttering "No—no—no—no—" in a meaningless voice. The limp weight of the psychiatrist leaned against his leg and then slipped down and pressed across the toes of his shoes.

"Helen," Alec called clearly, "Helen, you are dying. You have cancer."

She answered only with a wordless animal whimper. Alec looked away. The gleaming white walls began to lean at crazy angles. He shut his eyes and thought of darkness and silence. Presently the whimpering stopped. A voice faltered: "No, I am never going to d— No, I am not."

"Yes," he said firmly, "you are." The darkness ebbed. Alec opened his eyes. Helen had turned around and was watching him, a line of puzzlement on her forehead. "Really?" she asked childishly.

His face was damp, but he did not move to wipe it. "Yes," he stated, "absolutely certain. Cancer, incurable cancer."

"Cancer," she murmured wonderingly. "Where?"

He had that answer ready. He had picked it from an atlas of anatomy as an inaccessible spot, hard to confirm or deny, impossible to operate for. He told her.

She considered for a second, a vague puzzlement wrinkling her face. "Then . . . I can't do anything about it. It would happen just the same. It's there now." She looked up absently, rubbing a hand across her forehead. "The deadline?"

"It's very small and encysted." Casually he waved a hand. "Maybe even ten—twenty years."

Thinking, she got out of bed and stood looking out the window, her lips pursed as if she were whistling.

Alec turned to watch her, a polite smile fixed on his lips. He could feel the doctor's weight shifting as his head cleared.

"Cells," Helen murmured, once, then exclaimed suddenly to herself. "Of course not!" She chuckled, and chuckling spoke in her own warm voice, the thin note of fear gone. "Alec, you'll never guess what I have been doing. Wait until you hear the records!" She laughed delightedly. "A wild goose chase! I'm ashamed to face you. And I didn't see it until this minute."

"Didn't see what, honey?"

The doctor got to his knees and softly crawled away.

Helen swung around gayly. "Didn't see that all cells are mutable, not just germ cells but all cells. If they keep on multiplying—each cell with the same probability of mutation —and some viable mutations would be cancerous, then everybody— Work it out on a slide rule for me, Hon. I didn't discover immortality. Everybody who lives long enough will die of something with so many million cells in the body, with—"

She had been looking past him at the new idea, but now her gaze focused and softened. "Alec, you look so tired. You shouldn't be pale after all your tramping around in—" The mists of thought cleared. She saw him. "Alec, you're back."

And now there was no space or time separating them and she was warm and alive in his arms, nuzzling his cheek, whispering a chuckle in his ear. "And I was standing there lecturing you about cells! I must have been crazy."

He could hear the doctor padding up the hall with a squad of husky attendants, but he didn't care. Helen was back.

> *From too much love of living*
> *From hope and fear set free*
> *We thank with brief thanksgiving*
> *Whatever gods may be*
> *That no life lives for ever;*
> *That dead men rise up never;*
> *That even the weariest river*
> *Winds somewhere safe to sea.*
>
> Swinburne

THE SNOWBALL EFFECT

"ALL RIGHT," I said, "what is sociology good for?"

Wilton Caswell, Ph.D., was head of my Sociology Department, and right then he was mad enough to chew nails. On the office wall behind him were three or four framed documents in Latin that were supposed to be signs of great learning, but I didn't care at that moment if he papered the walls with his degrees. I had been appointed dean and president to see to it that the university made money. I had a job to do, and I meant to do it.

He bit off each word with great restraint: "Sociology is the study of social institutions, Mr. Halloway."

I tried to make him understand my position. "Look, it's the big-money men who are supposed to be contributing to the support of this college. To them, sociology sounds like socialism—nothing can sound worse than that—and an institution is where they put Aunt Maggy when she began collecting Wheaties in a stamp album. We can't appeal to them that way. Come on now." I smiled condescendingly, knowing it would irritate him. "What are you doing that's worth anything?"

He glared at me, his white hair bristling and his nostrils dilated like a war horse about to whinny. I can say one thing for them—these scientists and professors always keep themselves well under control. He had a book in his hand and I was expecting him to throw it, but he spoke instead:

"This department's analysis of institutional accretion, by the use of open system mathematics, has been recognized as an outstanding and valuable contribution to—"

The words were impressive, whatever they meant, but this still didn't sound like anything that would pull in money. I interrupted. "Valuable in what way?"

He sat down on the edge of his desk, thoughtful, apparently recovering from the shock of being asked to produce something solid for his position, and ran his eyes over the titles of the books that lined his office walls.

"Well, sociology has been valuable to business in initiating worker efficiency and group motivation studies, which they now use in management decisions. And, of course, since the depression, Washington has been using sociological studies of employment labor and standards of living as a basis for its general policies of—"

I stopped him with both raised hands. "Please, Professor Caswell! That would hardly be a recommendation. Washington, the New Deal and the present Administration are somewhat touchy subjects to the men I have to deal with. They consider its value debatable, if you know what I mean. If they got the idea that sociology professors are giving advice and guidance— No, we have to stick to brass tacks and leave Washington out of this. What, specifically, has the work of this specific department done that would make it as worthy to receive money as—say, a heart disease research fund?"

He began to tap the corner of his book absently on the desk, watching me. "Fundamental research doesn't show immediate effects, Mr. Halloway, but its value is recognized."

I smiled and took out my pipe. "All right, tell me about it. Maybe I'll recognize its value."

Prof. Caswell smiled back tightly. He knew his department was at stake. The other departments were popular with donors and pulled in gift money by scholarships and fellowships, and supported their professors and graduate students by research contracts with the government and industry. Caswell had to show a way to make his own department popular—or else. I couldn't fire him directly, of course, but there are ways of doing it indirectly.

He laid down his book and ran a hand over his ruffled hair. "Institutions—organizations, that is—" his voice became more resonant; like most professors, when he had to explain something he instinctively slipped into his platform lecture mannerisms, and began to deliver an essay— "have certain tendencies built into the way they happen to have been organized, which cause them to expand or contract without reference to the needs they were founded to serve."

He was becoming flushed with the pleasure of explaining his subject. "All through the ages, it has been a matter of wonder and dismay to men that a simple organization—such as a church to worship in, or a delegation of weapons to a warrior class merely for defense against an outside enemy—will either grow insensately and extend its control until it is a tyranny over their whole lives, or, like other organizations set up to serve a vital need, will tend to repeatedly dwindle and vanish, and have to be painfully rebuilt.

"The reason can be traced to little quirks in the way they were organized, a matter of positive and negative power feedbacks. Such simple questions as, 'Is there a way a holder of authority in this organization can use the power available to him to increase his power?' provide the key. But it still could not be handled until the complex questions of interacting motives and long-range accumulations of minor effects could somehow be simplified and formulated. In working on the problem, I found that the mathematics of open system, as introduced to biology by Ludwig von Bertalanffy and George Kreezer, could be used as a base that would enable me to develop a specifically social mathematics, expressing the human factors of intermeshing authority and motives in simple formulas.

"By these formulations, it is possible to determine automatically the amount of growth and period of life of any organization. The UN, to choose an unfortunate example, is a shrinker type organization. Its monetary support is not in the hands of those who personally benefit by its governmental activities, but, instead, in the hands of those who would personally lose by an extension and encroachment of its authority on their own. Yet by the use of formula analysis—"

"That's theory," I said. "How about proof?"

"My equations are already being used in the study of limited size Federal corporations. Washington—"

I held up my palm again. "Please, not that nasty word again. I mean, where else has it been put into operation? Just a simple demonstration, something to show that it works, that's all."

He looked away from me thoughtfully, picked up the book and began to tap it on the desk again. It had some unreadable title and his name on it in gold letters. I got the distinct impression again that he was repressing an urge to hit me with it.

He spoke quietly. "All right, I'll give you a demonstration. Are you willing to wait six months?"

"Certainly, if you can show me something at the end of that time."

Reminded of time, I glanced at my watch and stood up.

"Could we discuss this over lunch?" he asked.

"I wouldn't mind hearing more, but I'm having lunch with some executors of a millionaire's will. They have to be convinced that by, 'furtherance of research into human ills,' he meant that the money should go to research fellowships for postgraduate biologists at the university, rather than to a medical foundation."

"I see you have your problems, too," Caswell said, conceding me nothing. He extended his hand with a chilly smile. "Well, good afternoon, Mr. Halloway. I'm glad we had this talk."

I shook hands and left him standing there, sure of his place in the progress of science and the respect of his colleagues, yet seething inside because I, the president and dean, had boorishly demanded that he produce something tangible.

I frankly didn't give a hoot if he blew his lid. My job isn't easy. For a crumb of favorable publicity and respect in the newspapers and an annual ceremony in a silly costume, I spend the rest of the year going hat in hand, asking politely for money at everyone's door, like a well-dressed panhandler, and trying to manage the university on the dribble I get. As far as I was concerned, a department had to support itself or be cut down to what student tuition pays for, which is a handful of over-crowded courses taught by an assistant lecturer. Caswell had to make it work or get out.

But the more I thought about it, the more I wanted to hear what he was going to do for a demonstration.

At lunch, three days later, while we were waiting for our order, he opened a small notebook. "Ever hear of feed-back effects?"

"Not enough to have it clear."

"You know the snowball effect, though."

"Sure, start a snowball rolling downhill and it grows."

"Well, now—" He wrote a short line of symbols on a blank

page and turned the notebook around for me to inspect it. "Here's the formula for the snowball process. It's the basic general growth formula—covers everything."

It was a row of little symbols arranged like an algebra equation. One was a concentric spiral going up, like a cross-section of a snowball rolling in snow. That was a growth sign.

I hadn't expected to understand the equation, but it was almost as clear as a sentence. I was impressed and slightly intimidated by it. He had already explained enough so that I knew that, if he was right, here was the growth of the Catholic Church and the Roman Empire, the conquests of Alexander and the spread of the smoking habit and the change of the unwritten laws of styles.

"Is it really as simple as that?" I asked.

"You notice," he said, "that when it becomes too heavy for the cohesion strength of snow, it breaks apart. Now in human terms—"

The chops and mashed potatoes and peas arrived.

"Go on," I urged.

He was deep in the symbology of human motives and the equations of human behavior in groups. After running through a few different types of grower and shrinker type organizations, we came back to the snowball, and decided to run the test by making something grow.

"You add the motives," he said, "and the equation will translate them into organization."

"How about a good selfish reason for the ins to drag others into the group—some sort of bounty on new members, a cut of their membership fee?" I suggested uncertainly, feeling slightly foolish. "And maybe a reason why the members would lose if any of them resigned, and some indirect way they could use to force each other to stay in."

"The first is the chain letter principle," he nodded. "I've got that. The other . . . ." He put the symbols through some mathematical manipulation so that a special grouping appeared in the middle of the equation. "That's it."

Since I seemed to have the right idea, I suggested some more, and he added some, and juggled them around in different patterns. We threw out a few that would have made the organization too complicated, and finally worked out an idyllically simple and deadly little organization setup where joining had all the temptation of buying a sweepstakes ticket, going in deeper was as easy as hanging around a race track, and getting out was like trying to pull free from a Malayan thumb trap. We put our heads closer together and talked lower, picking the best place for the demonstration.

"Abington?"

"How about Watashaw? I have some student sociological surveys of it already. We can pick a suitable group from that."

"This demonstration has got to be convincing. We'd better pick a little group that no one in his right mind would expect to grow."

"There should be a suitable club—"

Picture Professor Caswell, head of the Department of Sociology, and with him the President of the University, leaning across the table toward each other, sipping coffee and talking in conspiratorial tones over something they were writing in a notebook.

That was us.

"Ladies," said the skinny female chairman of the Watashaw Sewing Circle. "Today we have guests." She signaled for us to rise, and we stood up, bowing to polite applause and smiles. "Professor Caswell, and Professor Smith." (My alias.) "They are making a survey of the methods and duties of the clubs of Watashaw."

We sat down to another ripple of applause and slightly wider smiles, and then the meeting of the Watashaw Sewing Circle began. In five minutes I began to feel sleepy.

There were only about thirty people there, and it was a small room, not the halls of Congress, but they discussed their business of collecting and repairing second hand clothing for charity with endless, boring parliamentary formality.

I pointed out to Caswell the member I thought would be the natural leader, a tall well-built woman in a green suit, with conscious gestures and resonant, penetrating voice, and then went into a half doze while Caswell stayed awake beside me and wrote in his notebook. After a while the resonant voice roused me to attention for a moment. It was the tall woman holding the floor over some collective dereliction of the club. She was being scathing.

I nudged Caswell and murmured, "Did you fix it so that a shover has a better chance of getting into office than a non-shover?"

"I think there's a way they could find for it," Caswell whispered back, and went to work on his equation again. "Yes, several ways to bias the elections."

"Good. Point them out tactfully to the one you select. Not as if she'd use such methods, but just as an example of the reason why only *she* can be trusted with initiating the change. Just mention all the personal advantages an unscrupulous person could have."

He nodded, keeping a straight and sober face as if we were exchanging admiring remarks about the techniques of clothes repairing, instead of conspiring.

After the meeting, Caswell drew the tall woman in the green suit aside and spoke to her confidentially, showing her the diagram of organization we had drawn up. I saw the responsive glitter in the woman's eyes and knew she was hooked.

We left the diagram of organization and our typed copy of the new bylaws with her and went off soberly, as befitted two social science experimenters. We didn't start laughing until our car passed the town limits and began the climb for University Heights.

If Caswell's equations meant anything at all, we had given that sewing circle more growth drives than the Roman Empire.

Four months later I had time out from a very busy schedule to wonder how the test was coming along. Passing Caswell's office, I put my head in. He looked up from a student research paper he was correcting.

"Caswell, about that sewing club business—I'm beginning to feel the suspense. Could I get an advance report on how it's coming?"

"I'm not following it. We're supposed to let it run the full six months."

"But I'm curious. Could I get in touch with that woman— what's her name?"

"Searles, Mrs. George Searles."

"Would that change the results?"

"Not in the slightest. If you want to graph the membership rise, it should be going up in a log curve, probably doubling every so often."

I grinned. "If it's not rising, you're fired."

He grinned back. "If it's not rising you won't have to fire me—I'll burn my books and shoot myself."

I returned to my office and put in a call to Watashaw. While I was waiting for the phone to be answered, I took a piece of graph paper and ruled it off into six sections, one for each month. After the phone had rung in the distance for a long time, a servant answered with a bored drawl:

"Mrs. Searles' residence."

I picked up a red gummed star and licked it.

"Mrs. Searles, please."

"She's not in just now. Could I take a message?"

I placed the star at the thirty line in the beginning of the first section. Thirty members they'd started with.

"No, thanks. Could you tell me when she'll be back?"

"Not until dinner. She's at the meetin'."

"The sewing club?" I asked.

"No, sir, not that thing. There isn't any sewing club any more, not for a long time. She's at the Civic Welfare meeting."

Somehow I hadn't expected anything like that.

"Thank you," I said and hung up, and after a moment noticed I was holding a box of red gummed stars in my hand. I closed it and put it down on top of the graph of membership in the sewing circle. No more members . . . .

Poor Caswell. The bet between us was ironclad. He wouldn't let me back down on it even if I wanted to. He'd probably quit before I put through the first slow move to fire him. His professional pride would be shattered, sunk without a trace. I remembered what he said about shooting himself. It had seemed funny to both of us at the time, but . . . . What a mess that would make for the university.

I had to talk to Mrs. Searles. Perhaps there was some outside reason why the club had disbanded. Perhaps it had not just died.

I called back. "This is Professor Smith," I said, giving the alias I had used before. "I called a few minutes ago. When did you say Mrs. Searles will return?"

"About six-thirty or seven o'clock."

Five hours to wait.

And what if Caswell asked me what I had found out in the meantime? I didn't want to tell him anything until I had talked it over with that woman Searles first.

"Where is this Civic Welfare meeting?"

He told me.

Five minutes later, I was in my car, heading for Watashaw, driving considerably faster than my usual speed and keeping a careful watch for highway patrol cars as the speedometer climbed.

The town meeting hall and theater was a big place, probably with lots of small rooms for different clubs. I went in through the center door and found myself in the huge central hall where some sort of rally was being held. A political-type rally —you know, cheers and chants, with bunting already down on the floor, people holding banners, and plenty of enthusiasm and excitement in the air. Someone was making a speech up on the platform. Most of the people there were women.

I wondered how the Civic Welfare League could dare hold its meeting at the same time as a political rally that could pull its members away. The group with Mrs. Searles was probably holding a shrunken and almost memberless meeting somewhere in an upper room.

There probably was a side door that would lead upstairs.

While I glanced around, a pretty girl usher put a printed bulletin in my hand, whispering, "Here's one of the new copies." As I attempted to hand it back, she retreated. "Oh, you can keep it. It's a new one. Everyone's supposed to have it. We've just printed up six thousand copies to make sure there'll be enough to last."

The tall woman on the platform had been making a driving, forceful speech about some plans for rebuilding Watashaw's slum section. It began to penetrate my mind dimly as I glanced down at the bulletin in my hands.

"Civic Welfare League of Watashaw. The United Organization of Church and Secular Charities." That's what it said. Below began the rules of membership.

I looked up. The speaker, with a clear, determined voice and conscious, forceful gestures, had entered the home-stretch of her speech, an appeal to the civic pride of all citizens of Watashaw.

"With a bright and glorious future—potentially without poor and without uncared-for ill—potentially with no ugliness, no vistas which are not beautiful—the best people in the best planned town in the country—the jewel of the United States."

She paused and then leaned forward intensely, striking her clenched hand on the speaker's stand with each word for emphasis.

"All we need is more members. Now get out there and recruit!"

I finally recognized Mrs. Searles, as an answering sudden blast of sound half deafened me. The crowd was chanting at the top of its lungs: "Recruit! Recruit!"

Mrs. Searles stood still at the speaker's table and behind her, seated in a row of chairs, was a group that was probably the board of directors. It was mostly women, and the women began to look vaguely familiar, as if they could be members of the sewing circle.

I put my lips close to the ear of the pretty usher while I turned over the stiff printed bulletin on a hunch. "How long has the League been organized?" On the back of the bulletin was a constitution.

She was cheering with the crowd, her eyes sparkling. "I don't know," she answered between cheers. "I only joined two days ago. Isn't it wonderful?"

I went into the quiet outer air and got into my car with my skin prickling. Even as I drove away, I could hear them. They were singing some kind of organization song with the tune of "Marching through Georgia."

Even at the single glance I had given it, the constitution looked exactly like the one we had given the Watashaw Sewing Circle.

All I told Caswell when I got back was that the sewing

circle had changed its name and the membership seemed to be rising.

Next day, after calling Mrs. Searles, I placed some red stars on my graph for the first three months. They made a nice curve, rising more steeply as it reached the fourth month. They had picked up their first increase in membership simply by amalgamating with all the other types of charity organizations in Watashaw, changing the club name with each fusion, but keeping the same constitution—the constitution with the bright promise of advantages as long as there were always new members being brought in.

By the fifth month, the League had added a mutual baby-sitting service and had induced the local school board to add a nursery school to the town service, so as to free more women for League activity. But charity must have been completely organized by then, and expansion had to be in other directions.

Some real estate agents evidently had been drawn into the whirlpool early, along with their ideas. The slum improvement plans began to blossom and take on a tinge of real estate planning later in the month.

The first day of the sixth month, a big two-page spread appeared in the local paper of a mass meeting which had approved a full-fledged scheme for slum clearance of Watashaw's shack-town section, plus plans for rehousing, civic building, and rezoning. *And* good prospects for attracting some new industries to the town, industries which had already been contacted and seemed interested by the privileges offered.

And with all this, an arrangement for securing and distributing to the club members *alone* most of the profit that would come to the town in the form of a rise in the price of building sites and a boom in the building industry. The profit distributing arrangement was the same one that had been built into the organization plan for the distribution of the small profits of membership fees and honorary promotions. It was becoming an openly profitable business. Membership was rising more rapidly now.

By the second week of the sixth month, news appeared in the local paper that the club had filed application to incorporate itself as the Watashaw Mutual Trade and Civic Development Corporation, and all the local real estate promoters had finished joining en masse. The Mutual Trade part sounded to me as if the Chamber of Commerce was on the point of being pulled in with them, ideas, ambitions and all.

I chuckled while reading the next page of the paper, on which a local politician was reported as having addressed the club with a long flowery oration on their enterprise, charity, and civic spirit. He had been made an honorary member. If he allowed himself to be made a *full* member with its contractual obligations and its lures, if the politicians went into this too. . . .

I laughed, filing the newspaper with the other documents on the Watashaw test. These proofs would fascinate any businessman with the sense to see where his bread was buttered. A businessman is constantly dealing with organizations, including his own, and finding them either inert, cantankerous, or both. Caswell's formula could be a handle to grasp them with. Gratitude alone would bring money into the university in carload lots.

The end of the sixth month came. The test was over and the end reports were spectacular. Caswell's formulas were proven to the hilt.

After reading the last newspaper reports, I called him up.

"Perfect, Wilt, *perfect!* I can use this Watashaw thing to get you so many fellowships and scholarships and grants for your department that you'll think it's snowing money!"

He answered somewhat disinterestedly, "I've been busy working with students on their research papers and marking tests—not following the Watashaw business at all, I'm afraid. You say the demonstration went well and you're satisfied?"

He was definitely putting on a chill. We were friends now, but obviously he was still peeved whenever he was reminded that I had doubted that his theory could work. And he was using its success to rub my nose in the realization that I had been wrong. A man with a string of degrees after his name is just as human as anyone else. I had needled him pretty hard that first time.

"I'm satisfied," I acknowledged. "I was wrong. The formulas

work beautifully. Come over and see my file of documents on it if you want a boost for your ego. Now let's see the formula for stopping it."

He sounded cheerful again. "I didn't complicate that organization with negatives. I wanted it to *grow*. It falls apart naturally when it stops growing for more than two months. It's like the great stock boom before an economic crash. Everyone in it is prosperous as long as the prices just keep going up and new buyers come into the market, but they all knew what would happen if it stopped growing. You remember, we built in as one of the incentives that the members know they are going to lose if membership stops growing. Why, if I tried to stop it now, they'd cut my throat."

I remembered the drive and frenzy of the crowd in the one early meeting I had seen. They probably would.

"No," he continued. "We'll just let it play out to the end of its tether and die of old age."

"When will that be?"

"It can't grow past the female population of the town. There are only so many women in Watashaw, and some of them don't like sewing."

The graph on the desk before me began to look sinister. Surely Caswell must have made some provision for—

"You underestimate their ingenuity," I said into the phone. "Since they wanted to expand, they didn't stick to sewing. They went from general charity to social welfare schemes to something that's pretty close to an incorporated government. The name is now the Watashaw Mutual Trade and Civic Development Corporation, and they're filing an application to change it to Civic Property Pool and Social Dividend, membership contractual, open to all. That social dividend sounds like a Technocrat climbed on the band wagon, eh?"

While I spoke, I carefully added another red star to the curve above the thousand members level, checking with the newspaper that still lay open on my desk. The curve was definitely some sort of log curve now, growing more rapidly with each increase.

"Leaving out practical limitations for a moment, where does the formula say it will stop?" I asked.

"When you run out of people to join it. But after all, there are only so many people in Watashaw. It's a pretty small town."

"They've opened a branch office in New York," I said carefully into the phone, a few weeks later.

With my pencil, very carefully, I extended the membership curve from where it was then.

After the next doubling, the curve went almost straight up and off the page.

Allowing for a lag of contagion from one nation to another, depending on how much their citizens intermingled, I'd give the rest of the world about twelve years.

There was a long silence while Caswell probably drew the same graph in his own mind. Then he laughed weakly. "Well, you asked me for a demonstration."

That was as good an answer as any. We got together and had lunch in a bar, if you can call it lunch. The movement we started will expand by hook or by crook, by seduction or by bribery or by propaganda or by conquest, but it will expand. And maybe a total world government will be a fine thing —until it hits the end of its rope in twelve years or so.

What happens then, I don't know.

But I don't want anyone to pin that on me. From now on, if anyone asks me, I've never heard of Watashaw.

INCOMMUNICADO

The solar system is not a gentle place. Ten misassorted centers of gigantic pulls and tensions, swinging around each other in ponderous accidental equilibrium, filling space with the violence of their silent battle. Among these giant forces the tiny ships of Earth were overmatched and weak. Few could spend power enough to climb back to space from the vortex of any planet's field, few dared approach closer than to the satellite spaceports.

Ambition always overreaches strength. There will always be a power shortage. Space became inhabited by underpowered private ships. In a hard school of sudden death new skills were learned. In understanding hands the violence of gravitation, heat, and cold, became sustenance, speed, and power. The knack of traveling was to fall, and fall without resistance, following a free line, using the precious fuel only for fractional changes of direction. To fall, to miss and "bounce" in a zigzag of carom shots—it was a good game for a pool shark, a good game for a handball addict, a pinball specialist, a kinetics expert. . . .

"Kinetics expert" is what they called Cliff Baker.

At the sixth hour of the fourth week of Pluto Station project he had nothing more to worry about than a fragment of tune which would not finish itself. Cliff floated out of the master control room whistling softly and looking for something to do.

A snatch of Smitty's discordant voice raised in song came from a hatch as he passed. Cliff changed direction and dove through into the darkness of a glassite dome. A rubbery crossbar stopped him at the glowing control panel.

"Take a break, Smitty. Let me take over for a while."

"Hi, chief," said Smitty, his hands moving deftly at the panel. "Thanks. How come you can spare the time? Is the rest of the circus so smooth? No emergencies, everything on schedule?"

114

"Like clockwork," said Cliff. "Knock wood." He crossed fingers for luck and solemnly rapped his skull. "Take a half hour, but keep your earphones tuned in case something breaks."

"Sure." Smitty gave Cliff a slap on the shoulder and shoved off. "Watch yourself now. Look out for the psychologist." His laugh echoed back from the corridor.

Cliff laughed in answer. Obviously Smitty had seen the new movie, too. Ten minutes later when the psychologist came in, Cliff was still grinning. The movie had been laid in a deep-space construction project that was apparently intended to represent Pluto Station project, and it had been commanded by a movie version of Cliff and Mike; Cliff acted by a burly silent character carrying a heavy, unidentified tool, and Mike Cohen of the silver tongue by a handsome young actor in a wavy pale wig. In this version they were both bachelors and wasted much time in happy pursuit of a gorgeous blonde.

The blonde was supposed to be the visiting psychologist sent up by Spaceways. She was a master personality who could hypnotize with a glance, a sorceress who could produce mass hallucinations with a gesture. She wound up saving the Earth from Cliff. He was supposed to have been subtly and insanely arranging the Pluto Station orbit, so that when it was finished it would leave Pluto and fall on Earth like a bomb.

Cliff had been watching the movie through an eyepiece-earphone rig during a rest period, but he laughed so much he fell out of his hammock and tangled himself in guide lines, and the others on the rest shift had given up trying to sleep and decided to play the movie on the big projector. They would be calling in on the earphones about it soon, kidding him.

He grinned, listening to the psychologist without subtracting from the speed and concentration of handling the control panel. Out in space before the ship, working as deftly as a distant pair of hands, the bulldog construction units unwrapped floating bundles of parts, spun, pulled, magnetized, fitted, welded, assembling another complex perfect segment of the huge Pluto Station.

"I'd like to get back to Earth," said the psychologist in a soft tenor voice that was faintly Irish, like a younger brother of Mike. "Look, Cliff, you're top man in this line. You can plot me a short cut, can't you?" The psychologist, Roy Pierce, was a slender dark Polynesian who seemed less than twenty years old. During his stay he had floated around watching with all the innocent awe of a tourist, and proved his profession only in an ingratiating skill with jokes. Yet he was extremely likeable, and seemed familiar in some undefinable way, as if one had known him all his life.

"Why not use the astrogator?" Cliff asked him mildly.

"Blast the astrogator! All it gives is courses that swing around the whole rim of the System and won't get me home for weeks!"

"It doesn't have to do that," Cliff said thoughtfully. The segment was finished. He set the controls of the bulldogs to guide it to the next working sector and turned around, lining up factors in his mind. "Why not stick around? Maybe someone will develop a split personality for you."

"My wife is having a baby," Pierce explained. "I promised I'd be there. Besides, I want to help educate it through the first year. There are certain things a baby can learn that make a difference later."

"Are you willing to spend four days in the acceleration tank just to go down and pester your poor kid?" Cliff floated over to a celestial sphere and idly spun it back and forth through the planetary positions of the month.

"Of course."

"O.K. I think I see a short cut. It's a little risky, and the astrogator is inhibited against risk. I'll tell you later."

"You're stalling," complained Pierce, yanking peevishly at a bending crossbar. "You're the expert who keeps the orbits of three thousand flying skew bodies tied in fancy knots, and here I want just a simple orbit for one little flitter. You could tell me now."

Cliff laughed. "You exaggerate, kid. I'm only half the expert. Mike is the other half. Like two halves of a stage horse. I can see a course that I could take myself, but it has to go on automatic tapes for you. Mike can tell me if he can make a computer see it, too. If he can, you'll leave in an hour."

Pierce brightened. "I'll go pack. Excuse me, Cliff."

As Pierce shoved off towards the hatch, Mike Cohen came in, wearing a spacesuit unzipped and flapping at the cuffs, talking as easily as if he had not stopped since the last conversation. "Did you see the new movie during rest shift, Cliff? That hulking lout who played yourself—" Mike smiled maliciously at Pierce as they passed in the semi-dark. "Hi, Kid. Speaking of acts, who were you this time?"

"Michael E. Cohen," said the youth, as he floated out. He looked back to see Mike's expression and before shoving from sight added maliciously, "I always pick the character for whom my subject has developed the greatest shock tolerance."

"Ouch!" Mike murmured. "But I hope I have no such edged tongue as that." He gripped a crossbar and swung to a stop before Cliff. "The boy is a chameleon," he said, half admiringly. "But I wonder has he any personality of his own."

Cliff said flatly, "I like him."

Mike raised his villainous black eyebrows and spread his hands, a plaintive note coming into his voice. "Don't we all? It is his business to be liked. But who is it that we like? These mirror trained sensitives—"

"He's a nice honest kid," Cliff said. Outside, the constructor units flew up to the dome and buzzed around in circles waiting for control. Another bundle of parts from the asteroid belt foundry began to float by. Hastily Cliff seized a pencil and scrawled a diagram on a sheet of paper, then returned to the controls. "He wants to go back to Earth. Could you tape that course? It cuts air for a sling turn at Venus."

An hour later Mike and Cliff escorted the psychologist to his ship and inserted the control tapes with words of fatherly advice.

Mike said cheerfully: "You will be running across uncharted space with no blinker buoys with the rocks, so you had better stay in the shock tank and pray."

And Cliff said cheerfully, "If you get off course below Mars, don't bother signalling for help. You're sunk."

"You know, Cliff," Mike said, "too many people get cooked that way. Maybe we should do something."

"How about Mercury?"

"Just the thing, Cliff. Listen, Kid, don't worry. If you fall into the Sun, we'll build a rescue station on Mercury and name it after you."

A warning bell rang from the automatics, and the two

pushed out through the air lock into space with Cliff protesting. "That's not it. About Mercury I meant—"

"Hear the man complaining," Mike interrupted. "And what would you do without me around to finish your sentences for you?"

Eight hours later Mike was dead. Some pilot accidentally ran his ship out of the assigned lanes and left the ionized gas of his jets to drift across a sector of space where Mike and three assistants were setting up the nucleus of the station power plant.

They were binding in high velocities with fields that put a heavy drain on the power plants of distant ships. They were working behind schedule, working fast, and using space gaps for insulation.

When the ionized gas drifted in everything arced.

The busy engineers in all the ring of asteroids and metalwork that circled Pluto saw a distant flash that filled their earphones with a howl of static, and at the central power plants certain dials registered a sudden intolerable drain, and safety relays quietly cut off power from that sector. Binding fields vanished and circular velocities straightened out. As the intolerable blue flash faded, dull red pieces of metal bulleted out from the damaged sector and were lost in space. The remainder of the equipment began to drift in aimless collisions.

Quietly the emergency calls came into the earphones of all sleeping men, dragging them yawning from their hammocks to begin the long delicate job of charting and rebalancing the great assembly spiral.

One of the stray pieces charted was an eighty-foot asteroid nugget that Mike was known to have been working on. It was falling irrevocably towards Pluto. For a time a searchlight glinted over fused and twisted metal which had been equipment, but it came no closer and presently was switched out, leaving the asteroid to darkness.

The damage, when fully counted, was bad enough to require the rebalancing of the entire work schedule for the remaining months of the project: subtracting the work hours of four men and all work on the power plant that had been counted done; a rewriting of an intricate mathematical jigsaw puzzle of hours; skills; limited fuel and power factors; tools; and heavy parts coming up with inexorable inertia from the distant sunward orbits where they had been launched over a year ago.

No one took the accident too hard. They knew their job was dangerous, and were not surprised when sometimes it demonstrated that point. After they had been working a while Cliff tried to explain something to Danny Orlando—Danny Orlando couldn't make out exactly what, for Cliff was having his usual amusing trouble with words. Danny laughed, and Cliff laughed and turned away, his heavy shoulders suddenly stooped.

He gave only a few general directions after that, working rapidly while he talked over the phone as though trying to straighten everything singlehanded. He gave brief instructions on diverting the next swarm of parts and rocks coming up from the asteroid belt foundries, and then he swung his small tug in a pretzel loop around Pluto that tangented away from the planet in the opposite direction from Pluto's orbital swing. The ship was no longer in a solar orbit at balance, solar gravity gripped it smoothly and it began to fall in steady acceleration.

"Going to Station A," Cliff explained over the general phone before he fell out of beam range. "I'm in a hurry."

The scattered busy engineers nodded, remembering that as a good kinetics man Cliff could jockey a ship through the solar system at maximum speed. They did not wonder why he dared leave them without co-ordination, for every man of them was sure that in a pinch, maybe with the help of a few anti-sleep and think-quick tablets, he could fill Cliff's boots. They only wondered why he did not pick one of them to be his partner, or why he did not tape a fast course and send someone else for the man.

When he was out of beam range a solution was offered. "Survival of the fittest," said Smitty over the general phone. "Either you can keep track of everything at once or you can't. There is no halfway in this co-ordination game, and no one can help. My bet is that Cliff has just gone down to see his family, and when he gets back he'll pick the man he finds in charge."

They set to work, and only Cliff knew the growing disorder

and desperation that would come. He knew the abilities of the men on his team—the physicists, the field warp specialists, the metallurgists. There was no one capable of doing co-ordination. Without perfect co-ordination the project would fall apart, blow up, kill.

And he was leaving them. Gross criminal negligence. Manslaughter.

"Why did you leave the project?" Spaceways Commission would ask at the trial.

"I would be no use there." Not without Mike.

He sat in the stern of his ship in the control armchair and looked at the blend of dim lights and shadows that picked out the instrument panel and the narrow interior of the control dome. Automatically the mixture analyzed for him into over-lapping spheres of light blending and reflecting from the three light sources. There was no effort to such knowledge. It was part of sight. He had always seen a confusion of river ripples as the measured reverberations of wind, rocks, and current. It seemed an easy illiterate talent, but for nineteen years it had bought him a place on Station A, privileged with the company of the top research men of Earth who were picked for the station staff as a research sinecure, men whose lightest talk was a running flame of ideas. The residence privilege was almost an automatic honor to the builder, but Cliff knew it was more of an honor than he deserved.

After this the others would know.

Why did you leave the project? Incompetence.

Cliff looked at his hands, front and back. Strong, clumsy, almost apelike hands that knew all the secrets of machinery by instinct, that knew the planets as well as if he had held them and set them spinning himself. If all the lights of the sky were to go out, or if he were blind, he could still have cradled his ship in any spaceport in the system, but this was not enough. It was not skill as others knew skill, it was instinct, needing no learning. How hard to throw a coconut—how far to jump for the next branch—no words or numbers needed for that, but you can't tape automatics or give directions without words and numbers.

All he could give would be a laugh and another anecdote to
swell the collection.

"Did you see Cliff trying to imitate six charged bodies in a
submagnetic field?"

Sitting in the shock tank armchair of the tug, Cliff shut his
eyes, remembered Brandy's remarks on borrowing trouble, and
cutting tension cycles, and with an effort put the whole subject
on ice, detaching it from emotions. It would come up later. He
relaxed with a slightly lopsided grin. The only current problem was how to get Archy and himself back to Pluto before
the whole project blew up.

He left his ship behind him circling the anchorage asteroid
at a distance and speed that broke all parking rules, and he
knew how much drain the anchorage projectors could take.
They could hold the ship in for two hours, long enough for
him to get Archy and tangent off again with all the ship momentum intact.

High speeds are meaningless in space, even to a lone man
in a thin spacesuit. There was no sense of motion, and nothing
in sight but unmoving stars, yet the polarized wiring of his
suit encountered shells of faint resistance, shoves and a variety
of hums, and Cliff did not need his eyes. He knew the electro-
magnetic patterns of the space around Station A better than
he knew the control board of the tug. With the absent precision
of long habit he touched the controls of his suit, tuning its
wiring to draw power from the station carrier wave. As he
tuned in, the carrier was being modulated by a worried voice.

"Can't quite make out your orbit. Would you like a taxi
service? Answer please. We have to clear you, you know."

Cliff wide-angled the beam of his phone and flashed it in
the general direction of Station A for a brief blink of full
power that raised it to scorching heat in his hand. The flash
automatically carried his identification letters.

"Oh, is that *you*, Cliff? I was beginning to wonder if your
ship were heaving a bomb at us. O.K. clear. The port is open."
In the far distance before him a pinpoint of light appeared and
expanded steadily to a great barrel of metal rotating on a
hollow axis. Inside, invisible forces matched his residual
velocity to the station and deposited him gently in a storage
locker.

Cliff passed through the ultraviolet and supersonic steriliz-
ing stalls to the locker room, changed his sterilized spacesuit
for clean white shorts, and stepped out onto the public corri-
dors. They were unusually deserted. He managed to reach the
library without exchanging more than a distant wave with
someone passing far down a corridor.

There was someone in the reading room, but Cliff passed
hurriedly, hoping the man would not turn and greet him or
ask why he was there, or how was Mike— Hurriedly he
shoved through a side door, and was in the tube banks and
microfiles where the information service works were open to
Archy's constant tinkering.

There was a figure sitting cross-legged, checking some
tubes, but it was not Archy. It was a stranger.

Cliff tapped the seated figure on the shoulder and extended
a hand as the man turned. "My name is Cliff Baker. I'm one
of the engineers of this joint. Can I be of any help to you?"

The man, a small friendly Amerind, leaped to his feet and
took the hand in a wiry nervous clasp, smiling widely. He answered in Glot with a Spanish accent.

"Happy to meet you, sir. My name is McCrea. I am the new
librarian to replace Dr. Reynolds."

"It's a good job," said Cliff. "Is Archy around?"

The new librarian gulped nervously. "Oh, yes, Dr. Reynolds'
son. He withdrew his application for the position. Something
about music I hear. I don't want to bother him. I am not used
to the Reynolds' system, of course. It is hard to understand.
It is sad that Dr. Reynolds left no diagrams. But I work hard,
and soon I will understand." The little man gestured at his
scattered tools and half-drawn tentative diagrams and gulped
again. "I am not a real, a *genuine* station research person, of
course. The commission they have honored me with is a
temporary appointment while they—"

Cliff had listened to the flow of words, stunned. "For the
luvva Pete!" he exploded. "Do you mean to say that Archy
Reynolds has left you stewing here trying to figure out the
library system, and never raised a hand to help you? What's
wrong with the kid?"

He smiled reassuringly at the anxious little workman. "Listen," he said gently. "He can spare you ten minutes. I'll get Archy up here if I have to break his neck."

He strode back into the deserted library, where one square stubborn man sat glowering at the visoplate on his desk. It was Dr. Brandias, the station medico.

"Ahoy, Brandy," said Cliff. "Where's Archy? Where is everybody anyhow!"

Brandy looked up with a start. "Cliff. They're all down in the gym, heavy level, listening to Archy give a jazz concert." He seemed younger and more alert, yet paradoxically more tense and worried than normal. He assessed Cliff's impatience and glanced smiling at his watch. "Hold your horses, it will be over any minute now. Spare me a second and show me what to do with this contraption." He indicated the reading desk. "It's driving me bats!" The intonations of his voice were slightly strange, and he tensed up self-consciously as if startled by their echo.

Cliff considered the desk. It sat there looking expensive and useful, its ground glass reading screen glowing mildly. It looked like an ordinary desk with a private microtape file and projector inside to run the microfilm books on the reading screen, but Cliff knew that it was one of Reynolds' special working desks, linked through the floor with the reference files of the library that held in a few cubic meters the incalculable store of all the Earth's libraries, linked by Doc Reynolds to the service automatics and the station computer with an elaborate control panel. It was comforting to Cliff that a desk should be equipped to do his calculating for him, record the results and photograph and play back any tentative notes he could make on any subject. Reynolds had made other connections and equipped his desks to do other things which Cliff had never bothered to figure out, but there was an irreverent rumor around that if your fingers slipped on the controls it would give you a ham sandwich.

"Cliff," Brandy was saying, "if you fix it, you're a life saver. I've just got the glimmering of a completely different way to control the sympathetic system and take negative tension cycles out of decision and judgment sets, and—"

Cliff interrupted with a laugh, "You're talking out of my frequency. What's wrong with the desk?"

"It won't give me the films I want," Brandy said indignantly. "Look, I'll show you." The doctor consulted a list of decimal index numbers on a note pad, and rapidly punched them into the keyboard. As he did so the board gave out a trill of flute-like notes that ran up and down the scale like musical morse. "And all that noise—" Brandy grumbled. "Doc kept turning it up louder and louder as he got deafer and deafer before he died. Why doesn't somebody turn it down?" He finished and pushed the total key to the accompaniment of a sudden simultaneous jangle of notes. The jangle moved into a high twittering, broke into chords and trailed off in a single high faint note that somehow seemed as positive and final as the last note of a tune.

Cliff ignored it. All of Reynolds' automatics ran on a frequency discrimination system, and Doc Reynolds had liked to hetrodyne them down to audible range so as to keep track of their workings. Every telephone and servo in the station worked to the tune of sounds like a chorus of canaries, and the people of the station had grown so used to the sound that they no longer heard it. He looked the panel over again.

"You have the triangulation key in," he told Brandias, and laughed shortly. "The computer is taking the numbers as a question, and it's trying to give you an answer."

"Sounds like a Frankenstein," Brandy grinned. "Everything always works right for engineers. It's a conspiracy."

"Sure," Cliff said vaguely, consulting his chrono. "Say, what's the matter with your voice?"

The reaction to that simple question was shocking; Dr. Brandias turned white. Brandy, who had taught Cliff to control his adrenals and pulse against shock reaction, was showing one himself, an uncontrolled shock reaction triggered to a random word. Brandy had taught that this was a good sign of an urgent problem suppressed from rational calculation, hidden, and so only able to react childishly in irrational identifications, fear sets triggered to symbols.

The square, practical looking doctor was stammering, looking strangely helpless. "Why . . . uh . . . uh . . . nothing." He turned hastily back to his desk.

The news service clicked into life. "The concert is over," it announced.

Cliff hesitated for a second, considering Brandias' broad stooped back, and remembering what he had learned from the doctor's useful lesson on fear. What could be bad enough to frighten Brandy? Why was he hiding it from himself?

He didn't have time to figure it out. He had to get hold of Archy. "See you later." Poor Brandy. Physician, heal thyself.

People were streaming up from the concert.

He strode out into the corridor and headed for the elevator, answering the hails of friends with a muttered greeting. At the door of the elevator Mrs. Gibbs stepped out, trailing her husband. She passed him with a gracious "Good evening, Cliff."

But Willy Gibbs stopped. "Hi, Cliff. Did you see the new movie? You fellows up around Pluto sure got the breaks." Oddly the words came out in a strange singsong that robbed them of meaning. As Cliff wondered vaguely what was wrong with the man, Mrs. Gibbs turned and tried to hurry her husband with a tug on his arm.

Willy Gibbs went on chanting. "There wasn't even an extra to play me in this one." The ecologist absently acknowledged his wife's repeated nudge with an impatient twitch of his shoulder. The shoulder twitched again, reasonlessly, and kept on twitching as the ecologist's voice became jerky. "It's . . . risks . . . that . . . appeal to . . . them. Maybe I . . . should . . . write . . . an article . . . about . . . my . . . man . . . eating . . . molds . . . or *reep beep tatatum la* kikikinoo *stup*."

Mrs. Gibbs glared icily at her husband, and Willy Gibbs suddenly went deep red. "Be seeing you," he muttered and hurried on. As the elevator door slid closed Cliff thought he heard a burst of whistling, but the door shut off his view and the elevator started softly downward.

He found Archy in the stage rehearsal room at 1.6 G. As he opened the door a deep wave of sound met him.

Eight teen-age members of the orchestra sat around the room, their eyes fixed glassily on the drummer. Archy Reynolds sat surrounded by drums, using his fingertips with an easy precision, filling the room with a vibrating thunder that modulated through octaves like an impossibly deep and passionate voice.

The sound held him at the door like a thick soft wall.

"Archy," he said, pitching his voice to carry over the drums. The cold eyes in the bony face flickered up at him. Archy nodded, flipped the score over two pages, and the drumbeat changed subtly. A girl in the orchestra lifted her instrument and a horn picked up the theme in a sad intermittent note, as the drumbeat stopped. Archy unfolded from his chair and came over with the smallest drum still dangling from one bony hand. Behind him the horn note rose up instantly and a cello began to whisper.

He had grown tall enough to talk to Cliff face to face, but his expression was cold and remote.

"What is it, Mr. Baker?"

"Brace yourself Jughead," Cliff said kindly, wondering how Archy would take the shock. The kid had always wanted to go along on a project. It was funny that now he would go to help instead of watch. He paused, collecting words. "How would you like to go up to Pluto Station and be my partner for a while?"

Archy looked past him without blinking, his bony face so preoccupied that Cliff thought he had not heard. He began again. "I said, how would you like—"

The horn began to whimper down to a silence, and the orchestra stirred restlessly. Archy shifted the small drum under his arm and laid his fingertips against it.

"No," he said, and walked back to his place, his fingers making a shuffling noise on the drum that reminded Cliff of a heart beating. The music swelled up again, but it was strange. Cliff could see someone striking chords at the piano, a boy with a flute—all the instruments of an orchestra sounding intermittently, but they were unreal. The sound was not music, it was the jumbled voices of a dream, laughing and muttering with a meaning beyond the mind's grasp.

A dull hunger to understand began to ache in his throat, and he let his eyes half close, rocking on his feet as the dreamlike clamor of voices surged up in his mind.

Instinct saved him. Without remembering having moved

he was out in the hall, and the clean slam of the soundproofed
door cut off the music and left a ringing silence.

At Pluto Station a field interacted subtly with fields out of
its calculated range, minor disturbances resonated and built,
and suddenly the field moved. Ten feet to one side, ten feet
back.

"Medico here," said Smitty on a directed beam, tightening
the left elbow joint of his spacesuit with his right hand. He was
using all the strength he had, trying to stop the jet of blood
from where his left hand had been. Numbly he moved back
as the field began to swing towards him again. He hummed
two code notes that switched his call into general beam, and
said loudly and not quite coherently: "Oscillation build up, I
think. Something wrong over here. I don't get it."

The hall was painted soberly in two shades of brown, with a
faint streak of handprints running along the wall and darken-
ing the doorknobs. It looked completely normal. Cliff shook
his head to shake the ringing out of his ears, and snorted,
"What the Sam Hill!" His voice was reassuringly sane, loud
and indignant. Memory came back to him. "He said no. He
said no!"

"What now?" He strode furiously toward the public elevator.
"Watch your temper," he cautioned himself. "For Pete's sake!
Stop talking to yourself. Archy will listen when it's explained
to him. Wait till he's through." Eight more minutes. They
were only going over a flubbed phrase from the concert.

A snatch of the tune played by the flute came back to him,
with a familiar ring. He whistled it tentatively, then with more
confidence. It sounded like the Reynolds' automatics running
through its frequency selection before giving service. The elevator stopped at the gym level and loaded on some people.
They crowded into the elevator, greeted Cliff jerkily, and then
stood humming and whistling and twitching with shame-faced
grins, avoiding each other's eyes. They all sounded like the
Reynolds' automatics, and all together they sounded like the
bird cage at the zoo.

"What the devil," muttered Cliff as the elevator loaded
and unloaded another horde of grinning imbeciles at every

level. "What's going on!" Cliff muttered, beginning to see the scene through a red haze of temper. "What's going on!"

At one G he got off and strode down the corridor, cooling himself off. By the time he reached the door marked *Baker* he had succeeded in putting it out of his mind. With a brief surge of happiness he came into the cool familiar rooms and called, "Mary."

Bill, his ten-year-old, charged out of the kitchen with a half-eaten sandwich in his hand, shouting.

"Pop! Hey, I didn't know you were coming!" He was grabbed by Cliff and swung laughing towards the ceiling. "Hey! Hey! Put me down. I'll drop my sandwich."

Laughing, Cliff threw him onto the sofa. "Go on, you always have a sandwich. It's part of your hand."

Bill got up and took a big bite of the sandwich, fumbling in his pocket with the other hand. "Hm-m-m," he said unintelligibly, and pulled out a child's clicker toy, and began clicking it. He gulped, and said, in a muffled voice, "I've got to go back to class. Come watch me, Pop. You can give that old teacher a couple of tips, I bet."

There was something odd about the tones of his voice even through the sandwich, and the clicker clicked in obscure relation to the rhythm of his words.

Cliff tried not to notice. "Where's your mom?"

Bill swayed up and down gently on his toes, clicking rapidly, and singing, *"Reeb* beeb. At work, Pop. The lab head has a new lead on something, and she works a lot. Foo *doo.*"

Cliff exploded.

"Don't you click at me! Stand still and talk like a human being!"

Bill went white and stood still.

"Now explain!"

Bill swallowed. "I was just singing," he said, almost inaudibly. "Just singing."

"It didn't sound like singing!"

Bill swallowed again. "It's Archy's tunes. Tunes from his concerts. Good stuff. I . . . we sing them all the time. Like opera, sort of."

"Why?"

"I dunno, Pop. It's fun, I guess. Everybody does it."

Cliff could hear a faint singsong note in the faltering voice. "Can you stop? Can *anyone* stop?"

"I dunno," Bill mumbled. "For Pete's sake, Pop, stop shouting. When you hear tunes in your head it doesn't seem right not to sing them."

Cliff opened the door and then paused, hanging on to the knob.

"Bill, has Archy Reynolds done anything to the library system?"

"No." Bill looked up with a wan smile. "He's going to be a great composer instead. His pop's tapes are all right. You know, Pop, I just noticed, I *like* the sound of the automatics. They sound hep."

"Hep," said Cliff, closing the door behind him, moving away fast! He had to get out of there. He couldn't afford to think about mass insanity, or about Bill, or Mary, or the Reynolds' automatics. His problem was to get Archy up to Pluto Station. He had to stick to it, and keep from thinking questions. He looked at his chrono. The first deadline for leaving was coming too close. No use mincing words with Archy. He'd let him know that he was needed.

Archy was not at the rehearsal room. He was not at the library. Cliff dialed the Reynolds' place, and after a time grew tired of listening to the ringing and hung up. The time was growing shorter. He picked up the phone again and looked at it. It buzzed inquiringly in his hand, an innocent looking black object with an earphone and mouthpiece, which was part of the strange organization of computer, automatic services, and library files which Doc Reynolds had left when he died. Cliff abandoned questions. He did not bother to dial.

"Ring Archy Reynolds, wherever he is," he demanded harshly. "Get me Archy Reynolds. Understand? Archy Reynolds." It might work.

The buzz stopped. The telephone receiver trilled and clicked for a moment in a whisper, playing through a scale, then it started ringing somewhere in Station A. Waiting, Cliff tried to picture Archy, but could bring back only an image of a thin twelve-year-old kid who tagged after Mike and him, asking questions, always the right questions, begging to be taken for space rides, looking up at him worshipfully.

The sound of Archy's voice dispelled the images and brought a clear vision of a preoccupied adult face. "Yes?"

"Archy," Cliff said, "you're *needed* up at Pluto Project. It's urgent. I haven't time to explain. We have ten minutes to get going. I'll meet you at the spacelock."

He didn't call Cliff "Chief" any more.

"I'm busy, Mr. Baker," said the impersonal voice. "My time is taken up with composing, conducting, and recording."

"It's a matter of life and death. I couldn't get anyone else in time. You can't refuse, Jughead."

"I can."

Cliff thought of kidnaping. "Where are you?"

The click of the phone was final. Cliff looked at the receiver in his hand, not hanging up. It was buzzing innocently. *The intonations of Archy's voice had been an alien singsong.* "Where is Archy Reynolds?" Cliff said suddenly. He gave the receiver a shake. It buzzed without answering. Cliff hung up jerkily. "How did you know?" he asked the inanimate phone.

Abruptly Cliff's chrono went off, loudly ringing out the deadline. A little later, eighteen miles away in space his ship would automatically begin to apply jet brakes. After that moment there would not be another chance to take off for Pluto Station for seven hours. It was too late to do anything. There was no need to hurry now, no need to restrain questions and theories; he could do what he liked.

The Reynolds' tapes. He was moving, striding down the hall, knowing he had himself under control, and his expression looked normal.

Someone caught hold of his sleeve. It was a stranger, meticulously dressed, looking odd in a place where no one wore much more than shorts.

"What?" Cliff asked abruptly, his voice strained.

The stranger raised his eyebrows. "I am from the International Business Machine Corporation," he stated, being politely reproving. "We have heard that a Martin Reynolds, late deceased, had developed a novel subject-indexing system—"

Cliff muttered impatiently, trying to move on, but the

business agent was persistent. Presumably he was tired of being put off with jibbering. He gripped Cliff's arm doggedly, talking faster.

"We would like to inquire about the patent rights—" The agent was brought to a halt by a sudden recognition of the expression on Cliff's face.

"Take your hand off my arm," Cliff requested with utmost gentleness, "I am busy." The I.B.M. man dropped his hand hurriedly and stepped back.

Ten minutes later, McCrea, the South American, stuck his head into the reading room and saw Cliff sitting at a reference desk.

"Hi," Cliff called tonelessly, without altering the icy speed with which he was taking numbers from a Reynolds' decimal index chart and punching them into the selection panel. The speaker on the wall twittered unceasingly, like a quartet of canaries.

"*Que pasa?* What happens, I mean," asked the librarian, smiling ingratiatingly.

Cliff hit the right setting. Abruptly all twittering stopped. Smiling tightly, Cliff reached for the standard Dewey-Whitehead index to the old library tapes. They were probably still latent in the machine somewhere. It wouldn't take much to resurrect them and restore the station to something resembling a normal inanimate machine with a normal library, computer, and servomech system. Whatever was happening, it would be stopped.

The wall speaker clicked twice and then spoke loudly in Doc Reynolds' voice.

"Sorry. You have made a mistake," he said. But Doc Reynolds was dead.

In the next fraction of a second Cliff began and halted three wild incomplete motions, and then gripped the edge of the desk with both hands and made himself listen. It was only a record. Doc Reynolds must have set it in years before as a safeguard.

"This setting is dangerous to the control tapes," said the recorded voice kindly. "If you actually need data on Motive-320 cross symbols 510.2, you had better consult me for a

safe setting. If I'm not around you can get help from either
Mike Cohen or the kid. If you need Archy you'll find him
back in the tube banks, or in the playground at .5 G or—"

With a violent sweep of his arm, Cliff wiped the panel clean
of all setting, and stood up.

"Thanks," said the automatics mechanically. There was
no meaning in the vodar voice. It always switched off with that
word.

The little American touched his arm, asking anxiously,
"Que pasa? Que tiene usted?"

Cliff looked down at his hands and found them shaking.
He had almost wiped off the Reynolds' tapes with them. He
had almost destroyed the old librarian's life work, and crippled
the automatic controls of Station A, merely from a rage and a
wild unverified suspicion. The problem of the madness of
Station A was a problem for a psychologist, not for a blun-
dering engineer.

He used will power in the right direction as Brandy had
shown all the technicians of the station how to use it, and
watched the trembling pass. "Nada," he said slowly. "Abso-
lutamente nada. Go take in a movie or something while I
straighten this mess out." He fixed a natural smile on his face
and headed for the control room.

Pierce was due to be passing the station in beam range.

Cliff had preferred taking the psychologist at face value,
but now he remembered Pierce's idle talk, his casual depar-
ture, apparently leaving nothing done and nothing changed,
and added to that Spaceway's known and immutable policy of
hiring only the top men in any profession, and using them to
their limit.

The duty of a company psychologist is a simple thing, to
keep men happy on the job, to oil the wheels of efficiency and
co-operation, to make men want to do what they had to do. If
there were no visible signs of Pierce having done anything, it
was only because Pierce was too good a craftsman to leave
traces—probably good enough to solve the problem of Station A and straighten Archy out.

In the control room Cliff took a reading on Pierce's ship
from blinker buoy reports. In four minutes the station auto-

matics had a fix on the ship and were trailing it with a tight light beam. "Station A calling flitter AK 48 M. Hi Pierce."

"Awk!" said a startled tenor voice from the wall speaker. "Is that Cliff Baker? I thought I left you back at Pluto. Can you hear me?" Behind Pierce's voice Cliff could hear a murmur of other voices.

"I hear too many."

"I'm just watching some stories. I've been bringing my empathy up with mirror training. I needed it. Association with you people practically ruined me as a psychologist. I can't afford to be healthy and calm; a psychologist isn't supposed to be sympathetic to square-headed engineers, he's supposed to be sympathetic to unhealthy excitable people."

"How's your empathy rating now?" Cliff asked, very casually.

"Over a hundred per cent, I think," Pierce laughed. "I know that's an idiotic sensitivity, but it will tone down later. Meanwhile I'm watching these stereos of case histories, and living their lives so as to resensitize myself to other people's troubles." His voice sharpened slightly. "What did you call for?"

Cliff dragged the words out with effort. "Something strange is happening to everybody. The way they talk is . . . I think it is in your line."

"Send for a psychiatrist," Pierce said briskly. "I'm on my vacation now. Anna and I are going to spend it at Manhattan Beach with the baby."

"But the delay—?"

"Are they in danger?" Pierce asked crisply.

"I don't know," Cliff admitted, "but they all—"

"Are they physically sick? Are they even unhappy?"

"Not exactly," Cliff said unwillingly. "But it's . . . in a way it's holding up Pluto Project."

"If I went over now, I couldn't reach Earth in time."

"I suppose so," Cliff said slowly, beginning to be angry, "but the importance of Station A and Pluto Station against one squalling baby—"

"Don't get mad," said Pierce with unexpected warmth and humor. "Ann and I think this is a special baby, it's important, too. Say that every man's judgment is warped to his profession, and my warp is psychology. My family tree runs to psychology, and we are working out ways of raising kids to the talent. Anna is a first cousin; we're inbreeding, and we might have something special in this kid, but he needs my attention. Can you see it my way, Cliff?" His voice was pleading and persuasive. "Communication research is what my family runs to, and communication research is what the world needs now. I'd blow up Pluto Station piece by piece for an advance in semantics! Cultural lag is reaching the breaking point, and your blasted space expansion and research are just adding more rings to the twenty-ring circus. It is more than people can grasp. They can't learn fast enough to understand, and they are giving up thinking. We've got to find better ways of communication, before it gets out of hand." Pierce sounded very much in earnest, almost frightened. "You should see the trend curves on general interest and curiosity. They're curving *down*, Cliff, all down."

"Let's get back to the subject," Cliff said grimly. "What about your duty to Pluto Station?"

"I'm on my vacation," said Pierce. "Send to Earth for a psychiatrist."

"I thought you were supposed to be sympathetic! Over a hundred per cent you said."

"Eye sympathy only," Pierce replied, a grin in his voice. "Besides, I'm still identified with the case in the stereo I'm watching, a very hard efficient character, not sympathetic at all."

Cliff was silent a moment, then he said, "Your voice is coming through scrambled. Your beam must be out of alignment. Set the signal beam dial for control by the computer panel, and I'll direct you." Enigmatic scrapings and whirrings came over the thousands of mile beam to Pierce.

With a sigh he switched off the movie projector and moved to the control panel, where Cliff's voice directed him to manipulate various dials.

"O. K. You're all set now," Cliff said. "Let's check. You have the dome at translucent. Switch it to complete reflection on the sun side and transparency on the shadow side, turn on your overhead light and stand against the dark side."

"What's all this rigmarole?" Pierce grumbled. With the blind faith of a layman before the mysteries of machinery, he cut off the steady diffused glow of sunlight, and stood back against the dark side, watching the opposite wall. The last shreds of opacity faded and vanished like fog, and there was only black space flecked with the steady hot brightness of the distant stars. The bright shimmer of the parabolic signal-beam mirror took up most of the view. It was held out and up to the fullest extension of its metallic arm, so that it blocked out a six-foot circle of sky. Pierce looked at it with interest, wondering if he had adjusted it correctly. Its angle certainly looked peculiar.

As he looked, the irregular shimmering light began to confuse his eyes. He suddenly felt that there were cobwebs forming between himself and the reflector. Instinctively Pierce reached out a groping hand, squinting with the effort to see.

His eyes found the focus, and he saw his hand almost touching a human being!

The violence with which he yanked his hand back threw him momentarily off balance. He fought for equilibrium while his eyes and mind went through a wrenching series of adjustments to the sight of Cliff Baker, only three feet high, floating in the air within reach of his hand. The effort was too great. At the last split second he saved himself from an emotional shock wave by switching everything off. A blank unnatural calm descended, and he said:

"Hi, Cliff."

The figure moved, extending a hand in a reluctant pleading gesture. Under a brilliant overhead light its expression looked strained and grim. "Pierce, Pierce, listen. This is trouble. You have to help." There was no mistaking the sincerity of the appeal. To the trained perception of the psychologist the relative tension of every visible muscle was characteristic of tightly controlled desperation, but to the intensified responsiveness of his feelings the personality and attitude of Cliff Baker burned in like hot iron, shaping Pierce's personality to its own image. Instinctively Pierce tried to escape the intolerable inpour of tension by crowding back against the wall, but the figure followed, expanding nightmarishly.

Then abruptly it vanished. It had been some sort of a

stereo, of course. For a long moment the psychologist leaned against the curved wall with one hand guarding his face, waiting for his heart to find a steady beat again, and his thoughts to untangle.

"Over a hundred . . . a hundred per cent. Cliff, you don't— What kind of a—"

"The projection?" The engineer's voice spoke cheerfully from the radio. "Just one of the things you can do with a tight-beam parabolic reflector. Some of the boys thought it up to scare novices with, but I never thought it would be useful for anything!"

"Useful! Cliff!" Pierce protested. "You don't know what you did!"

The engineer chuckled again. "I didn't mean to scare you," he said kindly. "I was trying something else. Eye sympathy you said— How do you feel about finding out what's wrong at Station A?"

"How do you expect me to feel?" Pierce groaned. "Go on, tell me what to do!"

"Come find out what it is, and cure them. And work on Archy Reynolds first."

There was a long pause, and when Pierce spoke, his feelings had changed again. "No, blast it! You can't have me like that. I can't just do what you want without thinking! It's phony. No station full of people goes crazy together. I don't believe it."

"I saw it," Cliff answered grimly.

"You *say* you saw it. And you force me to go to cure them —without explanation, without saying why it is important. What has it to do with Pluto Station? It isn't like you to force anybody to do anything, Cliff. It's not in your normal pattern! It isn't like you to cover and avoid explanations."

"What are you driving at?" Cliff said uneasily. "Let me tell you how to set the controls to head for Station A. You have to get here fast!"

"Covering up something. There's only one situation I know of that would make you try to cover." Pierce's voice sharpened with determination. "It must have happened. Listen, Cliff, I'm going to give this to you straight. I know the inside of your head better than you do. I know how you feel about those fluent fast-talking friends of yours at the station and on the job. You're afraid of them—afraid they'll find out you're just a dope. Something has happened at Pluto Station project, and it is still happening—something *bad*, and you think it is *your* fault, you don't know it, but you feel guilty. You're trying to cover up. Don't do it. Don't cover up!"

"Listen," Cliff stammered, "I—"

"Shut up," Pierce said briskly. "This is shock treatment. One level of your personality must have cracked. It would under that special stress. You had an inferiority complex a yard wide. You're going to reintegrate fast on another level right now. File away what I said and listen for the next shock. *You aren't a dope. You're an adjustable analogue.*"

"A what?"

"An adjustable analogue. You think with kinesthetic abstractions. Other people are arithmetic computers. They think with arbitrarily related blocks of memorized audio-visual symbols. That's why you can't talk with them. Different systems."

"What the devil—"

"Shut up. You'll get it in a minute. I ought to know this. I was matched into your feelings for half an hour at a time at Pluto Station. It took me four days to figure out what happened. Your concepts aren't visual, they are kinesthetic. You don't handle the problems of dynamics and kinetics with arbitrary words and numbers related by some dead thinker, you use the raw direct experience that your muscles know. You *think* with muscle tension data. I didn't dare follow you that far. I don't even guess what primitive integration center you have reactivated for that kind of thinking. I can't go down there. My muscle tension data abstracts in the forebrain. That's where I keep my motives and my ability to identify with other people's motives. If I borrowed your ability, I might start identifying with can openers."

"What the—"

"Pipe down," said Pierce, still talking rapidly. "You're following me and you know it. You aren't stupid but you're conditioned against thinking. You don't admit half you know. You'd rather kid yourself. You'd rather be a humble dope and have friends, than open your eyes and be an alien and a stranger. You'd rather sit silent at a station bull session and kick yourself for being a dope, than admit that they are word-juggling, talking nonsense. Listen, Cliff—you are not a dope. You may not be able to handle the normal symbol patterns of this culture, but you have a structured mind that's integrated right down to your boots! You can solve this emergency yourself. So what if your personality has been conditioned against thinking? Everybody knows the standard tricks for suspending conditioning. Put in cortical control, solve the problem first, whatever it is, and then be dumb afterwards if that's what you want!"

After a moment Cliff laughed shakily. "Shock treatment, you call it. Like being whacked over the head with a sledge hammer."

"I think I owed you a slight shock," Pierce said grimly. "May I go?"

"Wait a sec, aren't you going to help?"

Pierce sounded irritable. "Help? Help what? You have more brains than I have, solve your own problems: pull yourself together, Cliff, and don't give me any more of this raving about a whole station full of people going bats! It's not true!" He switched off.

Cliff sat down on the nearest thing resembling a chair, and made a mental note never to antagonize psychologists. Then he began to *think*.

Once upon a time the New York Public Library shipped a crate of microfilm to Station A. The crate was twenty by twenty and contained the incredible sum of the world's libraries. With the crate they shipped a librarian, one M. Reynolds to fit the films into an automatic filing system so that a reader could find any book he sought among the uncounted other books. He spent the rest of his life trying to achieve the unachievable, reduce the system of filing books to a matter of perfect logic. In darker ages he would have spent his life happily arguing the number of bodiless angels that could dance on the point of a pin.

The station people became used to seeing him puttering around, assisted by his little boy, or reading the journal of symbolic logic, or, temporarily baffled, trying to clear his mind by playing games of chess and cards, in which he beat all comers.

Once he grew excited by the fact that computers worked on a numerical base of two, and sound on the log of two. Once he grew interested in the station's delicate system of automatic controls and began to dismantle it and change the leads. If he had made a wrong move, the station would have returned to its component elements, but no one bothered him. They remembered the chess games, and left the automatics to him. They were satisfied with the new reading desks, and after a while there was a joke that if you made a mistake they would give you a ham sandwich, and a joke that the automatics would deliver pretty girls and blow up if you asked for a Roc's egg, but still no one realized the meaning of Doc Reynolds' research.

After all, it was simply the proper classification of subjects, and a symbology for the library keyboard that would duplicate the logical relations of the subjects themselves. No harm in that. It would just make it easier for the reader to find books—wouldn't it.

Once again Cliff stood under the deep assault of sound. This time it was tapes of two of Archy's best jazz concerts, strong and wild. Once again the rhythms fitted themselves into the padded beat of his heart, the surge of blood in his ears, and other, more complex rhythms of the nerves, subtly altering and speeding them in mimicry of the pulse of emotions, while flute notes played, with the sound of Reynolds' automatics, automatics impassioned, oddly fitting and completing the deeper surges of normal music.

Cliff stood, letting the music flow through him, subtly working on the pattern of his thought. Suddenly it was voices, a dreamlike clamor of voices surging up in his mind and closing over him in a great shout, and then passing, and then the music was just music, very good music *with words*. He listened calmly, with enjoyment.

It ended, and he left the room and went whistling down the corridor walking briskly, working off some energy. It was the familiar half ecstatic energy of learning, as if he had met a new clarifying generalization that made all thought much simpler. It kept hitting him with little sparks of laughter as if the full implication of the idea still automatically carried their chain reaction of integration into dim cluttered corners of the mind releasing them from redundancy and the weariness of facts.

He passed someone he knew vaguely, and lifted a hand in casual greeting.

"Reep beeb," he said.

It was a language.

The people of Station A did not know that it was a language, they thought they were going pleasantly cuckoo, but he knew. They had been exposed a long time to the sound of Reynolds' machines. Reynolds had put in the sound system and brought it down to audible range to help himself keep track of the workings of it, and the people of Station A for five years had been exposed to the sounds of the machine translating all their requests into its own symbolic perfect language before translating it back into action, or service, or English or mathematics.

It had been an association in their minds, and latent, but when Archy included frequency symbol themes in his jazz, they had come away humming the themes, and it had precipitated the association. Suddenly they could not stop humming and whistling and clicking, it seemed part of their thought, and it clarified thinking. They thought of it as a drug, a disease, but they knew they liked it. It was seductive, irresistible, and frightening.

But to Cliff it was a language, emotional, subtle and precise, with its own intricate number system. He could talk to the computers with it.

Cliff sat before the computer panel of his working desk. He did not touch it. He sat and hummed to himself thoughtfully, and sometimes whistled an arpeggio like a Reynolds' automatic making a choice.

A red light lit on the panel. Pluto had been contacted and had reported. Cliff listened to the spiel of the verbal report first as it was slowed down to normal speed. "I didn't know you could reach us," said the medico. "Ole is dead. Smitty has one hand, but he can still work. Danny Orlando—

Jacobson—" rapidly the doctor's weary voice went through the list reporting on the men and the hours of work they would be capable of. Then it was the turn of the machinery and orbit report. The station computer translated the data to clicks and scales and twitters, and slowly the picture of the condition of Pluto Station project built up in Cliff's mind.

When it was complete, he leaned back and whistled for twenty minutes, clicking with a clicker toy and occasionally blowing a chord on a cheap harmonica he had brought for the use, while the calculator took the raw formulas and extrapolated direction tapes for all of Pluto Station's workers and equipment.

And then it was done. Cliff put away the harmonica, grinning. The men would be surprised to have to read their instructions from directional tapes, like mechanicals, but they could do it.

Pluto Station Project was back under control.

Cliff leaned back, humming, considering what had been done, and while he hummed the essentially musical symbology of the Reynolds' index sank deeper and deeper into his thoughts, translating their natural precision into the precision of pitch, edging all his thinking with music.

On Earth teemed the backward human race, surrounded by a baffling civilization, understanding nothing of it, neither economics nor medicine or psychology, most of them baffled even by the simplicity of algebra, and increasingly hostile to all thought. Yet through their days as they worked or relaxed, the hours were made pleasant to them by music.

Symphony fans listened without strain while two hundred instruments played, and would have winced if a single violin struck four hundred forty vibrations per second where it should have reached four hundred forty-five. Jazz fans listened critically to a trumpeter playing around with a tune in a framework of six basic rhythms whose relative position shifted mathematically with every note. Jazz, symphony or both, they were all fans and steeped in it. Even on the sidewalks people walked with their expressions and stride responding to the unheard music of the omnipresent earphones.

The whole world was steeped in music. Saturated in music

of a growingly incredible eloquence and complexity, of a precision and subtlety that was inexpressible in any other language or art, a complexity whose mathematics would baffle Einstein, and yet it was easily understandable to the ear, and to the trained sensuous mind area associated with it.

What if that part of the human mind were brought to bear on the simple problems of politics, psychology and science?

Cliff whistled slowly in an ordinary non-index whistle of wonderment. No wonder the people of Station A had been unable to stop! They hummed solving problems, they whistled when trying to concentrate, not knowing why. They thought it was madness, but they felt stupid and thick-headed when they stopped, and to a city full of technicians to whom problem solving was the breath of life, the sensation of relative stupidity was terrifying.

The language was still in the simple association baby-babbling stage, not yet brought to consciousness as a language, not yet touching them with a fraction of its clarifying power—but it was raising their intelligence level.

Cliff had been whistling his thoughts in index, amused by the library machine's reflex bookish elaboration of them, for its association preferences had been set up by human beings, and they held a distinct flavor of the personalities of Doc Reynolds and Archy. But now, abruptly the wall speaker twittered something that carried an over-positive opinion in metaphor. "Why be intelligent? Why communicate when you are surrounded by cows? It would drive you even more bats to know what they think." The remark trailed off and scattered in twittering references to cows, bats, nihilism, animals, low order thinking and Darwin, which were obviously association trails added by the machine, but the central remark had been Archy himself. Somewhere in the station Archy was tinkering idly and unhappily with the innards of his father's machine, whistling an unconsciously logical jazz counterpoint to one of the strands of twittering that bombarded his ears.

It was something like being linked into Archy's mind without Archy being aware of it. Cliff questioned, and suggested topics. The flavor of the counterpoint was loneliness and anger. The kid felt that Cliff and Mike had deserted him in some way, for his father had died when he was in high

school, and Cliff and Mike had long given up tutoring him
and turned him over to his teachers. His father had died, and
Cliff and Mike were not around to talk with or ask advice, so
leaving Archy to discover in one blow of undiluted loneliness
that his mental immersion in science and logic was a wall
standing between him and his classmates, making it impossible
to talk with them or enjoy their talk, making it impossible for
his teachers to understand the meaning of his questions. Archy
had reacted typically in three years of tantrum, in which he
despairingly hated the world, hated theory and thinking, and
sought opiate in girls, dancing, and a frenzied immersion in
jazz.

He had not even noticed what his jazz had done to the
people who listened.

Cliff smiled, remembering the abysmal miseries of adoles-
cence, and smiled again. Everyone else in the station was
miserable, too. There was Dr. Brandias, who should have
been trying to solve the problem of the jazz madness, miserably turning over the pages of a light magazine in the next
cubicle, pretending not to notice Cliff's strange whistling and
harmonica blowing.

"Brandy."

The medico looked up and flushed guiltily. "How are you
doing, Cliff?"

"Come here. I've something to tell you."

It began with a lesson tour, pointing and describing an
index. It became a follow-the-leader with each action in turn
described in index—and it progressed.

The I. B. M. man, doggedly looking for Archy Reynolds
through the suddenly deserted station, at last wandered in to
the huge gym at 1.3 G and was horrified to see Archy
Reynolds and Cliff Baker leading the entire staff of Station
A in a monstrous conga line. Archy Reynolds was beating a
drum with one hand and clicking castanets with the other,
while the big sober engineer blew weird disjointed tunes on a
toy harmonica and the line danced wildly. The I. B. M. man
shut his eyes, then opened them grimly.

"Mr. Reynolds," he called. He was a brave man, and
tenacious. "Mr. Reynolds."

Archy stopped and the whole dance stopped with him in deadly silence, frozen in mid step.

"What can I do for you?"

The I. B. M. man pulled three reels of tape from his brief case. "Senor McCrea showed me Dr. Reynolds' basic tapes, and I took a transcription. Now about the patent rights—" He took a deep breath and swung his glance doggedly across the host of watching faces back to the lean impassive face of the young man who held the rights to Reynolds' tapes. "Could we discuss this in private?"

Instead of replying, the young man exchanged a glance with Cliff Baker, and they both began whistling rapidly, then Archy Reynolds stepped back with a gesture of dismissal and Cliff Baker turned, smiling.

"One condition," he said, and now the intonations of his deep, hesitant voice were as alien as the voices of all others of the station, although earlier in the hall he had sounded comparatively sane to the I. B. M. man. "Only one condition, that I. B. M. leave the sound-frequency setup Reynolds has in his plans at audible volume, no matter how useless the yeeps seem to an engineer. Except for that, it's all yours." He smiled and the people in the lines behind him began restlessly swaying from one foot to another. Archy Reynolds began to pound on his drum.

"What?" gasped the I. B. M. man.

"You can have the patent rights," Cliff replied over the din. "It's all yours!"

The dance was beginning again, the huge line slowly mimicking the actions of the leaders. As the I. B. M. man hesitated at the door, staring back at the strange sight, Cliff Baker was showing his wife some intricate step, and the others mimicked in pairs.

The big engineer glanced toward the door, hesitated and hummed, clicked and whistled weirdly in a moment of complete stillness, then threw back his head and laughed. All eyes in the assemblage swiveled and came to rest on the I. B. M. man, and all through the hall there was a slow chuckle of laughter growing towards a howl.

Madness!

He stumbled through the door and fled, carrying in his brief case the human race.

FEEDBACK

"WHY DID LEONARDO write backward?" The year was 1995. A pupil had asked the question.

William Dunner switched on the lights suddenly, showing the class of ten- and twelve-year-olds blinking in the sudden glare.

"He was in danger of his life," he said seriously. "Here"— he tapped the pointer against the floor—"give that last slide again."

The pupil at the back of the room worked the slide lever, and Da Vinci's *Last Supper*, which still showed dimly on the screen, vanished with a click and was replaced by an enlarged sketch of a flying machine. Under the sketch was time-dimmed writing, the words oddly curled and abbreviated. It was backward, as if the slide had been put in the wrong way.

"He was writing ideas that no one had ever written before," said William Dunner. The teacher was tall, angular, and somewhat awkward in his stance. He stared at the faded cryptic writing, selecting his words with the care of someone selecting footsteps along the edge of a precipice. "Da Vinci had seen things that should not have been there—the symmetry of sound waves—the perfect roundness of ripples spreading through each other, and, high up on a mountain he had found sea shells, as if the sea and the land had not always been where they were, but had changed places, and perhaps some day the sea would again close over the mountain top, and mountains rise from the depth of the sea. These thoughts were against the old beliefs, and he was afraid. Other men, later, saw new truths about nature. They were not so brilliant as he, but they risked their lives to teach and write them, and they gave us the new world of science we have today. Leonardo had great thoughts, but he wrote them down in silence and hid them in code, for if the people guessed what he thought, they might come and burn him, as they had burned some of his paintings. He was afraid."

145

He tapped the base of the pointer on the floor and the slide vanished with a click and was replaced by the *Last Supper*. Again the dim figure of Christ sat at the long table with his friends.

A chubby little girl put up her hand.

"Yes, Marilyn?"

"Were they Fascists? I mean, the people that Leonardo was scared of?" It was an obvious identification. Fascists tortured people and suppressed ideas. The pupils who knew a little more history stirred and giggled to show that they knew better.

"Stand up, please," he said gently. She stood up. It did not matter what the question or answer was, as long as they stood up. Standing up while the class sat, being alone on stage in the drama club he had started for them: learning to stand and think alone.

"No, not Fascism. It wasn't their government which made them cruel." Mr. Dunner made a slight sad clumsy gesture with the hand that held the pointer. "You might say it is a democratic thing, for in defending the old ways people feel that they are defending something worthy and precious." He ran his gaze across their faces as though looking for something, and said firmly, "Logically, of course, nothing is wrong which does not injure a neighbor, but if you attack a man's beliefs with logic, he sometimes feels as if you are attacking his body, as if you are injuring him. In Leonardo's time they held very many illogical beliefs which were beginning to crumple, so they felt constantly insecure and attacked, and they burned many men, women and children to death for being in league with Satan, the father of doubts."

In the painting on the screen the figure of Christ sat at the long table. The paint was blotched and cracked and his face almost hidden.

Mr. Dunner turned to it. "No, it need not be Fascism. The rulers of a corrupt government may have no beliefs or ideals left to defend. The Roman government would have pardoned Christ, the bringer of a new belief, but it was his own people who slew him, preferring to pardon a robber and murderer instead."

He pointed with the stick. "He is eating with his disciples.

He has just said "One of you will betray me." Observe the composition of—"

There was a slight stirring and whispering of disapproval. The things he had said were puzzling and almost violent, and sounded different from things they had been taught were true. They did not want him to return to the usual kind of lecture. A question was passed among them in quick murmuring and agreement. A boy raised his hand.

"Yes, Johnny?"

"Why is it democratic?" He was almost defiant. "Burning people."

"Because it was an expression of the majority will. The majority of people have faith that the things they already believe are true, and so they will condemn anyone who teaches different things, believing them to be lies. All basic progress must start with the discovery of a truth not yet known and believed. Unless those who have new ideas and different thoughts be permitted to speak and are protected carefully by law, they will be attacked, for in all times men have confused difference with criminality."

The murmur began again, and the boy put up his hand.

"Yes, Johnny?"

"I *like* inventors. I like inventions. I like things to change." He was speaking for the class. It was a question about people disliking changes. The teacher hesitated oddly.

"Stand up please."

The boy stood up. He had a thin oval face with large brown eyes which he narrowed to hide his nervousness. The other children in the class turned in their seats to look at him.

"You said you like things different," the teacher reminded him. "That's a good trait, but do you like to *be* different yourself? Do you like to stand up when the others are sitting down?" The boy licked his lips, glancing from the side of his eyes at the classmates seated around him, his nervousness suddenly increased.

Mr. Dunner turned to the blackboard and wrote "sameness."

"Here is the sameness of mass production, and human equality, and shared tastes and dress and entertainment, and basic education equalized at a high level, and forgotten prejudices, and the blending of minorities, and all the other good things of democracy. The sameness of almost everybody doing the same thing at once. Some of the different ones who are left notice their difference and feel left out and alone. They try to be more like the others." He curved a chalk arrow, and wrote "conformity." Johnny, still standing, noticed that Mr. Dunner was nervous, too. The chalk line wavered.

The arrow curved through "conformity" and back to the first word in a swift circle. "And then those who are left feel more conspicuous and lonesome than ever. People stare and talk about them. So *they* try to be more like the others. And then everybody is so much like everybody else that even a very tiny necessary difference looks peculiar and wrong. The unknown and unfamiliar is feared or hated. All differences, becoming infrequent, look increasingly strange and unfamiliar, and shocking, and hateful. Those who want to be different hide themselves and pretend to be like the others."

He moved the chalk in swift strokes. The thickening circle of arrows passed through the words: sameness, conformity, sameness, conformity, sameness. . . .

He stepped back and printed in the middle of the circle, very neatly, "STASIS."

He turned back to the class, smiling faintly. "They are trapped. And they don't know what has happened to them."

He turned back to the blackboard, and drew another circle thoughtfully. This one wavered much more. "These are feed-back circles. All positive feedbacks are dangerous. Not just man but other social animals have an instinct to follow, and can fall into the trap. Even the lowly tent caterpillars are in danger from it, for they crawl after each other in single file, and if the leader of a line happens to turn back and find before him the end of his own line, he will follow it, and the circle of caterpillars will keep crawling around and around, growing hungry and exhausted, following each other until they die."

Johnny licked his lips nervously, wishing Mr. Dunner would let him sit down.

Miraculously the teacher's eyes met his.

"I stand up," said Mr. Dunner softly to him alone. "If

everyone else went sledding, could you go skating alone, all by yourself?"

He could see that it was a real question: Mr. Dunner honestly wanted him to answer, as if he were an equal. Johnny nodded.

"It would take courage, wouldn't it? Sit down, Johnny."

Johnny sat down, liking the tall shy bony teacher more than ever. He was irritably aware of the stares and snickers of the others around him. As if he'd done something wrong! What did they think they were snickering at anyhow!

He leaned both elbows on the desk and looked at the teacher as if he were concentrating on the lecture.

The bell rang.

"Class dismissed," called Mr. Dunner unnecessarily and helplessly over the din of slamming desk tops and shouts as everybody rushed for the door.

Glancing back, Johnny saw the teacher still standing before the blackboard. Beside him the projected image of Leonardo's painting glowed dimly, forgotten, on the screen.

At his locker, Johnny slipped his arms into his jacket and grabbed his cap angrily. Why did they have to scare Leonardo? Grownups! People acted crazy!

Outside they were shouting, "Yeaaa-ahh yeaaa-ahh! Charlie put his cap on backward! Charlie put his cap on backward!" Charlie, one of his best pals, stood miserably pretending not to notice. His cap was frontward. He must have put it right as soon as they had started to call.

Johnny hunched his shoulders and walked through the ring as if he had not seen it, and it broke up unconcernedly in his wake into the scattering and clusters of kids going home. Johnny did not wait to get into a group. Stupid, they were all stupid! He wished he could have thought of something to tell them.

At home, stuffing down a sandwich in the kitchen, he came to a conclusion. "Mother, does everyone have to be like everyone else? Why can't they be different?"

It's started again, she thought. *I can't let Johnny get that way.*

Aloud she said, "No, dear, everyone can be as different as they like. This is a free country, a democracy."

"Then can Charlie wear his cap backward?"

It was an insane concept. She was tempted to laugh. "No, dear. If he did, he would be locked up."

He grew more interested. "Why? Why would they lock him up?"

"Because it would be crazy—" Her breath caught in her throat but she kept the sound of her voice level, and busied herself at the stove, her head down so that he wouldn't notice anything wrong.

"Why? Why would it be crazy?" The clear voice seemed too clear, as if someone could hear it outside the room, outside the walls, as if the whole town could hear. "Why can't I wear my cap backward—"

"It's crazy!" she snapped. The pan clattered loudly on the stove under the violence of her stirring. Always answer a child's questions with a smile. She swallowed with a dry mouth, and tried.

"I mean it would be queer. It's odd. You don't want to be odd, do you?" He didn't answer, and she plunged on, trying desperately to make him see it. "Only crazy people want to be odd. Crazy people and seditioners." She swallowed again. "Everyone likes to be like everyone else." Breathless, she waited, turning her head covertly to see if he understood. He had to understand! He couldn't talk like this in front of her friends, they might not understand, they might think that she—

She remembered the seditioner who had moved into town three years ago, a plane and tractor mechanic. He had seemed such a nice man on the outside, but he had turned out to be a seditioner, wanting to change something. People from the town had gone to show him what they thought of it, and someone had hit him too hard, and he had died. Johnny mustn't—

He looked sulky and unconvinced. "Mr. Dunner said everybody could be as different as they liked," he said. "He said it doesn't matter what you wear." He kicked the edge of the sink defiantly, something like desperation welling up in his voice. "He said being like other people is stupid, like caterpillars."

She thought, *Mr. Dunner now, the history teacher, another*

seditioner. That tall shy man. And he had been teaching the children for five years! Other people's children too. She turned off the stove and went numbly to the telephone.

While she was telephoning the fourth house, Johnny came out of the kitchen with his cap on and his jacket zipped, ready to go out and play. She lowered her voice. While she talked on the phone he went to the hall mirror, looked into it and carefully took his cap off, rotated it and replaced it backward, with the visor to the back and the ear tabs on his forehead. His eyes met hers speculatively in the mirror.

For a moment she did not absorb what he had done. She had never seen anyone wearing a hat wrong way before. It gave a horrible impression of a whole head turned backward, as if the back of his head were a featureless brown face watching her under the visor. The pale oval of his real face in the mirror seemed changed and alien.

Somehow a steel strength came to her. She remembered that the viewing screen was off. No one had seen. She said into the phone, as if starting a sentence, "Well, I think—" and put her finger on the lever, cutting the connection, and hung up.

Johnny was watching her. Rising, she slapped his face. Seeing the white hand marks, she realized that she had slapped harder than she had intended, but she was not sorry. It was for his sake.

The phone began ringing.

"Go upstairs—" she whispered, breathing hard. "Go to your room—" He went. She picked up the phone. "Yes, Mrs. Jessups, I'm sorry . . . I guess we were cut off."

Three calls, four calls, five calls.

When Bruce Wilson arrived home he heard the story. He listened, his hand clutching the bannister rail, the knuckles whitening.

When Pam finished he asked tightly, "Do you think a spanking would do any good?"

"No, he's all right now, he's frightened."

"Are you sure he's safe?"

"Yes." But she looked tired and worried. Johnny had been exposed to sedition. It remained to be seen if it would have any effect. Seditioners were always tarred and feathered, fired, driven out of their home, beaten, hanged, burned.

The telephone rang, Pam reached for it, then paused, glancing away from him. Her voice changed. "That will be the vigilantes, Bruce."

"I have to finish that report tonight. I'm tired, Pam."

"You didn't go last time. It wouldn't look right if you—"

"I guess I'd better go. It's my duty anyhow."

They didn't look at each other. He answered the phone.

They screamed and shouted, pushing, making threatening gestures at the man on the platform, lashing at him with the noise, trying to build his fear to the point where it would be visible and cowering. Someone in the crowd was waving a noose, shouting for his attention. Someone else was waving a corkscrew. He saw it.

They laughed at the comic horror of the threat, and laughed again at the man's expression as he realized what it was.

They were in a clearing among trees which was the town picnic grounds. At the center, before the mob, was the oration platform, built around the base of the giant picnic oak.

On the rear of the platform the judges of the occasion finished arranging themselves and were ready.

"Silence."

The mob quieted.

"William C. Dunner, you are accused of teaching sedition —malign and unworthy doctrines—to our children, violating the trust placed in you." He did not reply.

"Have you anything to say in your defense?"

The fluorescent lamp shone on the people grouped on the platform. Below, the light gleamed across the upturned faces of the mob as they watched the tall, stooped man who stood disheveled in the light, his hands tied behind him and a smear of blood on one cheek. He shook his head in negation. "I wouldn't do anything against the children," he said. They heard the faltering voice unclearly. "I'm sorry if it seems to you that—"

"Do you or do you not teach subversion?"

The reply was clearer. "Not by my definition of the term, although I have heard usages that—"

"Are you or are you not a seditioner?"

"You would have to define—"

A thick-armed young man standing by was given a nod by one of the judges and stepped forward and knocked the prisoner down. He started clumsily struggling to get up, hampered by his tied hands.

"Just like a seditioner, trying to hide behind words," said someone behind Bruce in the crowd. Bruce nodded.

Seditioners must all be skilled with words as their weapon, for, though it had been twenty years since any hostile foreign power existed to assist and encourage treachery, there seemed to be more and more seditioners. It was impossible to open a paper without reading an item of their being tarred and feathered, beaten up or fired, of newer and stricter uniformity oaths with stricter penalties of jailing and fines for those who were found later expressing opinions different from those beliefs they had sworn to. Yet in spite of this the number of seditioners increased. Their creed must be terrifyingly seductive and persuasive.

And Johnny had been exposed to those words! The shy tall teacher who was supposed to be "so good with children," whom he and Pam had hospitably invited to dinner several times, had repaid their hospitality with treachery.

Bruce felt the anger rising in him, and the fear. It must never happen again!

"We've got to find every crawling seditioner in Fairfield right now, and get rid of them! We've got to get the names of the others from this sneak!"

"Take it easy," said the man on his left, whose name he remembered vaguely as Gifford. "We're getting to that now." The teacher had regained his feet and stood up to face the judges.

The questioning began again.

Off to one side a man had climbed to the rail and was tossing the knotted end of a rope towards a high thick branch of the oak above.

"William Dunner, were you, or were you not, directed to teach subversion and disloyalty to our children?"

"I was not."

"Are you associated with other seditioners in any way?"

"I know other people of my own opinion. I wouldn't call them seditioners though."

"Are you directed by any subversive or disloyal organization?"

"I hold a great deal of love and loyalty for the people of the United States," he answered steadily. "But right now I think you people here are being extremely childish. You—" He was struck across the mouth.

"Answer the question!"

"I am a member of no subversive or disloyal organization."

"Will you give the names of those associated with you in subversion?"

The end of the rope was slung again, and passed over the limb this time, coming suddenly writhing down to be captured dexterously by the man holding the other end. The hangman did not seem to be listening to the questions, or care what the answers would be.

"I will not. I'm sorry but it's impossible."

Gifford nudged Bruce. "He's sorry! He doesn't know how sorry he can get. He'll change his mind in a hurry."

Up on the platform the judges conferred ceremonially and Dunner waited, standing abnormally still. The finished noose was released, and swung down and past his face in a slow arc. In the crowd the man with the corkscrew waved it again, grinning. There was laughter.

The teacher's face was suddenly shiny with sweat.

The men who were the judges turned from their conferring.

"Our finding is treason. However, confess, throw yourself on the mercy of the court, give the names of your fellow traitors and we will extend clemency."

The disheveled tall man looked from one face to another for a time of silence. "Do you have to go through with this?" The voice barely reached the crowd. The judges said nothing. His eyes searched their faces.

"I have committed no crimes. I refuse to tell any names." His voice was clear and carrying, a teacher's voice, but he was terrified, they could see.

"The prisoner is remanded for questioning."

One of the judges made an imperious gesture and the

teacher was seized roughly on either side by two guards, and his jacket and shirt stripped off roughly and cut free from the bound arms. As the slashed clothing was tossed to one side, the crowd chuckled at the effective brutality of the gesture, and at the reaction of the teacher.

"A good vicious touch," Bruce grinned. "He's impressed."

"Scared," Gifford laughed. "We'll have him talking like a dictaphone. Watch what's next."

Something small was handed up onto the platform. Walt Wilson, who had volunteered for the questioning, held it up for all to see. It was a card of thumbtacks.

The teacher was shoved against the trunk of the oak and secured to it rapidly. The rope was looped around his elbows, and his ankles fastened together with another loop. He faced the crowd upright, helpless and unable to struggle, with the harsh bright light of the lantern shining in his face and the noose dangling where he could see it.

"Scared green," commented somebody near Bruce. "He'll tell us."

Walt Wilson stood waiting to one side until all was quiet, then he extracted a tack and leaned forward with it pointed at the bare, bony chest.

"What are the names of the seditioners in Fairfield?"

The teacher closed his eyes and leaned back against the tree. The crowd waited, their breaths suspended unconsciously, waiting for the whimpers and apologies and confession, ready to laugh. The teacher was already afraid. Tacks are small things, but they hurt, and they held an aura of ruthlessness that spoke of tortures to come that would frighten him more. There was no sound from him yet, as Walt reached for another tack, but he jerked when it touched him. They laughed and waited, and waited with increasing impatience.

Walt's smile was fading. People in the crowd called encouragement. "Go on Walt, more." Walt put in more. He ran out of tacks and was handed another card of them.

"He's being a martyr," Bruce said, considering the shiny pale face and closed eyes with irritation. "A martyr with tacks. Trying to hold out long enough to seem noble."

"Go on Walt!"

"He jumped that time," said someone behind Bruce. "He'll

run out of nobility before we run out of tacks." They laughed.

Walt retired to a corner and the young guard took his place. "Are you, or are you not, a seditioner?"

It went on.

The harsh bright light of the lantern beat on the figures on the platform: the cluster of people at the sides where it curved around the tree; in the middle, leaning back against the trunk, the bony ungainly figure of the teacher, dressed only in shoes and green slacks. The light caught a decorative glitter of metal from Dunner's chest.

"The names, Mr. Dunner, the names!"

One time he answered. "Nonsense," he said in his clear teacher's voice without opening his eyes.

There was no yielding in that answer, only an infuriating self-righteousness. They continued. The tacks were used up.

"Confess." Already he had wasted half an hour of their time.

He opened his eyes. "I have committed no crimes."

An angry sibilance of indrawn breath ran over the crowd. The questioner slapped his thick hand against the glittering chest, and Dunner's arms jerked, and he leaned his head back against the tree trunk watching them with an air of suffering and patience.

The hypocrisy was intolerable.

"Noble. He's being noble," Gifford growled. "Give him something to be noble about, why don't they?"

Someone handed up the corkscrew they had used to frighten the teacher with.

"Now we'll see," said someone on Bruce's left.

The tall bony teacher stood upright, looking with quick jerks of his head from the faces of the crowd to the man approaching with the thing in his hand. Without any pause or relenting the glittering small kitchen object was brought nearer to him. Suddenly he spoke, looking over their heads.

"If you'll examine the term 'seditioner' semantically, you will discover that it had lost its original meaning and become a negatively charged label for the term referent 'innova—' "

A sudden blow stopped him.

"The names please, Mr. Dunner."

"The names, please."

"Mr. Dunner! Who are the seditioners?"

"There are a number of them." He had answered! A sudden hush fell.

He spoke again. *"They are here."*

The questioner asked, "Which ones?" People in the crowd stirred uneasily, not speaking. The names coming would be a shock. Bruce glanced around uneasily. Which ones?

The teacher raised his head sickly and looked at them, turning his face slowly to look across the crowd, with a wild smile touching his lips. They couldn't tell whose face his eyes touched— He spoke softly in that clear, carrying teacher's voice.

"Oh, I know you," he said. "I've talked to you and I know your minds, and how you've grown past the narrow boundaries of what was considered enlightened opinion and the right ways —forty years ago. I know how you hate against the unchanging limits, and fight yourselves to pretend to think like the contented ones around you, chaining and smothering half your mind. And I know the flashes of insane rage that come to you from nowhere when you are talking and living like the others live; rage against the world that smothers you; rage against the United States; rage against all crowds; rage against whoever you are with—even if it is your own family; rage like being possessed!" Bruce suddenly felt that he couldn't breathe. *And it seemed to him that William Dunner was looking at him, at Bruce Wilson.* The gentle, inhumanly clear voice flowed on mercilessly.

"And how terror comes that the hatred will show, that the rage will escape into words and betray you. You force the rage down with the frenzy of terror and hide your thoughts from yourself, as a murderer conceals his reddened hands. You are comforted and reassured, moving with a crowd, pretending that you are one of them, as contented and foolish as they." He nodded slightly, smiling.

But Bruce felt as if the eyes were burning into his own, plunging deep with a torturing dagger of cold clear vision. He stood paralyzed, as if there were a needle in his brain—feeling it twist and go deeper with the words.

The man leaning against the tree nodded, smiling. "I've

had dinner with all of them one time or another. And I know you, oh hidden seditioners, and the fear of being known that drives you to act your savagery and hatred against those of us who become known." He smiled vaguely, leaning his head back against the tree, his voice lower. "I know you—"

The husky questioner jogged him, asking harshly—

"Who are they?"

Bruce Wilson waited for the names, and incredibly, impossibly, *his* name. It would come. He stood unmoving as if he were a long way away from himself, his eyes and ears dimmed by the cold weight of his knowledge. He waited. There was no use moving. There was no place to go, no way to escape. From all the multitude of the people of Fairfield there came no sound.

The teacher raised his head again and looked at them. He chuckled almost inaudibly in a teasing gentle chuckle that seemed to fill the world.

"All of you."

Bruce grasped at the words and found that they were nonsense, meaningless— Swaying slightly he let out a tiny hysterical chuckle.

Like a meaningless thing he saw the questioner swing an instantaneous blow that rammed the teacher's head against the tree and sent him toppling slowly forward to dangle from the ropes at his elbows.

Around him were strange noises. Gifford was clapping him on the back, shouting in his ear. "Isn't that funny! Ha ha! Isn't that crazy! The guy's insane!" Gifford's eyes stared frightened out of a white face. He shouted and laughed.

"Crazy!" shouted Bruce back, and laughed loudly and shouted, "What crazy nonsense! We'll get the truth out of him yet." It had all been a dream, a lie. He could not remember why he was shaking. He had nothing to fear, he was one of the vigilantes, laughing with them, shouting against the teacher, hating the teacher. . . .

They revived William Dunner and he leaned back against the tree with his eyes closed, not speaking or answering, his body glittering with tacks. He must have been in pain. The crowd voices lashed at those on the platform. "Make him answer!" "Do something!" Bruce took out his pocket lighter and handed it up.

They took the pocket lighter.

The teacher leaned against the tree he was tied to, eyes closed with that infuriating attitude of unresentful patience, not seeing what was coming, probably very smug inside, laughing at how he had tricked them all, probably thinking—

Thinking—

Behind the closed eyes, vertigo, spinning fragments of the world. NAMES, MR. DUNNER. NAMES, MR. DUNNER. The yammering of insane voices shouting fear and hate and defensive rationalization. The faces which had been friendly, their mouths stretched open, shouting, their heavy fists coming— Impressions of changes of expression and mood passing over a crowded sea of upturned faces, marionettes being pulled by the nerve strings of one imbecile mind. Whirling and confusion—pain.

Somewhere far down in the whirlpool lay the quiet cool voice that would bring help.

He went down to it.

He was young, listening to the cool slow voice. The instructor standing before the class saying quietly: "It is easy. Your adult bodies have already learned subtle and precise associations of the cause and effect chains of sensations from within the body. The trick of making any activity voluntary is to bring one link of the chain to consciousness. We bring up the end link by duplicating its sensations."

And a little later the instructor sitting on the edge of his cot with a tray of hypos, picking one up, saying softly, "This one is for you, Bill, because you're such a stubborn fool. We call it suspenser." The prick of the needle in his arm. The voice continuing. "One of your steroids. It can produce coma with no breathing or noticeable pulse. Remember the taste that will come on your tongue. Remember the taste. Remember the sensations. You can do this again." The voice was hypnotic. "If you ever need to escape, if you ever need to play possum to escape, you will remember."

The needle was withdrawn. After a time the voice of the instructor was at the next cot, speaking quietly while the blackness came closing in, his heartbeat dimming, dwindling, the strange familiar taste—

Somewhere out of time came pain, searing and incredible.

Ignore it. . . ignore it—Concentrate on the taste. The taste—The heartbeat dwindling—Out of the dreaming distance a face swam close, twisted by some odd mixture of emotions.

"Confess. Get it over with."

Heartbeat dwindling—

He managed a whisper: "Hello, Bruce." A ghost of laughter touched lightly. "I know . . . you—" A small boy taunt, mocking and then sad. The face jerked itself away and then pain came again, but it was infinitely distant now, and he was floating slowly farther and farther away down a long tunnel—

Night wind stirred across the empty picnic ground. It had been deserted a long time—the light and sound and trampling footsteps gone away, leaving a little whimper of wind. Stars glittered down coldly.

Up on the platform something moved.

When Dr. Bayard Rawling, general practitioner and police coroner, came home at five a. m., he saw the humped form of a man sitting on his doorstep in the dark. He approached and bent forward to see who it was.

"Hello, Bill."

Dunner stirred suddenly as if he had been over the edge of sleep.

"Hello, Doc."

Rawling was a stoutish kindly man. He sat down beside Dunner and picked up his wrist between sensitive fingertips. He spoke quietly. "It happened tonight, eh?"

"Yes, tonight."

"How was it?" The doctor's voice roughened slightly.

"Pretty bad."

"I'm sorry. I would have been there if I could." In his bag he carried a small supply of cortocananoxidase, the life suspender, "death," and a small jet hypo, a flesh-colored rubber ball with a hollow needle which could be clenched in a fist with the needle between the fingers and injected with the appearance of a blow. Perhaps many doctors had carried such a thing as a matter of mercy since the hangings and burnings had begun.

"I know," Dunner smiled faintly in the dark.

"I was working on a hard delivery. No one told me about the trial."

" 'Sall right—I managed a trance. Took me a while though—Not very good at these things. Couldn't die fast enough." He whispered a chuckle. "Thought they'd kill me before I could die."

The doctor's fingertips listened to the thin steady pulse. "You're all right."

Dunner made an effort to get up and mumbled apologetically, "Let's get back to the picnic grounds and tie me up to be dead. My arms, strained hanging from those ropes."

The doctor rose and gave him a hand up. "Make it to the 'copter?"

"Well enough." He made an obvious effort and the doctor helped him. Once in, the doctor started the blades with a quick jerky motion.

"You aren't in fit shape to be dead and have a lot of boobs pawing you over and taking your fingerprints for six hours," he said irritably. "We'll chance substituting another corpse and dub it up to look like you. I knew you'd be in trouble. Cox at State University has had one your size and shape in a spare morgue drawer for four months now. He set it aside for me from dissection class." The ground dropped away. The doctor talked with spasmodic nervous cheerfulness. "Had any fillings lately?"

"No."

"I have your fingerprint caps. We'll duplicate the bruises and give it a face make-up, and they won't know the difference. There's not much time to get there and get it back before morning." He talked rapidly. "I'll have to photograph your damage. I'm going to drop you with Brown."

Working with nervous speed, he switched on the automatic controls and took out a camera from the glove compartment. "Let's see what they've done to you. Watch that altimeter. The robot's not working well."

The 'copter droned on through the sky and Dunner watched

the dials while Dr. Rawling opened the slit jacket and shirt and slid them off.

He stopped short and did not move for a moment: "What's that, burns?"

"Yes."

The doctor did not speak again until he had finished snapping pictures, slipped the tattered clothing back over Dunner's shoulders, turned off the light and returned to the controls. "Dig around in my bag and find the morphia ampoules. Give yourself a shot."

"Thanks." A tiny automatic light went on in the bag as it was opened and illuminated the neat array of instruments and drugs.

The doctor's voice was angry. "You know I'd treat you, Bill, if I had time."

"Sure." The light went out as the bag was closed.

"I've got to get that corpse back to the picnic grounds." The doctor handled the controls roughly. "People stink! Why bother trying to tell them anything?"

"It's not them."

"I know, it's the conformity circle! But it's their own circle, not yours. Let them stew in it." He pounded the wheel. "Forty years trading in my good 'copter every year for the same condemned 'copter with different trimmings. Every year trade in my comfortable suit for some crazy fashion and my good shoes for something that doesn't fit my feet, so I can look like everyone else." He pounded on the wheel. "And they don't even like it. People repeating each other like parrots, like parrots. They can't keep it up. It's got to crack. It's bound to stop." He turned plaintively. "But you can't stop a merry-go-round by getting ground up in the gears, Bill. Why not just ride it out?"

"It will end when enough people stand up in the open and try to end it." Dunner smiled. The 'copter landed with a slight jolt that made him suck in his breath suddenly.

"Don't preach at me," the doctor snarled, helping him out with gentle hands. "I'm just saying, quit it, Bill, quit it. Stifle their kids' minds, if that's what they want."

They stood out on the soft grass under the stars. Through the beginning pleasant distortion of the morphine, Dunner saw that the doctor was shouting and waving his arms. "If they want to go back to the middle ages, let 'em go! Let 'em go back to the Amoeba if that's what they want! You don't have to help them."

Dunner smiled.

"Go on, laugh," the doctor muttered. He climbed back into the 'copter abruptly. "If anyone wants to contact me, my copter phone is ML 5346. Can you make it to the house?"

"Yes, of course." Dunner guessed at the source of the doctor's upset. "You've been a great help, Doc. Nobody would expect you to do more than you've done."

"Of course," the doctor snarled, slamming the 'copter into gear. "Everything is just fine. It's a great world. People love the truth: they love teachers, and I'm a hero!"

He slammed the door, the 'copter taxied away to a little distance, then lifted into the sky with a heavy whispering rush of wind.

The teacher walked toward Brown's house. Stars swung in pleasant blurred loops through a quiet sky, and the past of screaming crowd and blows seemed very distant. He pushed the doorbell and heard it chime somewhere far away in the house, then remembered Doc waving his arms, and laughed weakly until the friendly door opened.

GAMES

RONNY WAS PLAYING by himself, which meant he was two tribes of Indians having a war.

"Bang," he muttered, firing an imaginary rifle. He decided that it was a time in history before the white people had sold the Indians any guns, and changed the rifle into a bow. "Wizzthunk," he substituted, mimicking from an Indian film on TV the graphic sound of an arrow striking flesh.

"Oof." He folded down onto the grass, moaning, "Uhhooh. . ." relaxing into defeat and death.

"Want some chocolate milk, Ronny?" asked his mother from the kitchen.

"No thanks," he called back, climbing to his feet to be another man. "Wizzthunk, wizzthunk," —he added to the flights of arrows as the best archer in the tribe. "Last arrow. Wizzzzz," he said, missing one enemy for realism. The best archer in the tribe spoke to other battling braves. "Who has more arrows? They are advancing. No time, I'll have to use my knife." He drew the imaginary knife, ducking an arrow as it wizzed past his head.

Then he was the tribal chief standing nearby on a slight hill, and he saw that too many of his warriors were dead, too few left alive. "We must retreat. We must not all die and leave our tribe without warriors to protect the women and children. Retreat, we are outnumbered."

Ronny decided that the chief was heroically wounded, his voice wavering from weakness. He had been propping himself against a tree to appear unharmed, but now he moved so that his braves could see he was pinned to the trunk by an arrow and could not walk. They cried out.

He said, "Leave me and escape. But remember. . . ." No words came, just the feeling of being what he was, a dying old eagle, a chief of warriors, speaking to young warriors who would need the advice of seasoned humor and moderation to

164

carry them through their young battles. He had to finish his speech, tell them something wise.

Ronny tried harder, pulling the feeling around him like a cloak of resignation and pride, leaning indifferently against the tree where the arrow had pinned him, hearing dimly in anticipation the sound of his aged voice conquering weakness to speak wisely what needed to be said. They had many battles ahead of them, and the battles would be against odds, with so many dead already.

They must watch and wait, be flexible and tenacious, determined and persistent—but not too rash; subtle and indirect—but not cowardly; and above all, be patient with the triumph of the enemy, and not maddened into suicidal attack.

His stomach hurt with the arrow wound, and his braves waited to hear his words. He had to sum a part of his life's experience in words. Ronny tried harder to make it real.

Then suddenly it was real.

He was an old man, guide and adviser in an oblique battle against great odds. He was dying of something, and his stomach hurt with a knotted ache, like hunger, and he was thirsty. He had refused to let the young men make the sacrifice of trying to rescue him. He was trapped in a steel cage, and dying, because he would not surrender to the enemy, nor cease to fight them. He smiled and said, "Do not be fanatical. Remember to live like other men, but remember to live like yourself. . . ."

And then he was saying things that could not be put into words, attitudes that were ways of taking bad situations that made them easier to smile at, complex feelings. . . .

He was an old man, trying to teach young men, and the old man did not know about Ronny. He thought sadly, how little he would be able to convey to the young men. He began to think sentences that were not sentences, but single alphabet letters pushing each other with signs, with a feeling of being connected like two halves of a swing, one side moving up when the other moved down, and like cogs and wheels interlaced inside a clock, only without the cogs, just the push.

It wasn't adding, and it used letters instead of numbers, but Ronny knew it was some kind of arithmetic.

And he wasn't Ronny.

He was an old man, in an oblique battle against great odds. His stomach hurt, and he was dying. Ronny was the old man and himself, both at once.

It was too intense. Part of Ronny wanted to escape and be alone, and that part withdrew and wanted to play something. Ronny sat on the grass and played with his toes like a much younger child.

Part of Ronny that was Doctor Revert Purcell sat on the edge of a prison cot, concentrating on secret, unpublished equations of biogenic stability which he wanted to pass on to the responsible hands of young researchers in the concealed—research chain. He was thinking, using the technique of holding ideas in the mind which they had told him was the telepathic sending of ideas to anyone ready to receive. It was difficult, and made more difficult by the uncertainty, for he could never tell if anyone was receiving. It was odd that he himself could never tell when he was sending successfully. Probably a matter of age. They had started to teach him new tricks when his mind had stiffened and lost the old limber ability to jump through hoops.

The water tap, four feet away, was dripping steadily, and it was hard for Purcell to concentrate, so intense was his thirst. He wondered if he could gather strength to walk that far. He was sitting up, and that was already success, but the effort to raise himself that far had left him dizzy and trembling. If he tried to stand, the effort would surely interrupt his transmitting of equations. All the data was not sent yet.

Would the man with the keys who looked in the door twice a day care whether Purcell died with dignity? He was the only audience, and his expression never changed when Purcell asked him to point out to the authorities that he was not being given anything to eat. It was funny to Purcell that he wanted the respect of any audience to his death, even of a watcher without expression and without response, who treated him as if he were already an inanimate, indifferent object.

Perhaps the man felt contempt for him. Perhaps the watcher would smile and respond only if Purcell said, "I have changed my mind. I will tell."

But if he said that, he would lose his own respect.

At the National BioChemical Convention, the reporter had asked him if any of his researches could be applied to warfare.

He had answered the reporter with no feeling of danger in what he said, knowing that what he did was common practice among research men, sure that he had an unchallengeable right to do it.

"Some of them can apply to warfare, but those I keep to myself."

The reporter remained deadpan. "For instance?"

"Well, I have to choose something that won't reveal how it's done now, but . . . ah . . . for example, a way of cheaply mass producing specific anti-toxins against any germ. It sounds harmless if you don't think about it, but actually it would make germ warfare the most deadly and inexpensive weapon yet developed, for it would make it possible to prevent the backspread of contagion into a country's own troops without much expense, they wouldn't bother to inoculate bystanders and neutral nations, that would let out to the enemy that—Well, there would be hell to pay if anyone ever let that technique out."

Then he added, trying to get the reporter to understand enough to change his cynical un-impressed expression. "You understand, germs are cheap—there would be a new plague to spread everytime some pipsqueak biologist mutated a new germ. It isn't even expensive or difficult."

The headline was: "Scientist Refuses to Give Secret of Weapon to Government."

Government men came with more reporters, and asked him if the headline was correct. When he confirmed it they pointed out that he owed a debt to his country. The research foundations where he had worked were subsidized by Government money. He had been deferred from military service during his youthful years of study and work so that he could become a productive scientist instead of having to fight or die on the battlefield.

"This might be so," he had said. "I am making an attempt to serve mankind by doing as much good and as little damage as possible. If you don't mind, I'd rather use my own judgment abut what constitutes service."

The statement seemed too blunt, and he recognized that it had implications that his judgement was superior to that of the Government. It probably was the most antagonizing thing that he could have said, but he could see no other possible statement, for it represented precisely what he thought.

There were bigger headlines about the interview.

Scientist Refuses to Give Secret. Patriotism Not Important Says Purcell. The evening and morning News Commentators mentioned the incident on the TV screens of the city.

When he stepped outside his building for lunch the next day, several small gangs of patriots were waiting to persuade him that patriotism was important. They fought each other to reach him.

The police rescued him after he had lost several front teeth and had one eye badly gouged. They then left him to the care of the prison doctor, in protective custody. Two days later, after having been questioned politely several times as to whether he considered it best to continue to keep important results of his researches secret, he was transferred to a place that looked like a military jail, and left alone. He was told that they were protecting him from threats against his life.

When someone came to ask him further questions about his attitude, Purcell felt quite sure that his imprisonment was illegal. He stated that he was going on a hunger strike until he was allowed to have visitors and see a lawyer.

The next time the dinner hour arrived, they gave him nothing to eat. There had been no food in the cell since, and that was probably two weeks ago. He was not sure just how long, for during part of the second week his memory had become garbled. He dimly remembered nightmares that might have been delirium. He might have been sick for more than one day.

Perhaps the military who wanted the antitoxins for germ warfare were waiting quietly for him to either talk or die. Perhaps they were afraid that someone else would get the information from him. Or perhaps no one cared if he lived or died, and they had stopped the food when he declared a hunger strike, and then forgotten he existed.

Ronny got up from the grass and went into the kitchen, stumbling in his walk like a beginning toddler.

"Choc-mil?" he said to his mother.

She poured him some, and teased gently, "What's the matter, Ronny—back to baby-talk?"

He looked at her with big solemn eyes and drank slowly, not answering. The chocolate milk was creamy and cool.

In the cell somewhere far away, Dr. Purcell, famous biochemist, began waveringly trying to rise to his feet, unable to remember hunger as anything that could ever be ended, but weakly wanting a glass of water. Ronny could not feed him with the chocolate milk. Even though this other person was also him, the body that was drinking was not the one that was thirsty.

Ronny wandered out into the back yard again, carrying the half-empty glass.

"Bang," he said deceptively, pointing with his hand in case his mother was looking. "Bang." Everything had to seem usual; he was sure of that. This was too big a thing, and too private, to tell a grownup.

On the way back from the sink, Dr. Purcell slipped and fell, and hit his head against the edge of the iron cot. Ronny felt the edge gashing through skin and into bone, and then a relaxing blankness inside his head, like falling asleep suddenly when they are telling you a fairy story, even though you really want to stay awake to find out what happened next.

"Bang," said Ronny vaguely, pointing at a tree. "Bang." He was ashamed because he had fallen down in the cell and hurt his head and become just Ronny again before he had finished sending out his equations. He tried to make believe he was alive again, but it didn't work.

You could never make-believe anything to a real good finish. They never ended neatly—there was always something unfinished, and something that would go right on after the end.

It would have been nice if the jailers had come in and he had been able to say something noble to them before dying, to show that he was brave.

"Bang," he said randomly, pointing his finger at his head, and then jerking his hand away as if it had burned him. He had become the wrong person that time. The feel of a bullet jolting the side of his head was startling and unpleasant, even though not real, and the flash of someone's vindictive anger and self-pity while pulling a trigger. . . . *My wife will be sorry she ever.* . . . Ronny didn't like that kind of make-believe. It was not safe to do it without making up a story first, so you know what is going to happen.

Ronny decided to be Indian braves again. They weren't very real, and when they were, they had simple straightforward emotions about courage and skill and pride and friendship that he always liked.

A man was leaning his arms on the fence, watching him. "Nice day." *What's the matter, kid, are you an esper?*

"Hul-lo." Ronny stood on one foot and watched him. *Just making-believe. I only want to play adventures. They make it too serious, having all these troubles.*

"Good countryside." The man gestured at the back yards, all opened in together with tangled bushes here and there to crouch behind, and trees to climb when the other kids were around to play with. *It can be the Universe if you pick and choose who to be, and don't let wrong choices make you shut yourself off from it. You can make yourself learn from this if you are strong enough. Who have you been?*

Ronny stood on the other foot and scratched the back of his leg with his toes. He didn't want to remember. He always forgot right away, but this grownup was confident and young and strong looking, like the young men in adventure stories, and besides he meant something when he talked, not like most grownups. Nobody else had ever asked him by talking the inside way.

"I was playing Indian." *I was an old chief, captured by enemies, trying to pass on to other warriors the wisdom of my life before I died.* He made believe he was the chief a little bit, to show the young man what he was talking about.

"Purcell!" The man drew in his breath between his teeth with a hiss, and his face paled. He pulled his feelings back from reaching Ronny, like holding his breath in. "Good game." *You can learn from him. Don't let him shut off, I beg you. You can let him influence you without being pulled off your*

*own course. He was a good man. You were honored, and I
envy the man you will be if you contacted him because of
basic similarity.*

The grownup put his hand over his own eyes. *But you are
too young. You'll block him out and lose him. Kids have to
grow and learn at their own speed.* He looked frightened.

He looked down at his hands on the fence, and his thoughts
struggled against each other. *I could prevent him. Not fair;
kids should grow at their own speed. But to shut out Purcell—
no. Maybe no one else so close to him anywhere, no one but
this little boy with Purcell's memories. He'd become—Not
fair, kids should grow up in their own directions. But Purcell,
someone special. . . . Ronny, how strong are you?* The young
man looked up, and met his eyes.

"Did you like being chief?"

Grownups always want you to do something. Ronny stared
back, clenching his hands and moving his feet uneasily.

The thoughts were open to him. *Do you want to be the old
chief again, Ronny? Be him often, so you can learn to know
what he knew?* (*And feel as he felt. It would be a stiff dose
for a kid.*) *It will be rich and exciting, full of memories and
skills.* (*But hard to chew. I'm doing this for Purcell, Ronny,
not for you. You have to make up your own mind.*)

"Did you like being chief, Ronny?"

His mother would not like it. She would feel the difference
in him, as much as if he had read one of the books she kept
away from him, books that were supposed to be for adults
only. The difference would hurt her. She liked him to be
little and young. He was being bad, like eating between
meals. But to know what grownups knew. . . .

He tightened his fists and looked down at the grass. "I'll
play chief some more."

The young man was still pale and holding half his feelings
back behind a dam, but he smiled. *Then mesh with me a
moment. Let me in.*

He was in with the thought, feeling Ronny's confused con-
sent, reassuring him by not thinking or looking around inside while sending out a single call. *Purcell, Doc,* that
found the combination key to Ronny's guarded yesterdays and

ten-minutes-agos. Then they were separate again, looking through their own eyes. *Ronny, I set that door, Purcell's memories, a little bit open. You can't close it, but feel like this about it*—Questioning, cool, a feeling of absorbing without words. . . . *It will give knowledge when you need it.*

The grownup straightened up and away from the fence, preparing to walk away. Behind a dam pressed grief and anger for the death of the man he called Purcell.

"And any time you want to be the old chief, when he was young, or when he was a kid like you, or any age, just make believe you are him."

Grief and anger pressed more strongly against the dam, and the man turned and left rapidly, letting his thoughts flicker and scatter through private memories that Ronny did not share, that no one shared, breaking thought contact with everyone so that the man could be alone in his own mind to have his feelings in private.

Ronny picked up the empty glass that had held his chocolate milk and went inside. As he stepped into the kitchen he knew what another kitchen had looked like for a five year old child who had been Purcell, sixty years ago. There had been an iron sink, and a brown and green-spotted faucet, and the glass had been heavy and transparent, like real glass.

Ronny reached up and put the colored plastic tumbler on the table.

"That was a nice young man, dear. What did he say to you?"

Ronny looked up at his Mamma, comparing her with the remembered Mamma of sixty years ago. He loved the other one too.

"He told me he's glad I play Indian."

PICTURES DON'T LIE

THE MAN FROM THE *News* asked, "What do you think of the aliens, Mister Nathen? Are they friendly? Do they look human?"

"Very human," said the thin young man.

Outside, rain sleeted across the big windows, blurring and dimming the view of the airfield where *they* would arrive. On the concrete runways, the puddles were pockmarked with rain, and the grass growing untouched between the runways of the unused airfield glistened wetly, bending before gusts of wind.

Back at a respectful distance from where the huge space-ship would land were the gray shapes of trucks, where TV camera crews huddled inside their mobile units, waiting. Farther back in the deserted sandy landscape, behind distant sandy hills, artillery was ranged in a great circle, and in the distance across the horizon, bombers stood ready at air fields, guarding the world against possible treachery from the first alien ship ever to land from space.

"Do you know anything about their home planet?" asked the man from the *Herald*.

The *Times* man stood with the others, listening absently; thinking of questions but reserving them. Joseph R. Nathen, the thin young man with the straight black hair and the tired lines on his face, was being treated with respect by his interviewers. He was obviously on edge and they did not want to harry him with too many questions. They wanted to keep his good will. Tomorrow he would be one of the biggest celebrities ever to appear in headlines.

"No, nothing directly."

"Any ideas or deductions?" *Herald* persisted.

"Their world must be Earth-like to them," the weary-looking young man answered uncertainly. "The environment evolves the animal. But only in relative terms, of course." He looked at them with a quick glance and then looked away evasively, his lank black hair beginning to cling to his fore-

173

head with sweat. "That doesn't necessarily mean anything."

"Earth-like," muttered a reporter, writing it down as if he had noticed nothing more in the reply.

The *Times* man glanced at the *Herald*, wondering if he had noticed, and received a quick glance in exchange.

The *Herald* asked Nathen, "You think they are dangerous, then?"

It was the kind of question, assuming much, which usually broke reticence and brought forth quick facts—when it hit the mark. They all knew of the military precautions, although they were not supposed to know.

The question missed. Nathen glanced out the window vaguely. "No, I wouldn't say so."

"You think they are friendly, then?" said the *Herald*, equally positive on the opposite tack.

A fleeting smile touched Nathen's lips. "Those I know are."

There was no lead in this direction, and they had to get the basic facts of the story before the ship came. The *Times* asked, "What led up to your contacting them?"

Nathen answered after a hesitation. "Static. Radio static. The Army told you my job, didn't they?"

The Army had told them nothing at all. The officer who had conducted them in for the interview stood glowering watchfully, as if he objected by instinct to telling the public anything.

Nathen glanced at him doubtfully. "My job is radio decoding for the Department of Military Intelligence. I use a directional pickup, tune in on foreign bands, record any scrambled or coded messages I hear, and build automatic decoders and descramblers for all the basic scramble patterns."

The officer cleared his throat, but said nothing.

The reporters smiled, noting that down.

Security regulations had changed since arms inspection had been legalized by the U.S. Complete information being the only public security against secret rearmament, spying and prying had come to seem a public service. Its aura had changed. It was good public relations to admit to it.

Nathen continued, "I started directing the pickup at stars in my spare time. There's radio noise from stars, you know.

Just stuff that sounds like spatter static, and an occasional squawk. People have been listening to it for a long time and researching, trying to work out why stellar radiation on those bands comes in such jagged bursts. It didn't seem natural."

He paused and smiled uncertainly, aware that the next thing he would say was the thing that would make him famous—an idea that had come to him while he listened—an idea as simple and as perfect as the one that came to Newton when he saw the apple fall.

"I decided it wasn't natural. I tried decoding it."

Hurriedly he tried to explain it away and make it seem obvious. "You see, there's an old intelligence trick: speeding up a message on a record until it sounds just like that, a short squawk of static, and then broadcasting it. Undergrounds use it. I'd heard that kind of screech before."

"You mean they broadcast at us in code?" asked the *News*.

"It's not exactly code. All you need to do is record it and slow it down. They're not broadcasting at us. If a star has planets, inhabited planets, and there is broadcasting between them, they would send it on a tight beam to save power." He looked for comprehension. "You know, like a spotlight. Theoretically, a tight beam can go on forever without losing power. But aiming would be difficult from planet to planet. You can't expect a beam to stay on target over such distances more than a few seconds at a time. So they'd naturally compress each message into a short half-second or one-second-long package and send it a few hundred times in one long blast to make sure it is picked up during the instant the beam swings across the target."

He was talking slowly and carefully, remembering that this explanation was for the newspapers. "When a stray beam swings through our section of space, there's a sharp peak in noise level from that direction. The beams are swinging to follow their own planets at home, and the distance between there and here exaggerates the speed of swing tremendously, so we wouldn't pick up more than a bip as it passes."

"How do you account for the number of squawks coming in?" the *Times* asked. "Do stellar systems rotate on the plane of the Galaxy?" It was a private question; he spoke impulsively from excitement.

The radio decoder grinned, the lines of strain vanishing from his face for a moment. "Maybe we're intercepting everybody's telephone calls, and the whole Galaxy is swarming with races that spend all day yakking at each other over the radio. Maybe the human type is a standard model."

"It would take something like that," the *Times* agreed. They smiled at each other.

The *News* asked, "How did you happen to pick up television instead of voices?"

"Not by accident," Nathen explained patiently. "I'd recognized a scanning pattern, and I wanted pictures. Pictures are understandable in any language."

Near the interviewers, a Senator paced back and forth, muttering his memorized speech of welcome and nervously glancing out the wide streaming windows into the gray sleeting rain.

Opposite the windows of the long room was a small raised platform flanked by the tall shapes of TV cameras and sound pickups on booms, and darkened floodlights, arranged and ready for the Senator to make his speech of welcome to the aliens and the world. A shabby radio sending set stood beside it without a case to conceal its parts, two cathode television tubes flickering nakedly on one side and the speaker humming on the other. A vertical panel of dials and knobs jutted up before them and a small hand-mike sat ready on the table before the panel. It was connected to a box-like, expensively cased piece of equipment with "Radio Lab, U.S. Property" stenciled on it.

"I recorded a couple of package screeches from Sagittarius and began working on them," Nathen added. "It took a couple of months to find the synchronizing signals and set the scanners close enough to the right time to even get a pattern. When I showed the pattern to the Department, they gave me full time to work on it and an assistant to help. It took eight months to pick out the color bands, and assign them the right colors, to get anything intelligible on the screen."

The shabby-looking mess of exposed parts was the original

receiver that they had labored over for ten months, adjusting and readjusting to reduce the maddening rippling plaids of unsynchronized color scanners to some kind of sane picture.

"Trial and error," said Nathen, "but it came out all right. The wide band-spread of the squawks had suggested color TV from the beginning."

He walked over and touched the set. The speaker bipped slightly and the gray screen flickered with a flash of color at the touch. The set was awake and sensitive, tuned to receive from the great interstellar spaceship which now circled the atmosphere.

Between the pauses in Nathen's voice, the *Times* found himself unconsciously listening for the sound of roaring, swiftly approaching rocket jets.

The *Post* asked, "How did you contact the spaceship?"

"I scanned and recorded a film copy of *Rite of Spring*, the Disney-Stravinsky combination, and sent it back along the same line we were receiving from. Just testing. It wouldn't get there for a good number of years, if it got there at all, but I thought it would please the library to get a new record in.

"Two weeks later, when we caught and slowed a new batch of recordings, we found an answer. It was obviously meant for us. It was a flash of the Disney being played to a large audience, and then the audience sitting and waiting before a blank screen. The signal was very clear and loud. We'd intercepted a spaceship. They were asking for an encore, you see. They liked the film and wanted more. . . ."

He smiled at them in sudden thought. "You can see them for yourself. It's all right down the hall where the linguists are working on the automatic translator."

The listening officer frowned and cleared his throat, and the thin young man turned to him quickly. "No security reason why they should not see the broadcasts, is there? Perhaps you should show them." He said to the reporters reassuringly, "It's right down the hall. You will be informed the moment the spaceship approaches."

The interview was very definitely over. The lank-haired, nervous young man turned away and seated himself at the radio set while the officer swallowed his objections and showed them dourly down the hall to a closed door.

They opened it and fumbled into a darkened room crowded with empty folding chairs and dominated by a glowing bright screen. The door closed behind them, bringing total darkness.

There was the sound of reporters fumbling their way into seats around him, but the *Times* man remained standing, aware of an enormous surprise, as if he had been asleep and wakened to find himself in the wrong country.

The bright colors of the double image seemed the only real thing in the darkened room. Even blurred as they were, he could see that the action was subtly different, the shapes subtly not right.

He was looking at aliens.

The impression was of two humans in disguise; humans moving oddly, half-dancing, half-crippled. Carefully, afraid the images would go away, he reached up to his breast pocket, took out his polarized glasses, rotated one lens at right angles to the other and put them on.

Immediately, the two beings came into sharp focus, real and solid, and the screen became a wide, illusively near window through which he watched them.

They were conversing with each other in a gray-walled room, discussing something with restrained excitement. The large man in the green tunic closed his purple eyes for an instant at something the other said and grimaced, making a motion with his fingers as if shoving something away from him.

Mellerdrammer.

The second, smaller, with yellowish-green eyes, stepped closer, talking more rapidly in a lower voice. The first stood very still, not trying to interrupt.

Obviously, the proposal was some advantageous treachery, and he wanted to be persuaded. The *Times* groped for a chair and sat down.

Perhaps gesture is universal: desire, a leaning forward; aversion, a leaning back; tension, relaxation. Perhaps these actors were masters. The scenes changed, a corridor, a parklike place in what he began to realize was a spaceship, a lecture room. There were others talking and working, speaking to the

man in the green tunic, and never was it unclear what was
happening or how they felt.

They talked a flowing language with many short vowels and
shifts of pitch, and they gestured in the heat of talk, their
hands moving with an odd lagging difference of motion, not
slow but somehow drifting.

He ignored the language, but after a time the difference in
motion began to arouse his interest. Something in the way
they walked. . . .

With an effort he pulled his mind from the plot and forced
his attention to the physical difference. Brown hair in short
silky crew cuts, varied eye colors, the colors showing clearly
because their irises were very large, their round eyes set very
widely apart in tapering light brown faces. Their necks and
shoulders were thick in a way that would indicate unusual
strength for a human, but their wrists were narrow and their
fingers long and thin and delicate.

There seemed to be more than the usual number of fingers.

Since he came in, a machine had been whirring and a voice
muttering beside him. He called his attention from counting
fingers and looked around. Beside him sat an alert-looking
man wearing earphones, watching and listening with hawklike
concentration. Beside him was a tall streamlined box. From
the screen came the sound of the alien language. The man
abruptly flipped a switch on the box, muttered a word into a
small hand-microphone and flipped the switch back with
nervous rapidity.

He reminded the *Times* man of the earphoned interpreters
at the UN. The machine was probably a vocal translator and
the mutterer a linguist adding to its vocabulary. Near the
screen were two other linguists taking notes.

The *Times* remembered the Senator pacing in the obser-
vatory room, rehearsing his speech of welcome. The speech
would not be just an empty pompous gesture. It would be
translated mechanically and understood by the aliens.

On the other side of the glowing window that was the stereo
screen, the large protagonist in the green tunic was speaking
to a pilot in a gray uniform. They stood in a brightly lit
canary-yellow control room in a spaceship.

The *Times* tried to pick up the thread of the plot. Already he was interested in the fate of the hero, and liked him. That was the effect of good acting probably, for part of the art of acting is to win affection from the audience, and this actor might be the matinee idol of whole solar systems.

Controlled tension, betraying itself by a jerk of the hands, a too-quick answer to a question. The uniformed one, not suspicious, turned his back and busied himself at some task involving a map lit with glowing red points, his motions sharing the same fluid dragging grace of the others, as if they were underwater or on a slow motion film. The other was watching a switch, a switch set into a panel, moving closer to it, talking casually—background music coming and rising in thin chords of tension.

There was a closeup of the alien's face watching the switch, and the *Times* noted that his ears were symmetrical half circles, almost perfect, with no earholes visible. The voice of the uniformed one answered, a brief word in a preoccupied deep voice. His back was still turned. The other glanced at the switch, moving closer to it, talking casually, the switch coming closer and closer stereoscopically. It was in reach, filling the screen. His hand came into view, darting out, closed over the switch—

There was a sharp clap of sound and his hand opened in a frozen shape of pain. Beyond him, as his gaze swung up, stood the figure of the uniformed officer, unmoving, a weapon rigid in his hand, in the startled position in which he had turned and fired, watching with widening eyes as the man in the green tunic swayed and fell.

The tableau held, the uniformed one drooping, looking down at his hand holding the weapon which had killed, and music began to build in from the background. Just for an instant, the room and the things within it flashed into one of those bewildering color changes which were the bane of color television, and switched to a color negative of itself, a green man standing in a violet control room, looking down at the body of a green man in a red tunic. It held for less than a second; then the color band alternator fell back into phase and the colors reversed to normal.

Another uniformed man came and took the weapon from

the limp hand of the other, who began to explain dejectedly in a low voice while the music mounted and covered his words and the screen slowly went blank, like a window that slowly filmed over with gray fog.

The music faded.

In the dark, someone clapped appreciatively.

The earphoned man beside the *Times* shifted his earphones back from his ears and spoke briskly. "I can't get any more. Either of you want a replay?"

There was a short silence until the linguist nearest the set said, "I guess we've squeezed that one dry. Let's run the tape where Nathen and that ship's radio boy are diddling around CQing and tuning their beams. I have a hunch the boy is talking routine ham talk and giving the old radio count, one-two-three-testing. If he is, we have number words."

There was some fumbling in the semi-dark and then the screen came to life again.

It showed a flash of an audience sitting before a screen and gave a clipped chord of some familiar symphony. "Crazy about Stravinsky and Mozart," remarked the earphoned linguist to the *Times*, resettling his earphones. "Can't stand Gershwin. Can you beat that?" He turned his attention back to the screen as the right sequence came on.

The *Post*, who was sitting just in front of him, turned to the *Times* and said, "Funny how much they look like people." He was writing, making notes to telephone his report. "What color hair did that character have?"

"I didn't notice." He wondered if he should remind the reporter that Nathen had said he assigned the color bands on guess, choosing the colors that gave the most plausible images. The guests, when they arrived, could turn out to be bright green with blue hair. Only the gradations of color in the picture were sure, only the similarities and contrasts, the relationship of one color to another.

From the screen came the sound of the alien language again. This race averaged deeper voices than human. He liked deep voices. Could he write that?

No, there was something wrong with that, too. How had Nathen established the right sound-track pitch? Was it a matter of taking the modulation as it came in, or some sort of hetrodyning up and down by trial and error? Probably.

It might be safer to assume that Nathen had simply preferred deep voices.

As he sat there, doubting, an uneasiness he had seen in Nathen came back to memory. The tightness and uncertainty of Nathen's gestures. . . . He was afraid of something.

"What I still don't get, is why he went to all the trouble of building a special TV set to pick up their TV shows, instead of just talking to them on the radio," the *News* complained aloud. "They're good shows, but what's the point?"

Nobody bothered to answer. Pictures can be understood. Pictures need no translation. Pictures don't lie. Nathen's reasoning was obvious to the others.

On the screen now was the obviously unstaged and genuine scene of a young alien working over a bank of apparatus. He turned and waved, and opened his mouth in the comical O shape which the *Times* was beginning to recognize as their equivalent of a grin, then went back to trying to explain something about the equipment, in elaborate awkward gestures and carefully mouthed words.

The *Times* got up quietly, went out into the bright, white stone corridor and walked back the way he had come, thoughtfully folding his stereo glasses and putting them away.

No one stopped him. Secrecy restrictions were ambiguous here. The reticence of the Army seemed a matter of habit, a reflex response of the Intelligence Department, in which all this had originated, rather than any reasoned policy of keeping the landing a secret.

The main room was more crowded than when he had left it. The TV camera and sound crew stood near their apparatus, the Senator had found a chair and was reading, and at the far end of the room eight men were grouped in a circle of chairs, arguing something with impassioned concentration. The *Times* recognized a few he knew personally, eminent names in science, workers in field theory.

A stray phrase reached him: "—reference to the universal constants as ratio—" It was probably a discussion of ways of converting formulas from one mathematics to another for a rapid exchange of information.

They had reason to be intent, aware of the flood of insights that novel viewpoints could bring if they could grasp them. He would have liked to go over and listen, but there was too little time left before the spaceship was due, and he had a question to ask.

The hand-rigged transceiver was still humming, tuned to the sending band of the circling ship, and the young man who had started it all was sitting on the edge of the TV platform with his chin resting in one hand. He did not look up as the *Times* approached, but it was the indifference of preoccupation, not discourtesy.

The *Times* sat down on the edge of the platform beside him and took out a pack of cigarettes, then remembered the coming TV broadcast and the ban on smoking. He put them away, thoughtfully watching the diminishing rain spray against the streaming windows.

"What's wrong?" he asked.

Nathen showed that he was aware and friendly by a slight motion of his head.

"*You* tell me."

"Hunch," said the *Times* man. "Sheer hunch. Everything sailing along too smoothly, everyone taking too much for granted."

Nathen relaxed slightly. "I'm still listening."

"Something about the way they move. . . ."

Nathen shifted to glance at him.

"That's bothered me, too."

"Are you sure they're adjusted to the right speed?"

Nathen clenched his hands out in front of him and looked at them consideringly. "I don't know. When I turn the tape faster, they're all rushing, and you begin to wonder why their clothes don't stream behind them, why the doors close so quickly and yet you can't hear them slam, why things fall so fast. If I turn it slower, they all seem to be swimming." He gave the *Times* a considering sidewise glance. "Didn't catch the name."

Country-bred guy, thought the *Times*. "Jacob Luke, *Times*," he said, extending his hand.

Nathen gave the hand a quick, hard grip, identifying the

name. "Sunday Science Section editor. I read it. Surprised to
meet you here."

"Likewise." The *Times* smiled. "Look, have you gone into
this rationally, with formulas?" He found a pencil in his
pocket. "Obviously there's something wrong with our judgement of their weight-to speed-to momentum ratio. Maybe
it's something simple like low gravity aboard ship, with magnetic shoes. Maybe they *are* floating slightly."

"Why worry?" Nathen cut in. "I don't see any reason to try
to figure it out now." He laughed and shoved back his black
hair nervously. "We'll see them in twenty minutes."

"Will we?" asked the *Times* slowly.

There was a silence while the Senator turned a page of his
magazine with a slight crackling of paper, and the scientists
argued at the other end of the room. Nathen pushed at his lank
black hair again, as if it were trying to fall forward in front
of his eyes and keep him from seeing.

"Sure." The young man laughed suddenly, talked rapidly.
"Sure we'll see them. Why shouldn't we, with all the Government ready with welcome speeches, the whole Army turned
out and hiding over the hill, reporters all around, newsreel
cameras—everything set up to broadcast the landing to the
world. The President himself shaking hands with me and
waiting in Washington—"

He came to the truth without pausing for breath.

He said, "Hell, no, they won't get here. There's some mistake somewhere. Something's wrong. I should have told the
brass hats yesterday when I started adding it up. Don't know
why I didn't say anything. Scared, I guess. Too much top rank
around here. Lost my nerve."

He clutched the *Times* man's sleeve. "Look, I don't know
what—"

A green light flashed on the sending-receiving set. Nathen
didn't look at it, but he stopped talking.

The loudspeaker on the set broke into a voice speaking in
the alien's language. The Senator started and looked nervously at it, straightening his tie. The voice stopped.

Nathen turned and looked at the loudspeaker. His worry
seemed to be gone.

"What is it?" the *Times* asked anxiously.

"He says they've slowed enough to enter the atmosphere now. They'll be here in five to ten minutes, I guess. That's Bud. He's all excited. He says holy smoke, what a murky-looking planet we live on." Nathen smiled. "Kidding."

The *Times* was puzzled. "What does he mean, murky? It can't be raining over much territory on Earth." Outside, the rain was slowing and bright blue patches of sky were shining through breaks in the cloud blanket, glittering blue light from the drops that ran down the windows. Murky? He tried to think of an explanation. "Maybe they're trying to land on Venus." The thought was ridiculous, he knew. The spaceship was following Nathen's sending beam. It couldn't miss Earth. "Bud" had to be kidding.

The green light on the set glowed again, and they stopped speaking, waiting for the message to be recorded, slowed, and replayed. The cathode screen came to life suddenly with a picture of the young man sitting at his sending-set, his back turned, watching a screen at one side which showed a glimpse of a huge dark plain approaching. As the ship plunged down toward it, the illusion of solidity melted into a boiling turbulence of black clouds. They expanded in an ink swirl, looked huge for an instant, and then blackness swallowed the screen. The young alien swung around to face the camera, speaking a few words as he moved, made the O of a smile again, then flipped the switch and the screen went gray.

Nathen's voice was suddenly toneless and strained. "He said something like break out the drinks, here they come."

"The atmosphere doesn't look like that," the *Times* said at random, knowing he was saying something too obvious even to think about. "Not Earth's atmosphere."

Some people drifted up. "What did they say?"

"Entering the atmosphere, ought to be landing in five or ten minutes," Nathen told them.

A ripple of heightened excitement ran through the room. Cameramen began adjusting the lens angles again, turning on mikes and checking them, turning on the floodlights. The scientists rose and stood near the window, still talking. The reporters trooped in from the hall and went to the windows to watch for the great event. The three linguists came in, trundling a large wheeled box that was the mechanical translator, supervising while it was hitched into the sound broadcasting system.

"Landing where?" the *Times* asked Nathen brutally. "Why don't you do something?"

"Tell me what to do and I'll do it," Nathen said quietly, not moving.

It was not sarcasm. Jacob Luke of the *Times* looked sidewise at the strained whiteness of his face, and moderated his tone. "Can't you contact them?"

"Not while they're landing."

"What now?" The *Times* took out a pack of cigarettes, remembered the rule against smoking, and put it back.

"We just wait." Nathen leaned his elbow on one knee and his chin in his hand.

They waited.

All the people in the room were waiting. There was no more conversation. A bald man in the scientist group was automatically buffing his fingernails over and over and inspecting them without seeing them, another absently polished his glasses, held them up to the light, put them on, and then a moment later took them off and began polishing again. The television crew concentrated on their jobs, moving quietly and efficiently, with perfectionist care, minutely arranging things which did not need to be arranged, checking things that had already been checked.

This was to be one of the great moments of human history, and they were all trying to forget that fact and remain impassive and wrapped up in the problems of their jobs as good specialists should.

After an interminable age the *Times* consulted his watch. Three minutes had passed. He tried holding his breath a moment, listening for a distant approaching thunder of jets. There was no sound.

The sun came out from behind the clouds and lit up the field like a great spotlight on an empty stage.

Abruptly the green light shone on the set again, indicating that a squawk message had been received. The recorder recorded it, slowed it, and fed it back to the speaker. The speaker clicked and the sound was very loud in the still, tense room.

The screen remained gray, but Bud's voice spoke a few words in the alien language. He stopped, the speaker clicked and the light went out. When it was plain that nothing more would occur and no announcement was to be made of what was said, the people in the room turned back to the windows. Talk picked up again.

Somebody told a joke and laughed alone.

One of the linguists remained turned toward the loud-speaker, then looked at the widening patches of blue sky showing out the window, his expression puzzled. He had understood.

"It's dark," the thin Intelligence Department decoder translated, low-voiced, to the man from the *Times*. "Your atmosphere is *thick*. That's precisely what Bud said."

Another three minutes. The *Times* caught himself about to light a cigarette and swore silently, blowing the match out and putting the cigarette back into its package. He listened for the sound of the rocket jets. It was time for the landing, yet he heard no blasts.

The green light came on in the transceiver.

Message in.

Instinctively he came to his feet. Nathen abruptly was standing beside him. Then the message came in the voice he was coming to think of as Bud. It spoke and paused. Suddenly the *Times* knew.

"We've landed." Nathen whispered the words.

The wind blew across the open spaces of white concrete and damp soil that was the empty airfield, swaying the wet, shiny grass. The people in the room looked out, listening for the roar of jets, looking for the silver bulk of a spaceship in the sky.

Nathen moved, seating himself at the transmitter, switching it on to warm up, checking and balancing dials. Jacob Luke of the *Times* moved softly to stand behind his right shoulder, hoping he could be useful. Nathen made a half motion of his head, as if to glance back at him, unhooked two of the earphone sets hanging on the side of the tall streamlined box that was the automatic translator, plugged them in and handed one back over his shoulder to the *Times* man.

The voice began to come from the speaker again.

Hastily, Jacob Luke fitted the earphones over his ears. He fancied he could hear Bud's voice tremble. For a moment it was just Bud's voice speaking the alien language, and then, very distant and clear in his earphones, he heard the recorded voice of the linguist say an English word, then a mechanical click and another clear word in the voice of one of the other translators, then another as the alien's voice flowed from the loudspeaker, the cool single words barely audible, overlapping and blending with it like translating thought, skipping unfamiliar words, yet quite astonishingly clear.

"Radar shows no buildings or civilization near. The atmosphere around us registers as thick as glue. Tremendous gas pressure, low gravity, no light at all. You didn't describe it like this. Where are you, Joe? This isn't some kind of trick, is it?" Bud hesitated, was prompted by a deeper official voice, and jerked out the words:

"If it is a trick, we are ready to repel attack."

The linguist stood listening. He whitened slowly and beckoned the other linguists over to him and whispered to them.

Joseph Nathen looked at them with unwarranted bitter hostility while he picked up the hand-mike, plugging it into the translator. "Joe calling," he said quietly into it in clear, slow English. "No trick. We don't know where you are. I am trying to get a direction fix from your signal. Describe your surroundings to us if at all possible."

Nearby, the floodlights blazed steadily on the television platform, ready for the official welcome of the aliens to Earth. The television channels of the world had been alerted to set aside their scheduled programs for an unscheduled great event. In the long room the people waited, listening for the swelling sound of rocket jets.

This time, after the light came on, there was a long delay. The speaker sputtered, and sputtered again, building to a steady scratching behind which they could barely sense a dim voice. It came through in a few tiny words and then wavered back to inaudibility. The machine translated in their earphones.

"Tried . . . seemed . . . repair. . . ." Suddenly it came in clearly. "Can't tell if the auxiliary blew, too. Will try it. We might pick you up clearly on the next try. I have the volume down. Where is the landing port? Where are you?"

Nathen put down the hand-mike and carefully set a dial on the recording box, and flipped a switch, speaking over his shoulder. "This sets it to repeat what I said the last time. It keeps repeating." Then he sat with unnatural stillness, his head still half turned, as if he had suddenly caught a glimpse of answer and was trying to understand it.

The green warning light cut in, the recording clicked and the playback of Bud's face and voice appeared on the screen.

"We heard a few words, Joe, and then the receiver blew again. We're adjusting a viewing screen to pick up the long waves that go through the murk and convert them to visible light. We'll be able to see out soon. The engineer says that something is wrong with the stern jets, and the captain has had me broadcast a help call to our nearest space base." He made the mouth O of a grin. "The message won't reach it for some years. I trust you, Joe, but get us out of here, will you?— They're buzzing that the screen is finally ready. Hold everything."

The screen went gray, and the green light went off.

The *Times* considered the lag required for the help call, the speaking and recording of the message just received, the time needed to reconvert a viewing screen.

"They work fast." He shifted uneasily, and added at random, "Something wrong with the time factor. All wrong. They work *too* fast."

The green light came on again immediately. Nathen half turned to him, sliding his words hastily into the gap of time as the message was recorded and slowed. "They're close enough for our transmission power to blow their receiver."

If it was on Earth, why the darkness around the ship? "Maybe they see in the high ultra-violet—the atmosphere is opaque to that band," the *Times* suggested hastily as the speaker began to talk in the young extraterrestrial's voice.

His voice *was* really shaking now. "Stand by for the description." They tensed, waiting. The *Times* brought a map of the state before his mind's eye.

"A half circle of cliffs around the horizon. A wide, muddy lake, swarming with swimming things. Huge, strange white foliage all around the ship, and incredibly huge pulpy monsters attacking and eating each other on all sides. We almost landed in the lake, right on the soft edge. The mud can't hold the ship's weight, and we're sinking. The engineer says we might be able to blast free, but the tubes are mud-clogged and might blow up the ship.— When can you reach us?"

The description fitted nowhere on the map of the state. It fitted nowhere on a map of Earth.

Pulpy monsters . . . *Times* thought of the Carboniferous era. Dinosaurs? Cliffs . . . a muddy lake . . . monsters . . . Where?

"Right away," Nathen said. "We can reach them right away." Nathen obviously had seen something.

"Where are they?" the *Times* asked him quietly.

Nathen pointed to the antenna position indicators. The *Times* let his eyes follow the converging imaginary lines of focus out the window to the sunlit airfield, the empty airfield, the white drying concrete runways and green waving grass where the lines met.

Where the lines met. The spaceship was there!

The fear of something unknown gripped him suddenly.

The spaceship was broadcasting again. *"Where are you? Answer if possible! We are sinking! Where are you?"*

He saw that Nathen knew. "What is it?" the *Times* asked hoarsely. "How will we get them out of there? Are they in another dimension, or the past, or in another world or what?"

Nathen was smiling bitterly, and *Times* remembered that he had a good friend in the spaceship.

"My guess is that they evolved on a high-gravity planet with a thin atmosphere near a blue-white sun. Sure they see in the ultra-violet. Blue-white stars are normal. Our sun is small and dim and yellow, not normal. Our atmosphere is so thick, like under water. . . ." He brought his gaze back to Jacob Luke of the *Times* without seeing him, seeing only some picture in his own mind. "We are giants, do you understand? Big, slow, stupid. . . ."

"Where is the spaceship?"

"Slow. . . ." Nathen laughed harshly. "A good joke on us, the weird place we live in, the thing it did to us."

The receiver squawked. The decoder machine caught the squawk, slowed it and replayed it immediately, spacing the tumbled frightened voice with cool English words.

"Where are you?" called the young voice from the alien spaceship. "Hurry, please, we're sinking."

The *Times* man took off the earphones and came to his feet. "We've got to hurry." He gripped Nathen's shoulder to get his attention. "Just tell me. Where are they?"

Nathen looked up into *Times*' face. "I want you to understand. We'll rescue them," he said quietly. "You were right about their way of moving, right about them moving at different speeds. This business I told you about them squawk-coding, speeding up their messages for better transmission. I was wrong."

"What do you mean?"

"They don't speed up their broadcasts."

"They don't—?"

Suddenly, in his mind's eye, the *Times* man began to see again the play he had just seen—but the actors were moving at blurring speed, the words jerking out in fluting, dizzying streams, thoughts and decisions passing with unnoticeable rapidity, rippling faces in a twisting blur of expressions, doors slamming wildly, shatteringly, as the actors leaped in and out of rooms.

No—faster, faster—he wasn't visualizing it as rapidly as it was, an hour of talk and action in one second of "squawk," a narrow peak of "noise" interfering with one single word of an Earth broadcast! Faster . . . faster. . . . It was impossible. Matter could not stand such stress. Inertia—momentum—abrupt weight. . . .

It was insane. "Why?" he asked. "How?"

Nathen laughed again, harshly. "Get them out? There isn't a lake or a big river within a hundred miles of here! Where did you think they were?"

A shiver of unreality went down the *Times* man's spine. Automatically and inanely, he found himself delving in his pocket for a cigarette while he tried to understand what had happened. "Where are they, then? Why can't we see their spaceship?"

Nathen picked up the microphone in a gesture that showed the bitterness of his disappointment.

"We'll need a magnifying glass for that."

— The End —

Printed in the United States
96209LV00002B/47/A

9 781587 151286